Other Books by Andrew Darlington

I WAS ELVIS PRESLEY'S BASTARD LOVE-CHILD
Eighteen interviews drawn from twenty years of Music
Journalism
(Headpress / Critical Vision – 2001)

EUROSHIMA MON AMOUR
Thirty-Two Science Fiction poems 'From the Inner Mind to the
Outer Limits'
(Hilltop Press – 2001)

**DON'T CALL ME NIGGER, WHITEY: SLY STONE AND
BLACK POWER**
Music Biography (Leaky Book Press – 2014)
http://www.leakyboot.com/

Andrew's website is:
www.andrewdarlington.blogspot.com

A
SAUCERFUL
OF
SECRETS

FOURTEEN STORIES
OF
FANTASY
WARPED SCI-FI
&
PERVERSE HORROR

ANDREW
DARLINGTON

PARALLEL UNIVERSE PUBLICATIONS

ISBN: 978-0-9935742-0-7
Parallel Universe Publications, 130 Union Road,
Oswaldtwistle, Lancashire, BB5 3DR, UK

CONTENTS

THE STRANGE LAUDANUM DREAM
OF BRANWELL BRONTË   7

LONDON BRIDGE IS FALLING DOWN,
FALLING DOWN, FALLING DOWN   17

THUESDAY TO FRYDAY   33

THE DOOR TO ANYWHERE   43

BEAST OF THE BASKERVILLES   56

DEREK EDGE AND THE SAUCERFUL
OF SECRETS   65

REFUGE   86

THE NON-EXPANDING UNIVERSE   96

GENDER-SHOCK   106

BIG BAD JOHN   119

TERMINATOR ZERO AND
THE DREAM DEMONS   128

A GROTESQUE ROMANCE   142

THIS WORLD HOLDS SPACE ENOUGH   156

AND THE EARTH HAS NO END   180

THE STRANGE LAUDANUM DREAM OF BRANWELL BRONTË

The inscription reads: "Patrick Branwell Brontë: 26 June 1817 – 24 September 1848, author of *Jane Eyre* (1847), *Wuthering Heights* (1847) and *The Tenant of Wildfell Hall* (1848)". Is this a vision of the Poet's own future?

It was the snowstorm – the highly localised snowstorm – that first intimated to him that all was not well. It was a warm day, albeit a little oppressively humid. Penistone hill casts tall shadows across gorse and wilting yellowing grass. There should not have been snow. But the poet was too lost in contemplation to take much notice. Neither did it resemble the snow's of winter 'fast whitening o'er the flinty ground', when it blizzards down from lowering skies to blanket the village and isolate it, sometimes for weeks on end, from Keighley or Oxenhope, and the towns beyond. Rather, it was a dry snow that falls on the folds of his jacket for a moment only, before fading away to nothing. And, having fallen, it leaves no trace upon the footpath or the grass verges where groundsel, speedwell and chickweed ignore its intervention.

It was the briefest swirl of snow. Stepping through into the brightness beyond he brushes his coat irritably, although there's nothing to brush away. He knows this path. He knows this path too well; it is a route he takes as part of his constitutional whenever the pressures of time allow. And there have not been too many prior engagements recently. Far too few of them for his ease of mind. A new portrait commission would be welcome. Dependent upon the subject being sufficiently interesting to justify the investment of his creative effort. The poet stands rather below middle height. His auburn hair brushed back from his forehead, as if in boastful exaggeration of the mental powers contained within. His spectacles perched upon the bridge of a nose a little too prominent for his liking. It wrinkles with evident distaste. His previous familiarity with the footpath does not allow for its sudden blockage by the metal sphere.

As if for the first time, with his forward direction denied, he paused and looked around him. The strangeness of the snow at last registering. And now, this. There is no logical reason why there should be a metal sphere at this precise location. No logical explanation at all for such an annoyance. Should he progress around it to the left, up the slight incline with the possibility of losing his footing and suffering a grazed shin or worse, or to the right where a patch of particularly virulent nettles discourages such an option? For a moment he merely stands without any conscious thought process at all. Then compromises by advancing one step only, before halting, to reconsider again. The sphere, taller than he is, is obviously artificial, girded by a series of studs that probably serve to bolt segments together, for there are also hairline patterns indicating it to be made up of hexagonal sections. But as for who is responsible for its construction, what their purpose might be, and most specifically why they have chosen to deposit it here to inconvenience the poet are questions for which he's unable to furnish a satisfactory response.

To retreat back the way he'd come is something not worthy of consideration. There are projects, ambitions and dreams aplenty which, having been commenced upon, he'd abandoned, leaving them unrealised. To add yet another failure to his accomplishments, even in so trivial a matter, is something he refuses to contemplate. Nevertheless, retracing his steps would hasten his return to the inviting hospitality of the Black Bull, convivial company and another glass of gin…?

It is at this point of deliberation that he becomes aware that he's no longer alone. A loose swirl of snow drifts past his shoulder. He hears the rapid beat of gauzy wings. Feels its soft flutter against his cheek. Half-turning, he does not believe the evidence of his senses. He closes his eyes determinedly. But when he re-opens them, the giant bee is still there. Even in his wildest laudanum dreams he could never have conjectured such a being.

Standing on the footpath beneath Penistone hill he finds

himself positioned midway between the metal sphere, and a man-tall bee. Well, not quite man-tall, for it is hovering at a point knee-high above the dried-mud path, but even that puts it level with the poet. Its giant wings flit almost faster than his eyes can trace, suspending the bizarre creature so close that, should he reach out, he could touch it. Although he doubted that such contact was possible. You cannot touch a nightmare. Such a phantasm is by nature untouchable. Reach out, it will surely dissolve as mist touched by sunlight. Yet it stubbornly continues to exist.

A startling miscellany of disturbing sound erupts, seemingly emanating from the creature's mid-point. From its lower thorax. He draws back, fearing a dreadful sting that will surely kill or paralyse him. Instead, it emits a burbling and a buzzing, sometimes resembling that of an electromagnetic telegraph device, oscillating in volume. Then words. "Heus." "Ba'ax ka wa'alik." "Salaam." "Hola". "Guuten takh." And finally, "My greetings, sir."

"So you are a talking manifestation?"

"Imperfectly I'm afraid. Forgive my pitiful inadequacy in this respect, Mr Brontë."

Which is the stranger? A giant bee? A giant talking bee? Or a giant talking bee that knows your name? "You know my name?"

"Please forgive my tactlessness in startling you. That was not our intention. Not our intention at all. Quite the reverse. In truth, I fear I was distracted. Distracted too long by the gorse-nectar. But as our subterfuge has obviously failed, I can at least hope to extend reassurance."

"Only the other night as I lay abed I was startled awake by the skeletal apparition of death itself, which reached out its bony hand to claim me. I have a sketch of it, 'Summoned by Death', should you care to see it? So I am not unfamiliar with horrors. Anyway, as I understand it, eminent scientists who have investigated the subject have declared it impossible for insects to exist beyond a certain limited size. Hence you cannot exist. Therefore I refuse to converse with that which is contrary to nature."

"Oddly enough, our scientists long insisted that hymenpotera-sized anthropoids were equally impossible. Clearly both learned parties were mistaken. Perhaps you would care to step inside our machine?"

He focused his gaze through his thick spectacles, into the mosaic compound eyes, the texture of metal gauze, seeking to find some evidence of expression. But could find none beyond facets glittering as wondrous gems. True, the antenna twitch with what seems to be a purposeful manner, although what that purpose could be he was unable to guess. But more than that, this monstrous mutation knows his name! That prompts fascination beyond unease.

"May I enquire of you sir, if – indeed you can be addressed as such – what aspect of my work has attracted the admiration of the bee-people? Although I try to make myself a name in the world of posterity, as yet I fear I have done little either great and good."

"Answers there will be..." The coiled proboscis twitched. A panel set into the metal sphere shifts in response. For the first time the poet experienced a shock of unease. Step into my lair...? A portal had opened in the sphere, unleashing the overwhelming fragrance of wax. He was tempted to peer within. Into an illogical honeycomb, polyhedral in its geometrical regularity. A yellow gloom in which there are other bees, two at least, perhaps more. Operating strange devices with their mandibles and bristly forelegs. Two steps takes the poet over the threshold, into what the creature has termed the machine. Maybe a mistranslation? After all, isn't the being speaking through some kind of voice-box animated by an electrical power-source? A degree of error could be expected.

The floor is spongy, and sticky. Resembling molasses. It adheres to the soles of his boots, while its viscosity oozes up over the welds and stitching. The bee-thing enters behind him. The portal closes. It's already too late to escape. He's trapped within a druggist's mad dream. There should have been fear. There should have been terror. But had he not seen greater horrors in the depths of drugged intoxication? He was still unsure if this encounter was anything more than some hallucination prompted by an opium-residue in his bloodstream.

The poet had sought, and entertained commissions as a portraitist. These creatures have rows of animated pictures, pictures that move in jerky blurs of colour, then flicker and darken. They pore over the shifting images as though they are

10

invested with some special significance. He watches with incomprehension. "Where are you from? Some hidden valley in Brazil? A place in the clouds? Or an imaginary realm such as the Gondal and Angria tales we conjured as children?"

"You will not understand. Beg my presumption. But if you imagine an onion. The layers of an onion that you shim away to reveal the layers beneath. Now think of each onion-layer as a world, one within the other, each a slight variant different from the others. We merely slip from one layer to another."

The portal winks open. Nothing has changed. As if he ever expected it would. The bee leads the way back out. He follows, through a brief swirl of snow. The sticky substance makes his first few paces adhere to the packed-mud of the path, but soon, as he walks, the effect wears off. The creature is leading him back towards the village. Yet, if that should have been reassuring, unease rises like an unpleasant bile in his gut. It's one thing to hallucinate demons, quite another to share them with his neighbours.

The main street slopes down past the Post Office, the apothecary, the Parsonage, and the Black Bull. It is familiar, how could it be otherwise? Except that within the usual drift of villagers, those he recognises, there are giant bees moving freely, murmuring, rustling, buzzing or chittering. Some of them wear colours. Others are harnessed with devices. Yet in every other respect, they are regular bees, two body-segments, upper and lower, in soft gold stripes. Their fuzzy cheeks beneath their bulbous cranium tufted with bristles, their wings vibrating tremulously. Only of giant size. How can such monstrosities even take flight? But they fly.

The poet turns to his winged guide questioningly. It explains, "Here, we are closer to a dimensional overlap, where bees and humans share the world amicably. Further this way are bee-continuums. Further that way, human ones. This is where they merge one into the other. But we bring you here for a specific purpose. A little further, if you please."

The parsonage. His home. But not quite the same. There's a statue constructed of polished Pennine stone. A figure in heroic stature, swirling cloak trapped in dramatic flourish. He does not recognise it. But bends to read the inscription. It says "Patrick Branwell Brontë: 26 June 1817 – 24 September 1848". Something lurches deep within his gut. No, this cannot be. This is surely his night-vision of being "Summoned by Death"? The skeletal figure of nightmare transfigured into this eloquent bee? He stumbles backwards sobbing aloud.

"My apologies, Sir. We should have protected you from this knowing. But I implore you to read the full inscription."

He reads on. "...author of *Jane Eyre* (1847), *Wuthering Heights* (1847), *The Tenant of Wildfell Hall* (1848) and other works of great literature".

"I do not understand." His voice little more than a whimper. A formation of giant bees angles above him, the low-pitched hum of their wings drowning his stammered words. They are heading towards a row of towers rising beyond the Parsonage cemetery. Hexagonal structures resembling the fever-dreams of derangement. There are bulbous airships navigating the fleecy clouds still higher.

"Sir, your novels were originally published under the pseudonym Currer, Ellis and Acton Bell. Following your demise, it was your surviving sister Charlotte who revealed the true authorship of the books, and so created the literary cult surrounding your works. This is surely something that you would wish to know? Is this not the case?"

"Yes... no, I don't know, I don't understand."

Further discussion was instantly curtailed by a loud popping squawk from the voice-synthesiser. "Ah! Slithy Toves. Hasten if you will, sir..." after which his bee-companion moved with agitated speed back up the cobbled main street. The poet does his best to keep up, repacing the way they'd come. His stolen glance back rewarded only by a confusion of images. A group of man-tall lizards...? A squadron of armed reptiles...? A military formation of saurian-beings brandishing projectile-weapons striding or waddling up from the lower extremity of the village towards the statue.

Safely back within the sealed sphere he stares curiously at his companions. "When we converse, who is it I am speaking to?"

A moment's pause, as though considering the question. "We do not have the same sense of individuality as you. So no, when we converse, you are not exactly speaking to the bee you see before you. Although our collective sense means that yes, at the same time, you are. The drone has no individual consciousness, other than as part of the colony, which is a collective hive-intelligence. So these words originate from within this sphere. But one trait we do share with you is curiosity. That is the motivation for the project on which we have embarked. We seek to resolve the legacy of various questions left by history. The fate of the Roman Ninth Legion after they marched north from Eboracum into Pictish Caledonia. The nature of the Nazarene's death. And, if you will excuse our discourtesy, the contested authorship of the novels the statue attributes to you. Unfortunately this entails a degree of intervention in other dimensions that the Slithy Toves forbid. In fairness, they are simply enforcing an inter-dimensional prohibition that we are… contravening. A ban that has some legitimacy in the face of trans-continuum Time Wars that are devastating worlds further down the layers. But we are a curious species. So we seek out inconvenient truths."

Familiarity has rendered the sickly-sweetness of the sphere's waxy aroma less offensive. While his companion's bumbling whirring strangeness in its golden ambience is no longer quite so disturbing. The bee's purring drone is even curiously hypnotic. "My demise. I witnessed my own death. I am but thirty years old. And I know the very day when approaching death will quench life's feeble ember."

"Nothing is certain. In the infinite cascade of levels the possible variations are endless. That is but one outcome. There may be others more favourable, or yet more disagreeable. There are worlds in which you are a mere footnote in the illustrious story of your sisters, Charlotte, Anne and Emily. In which you are considered little more than a feckless dilettante. Please, we make no judgement, we seek only truths."

The portal opens into chill darkness. They step outside into a world without motion, a land of dark abnormality silvered by a bright moon. But a moon from which a bite has been taken from its upper left portion, the familiar lunar face breaking into a spray of smaller moons. In its light he can barely discern a ruin-bedecked horizon of broken architecture. The path on which they stand is fractured with a crackling crispness of ice. The poet's breath leaves his open mouth in visible exhalations.

"In our urgency to depart it seems we have come further than we intended. The moon has suffered asteroidal impact, inducing climate change. We should not tarry here."

There can hardly be a weirder fate to befall a hapless poet. To be brought so thoroughly into confrontation with blind uncaring nature. Yet it is his introspection which predominates. "It is true that my sisters walk round and around the kitchen table, reading excerpts from their latest tales out loud to each other, so they can suggest changes and additions, so they can debate plot amendments and perfect the conversations between their characters. I have watched with amusement. When younger I would also participate. And yet…"

The phrase remained unspoken as a sudden squall of snow announces the materialisation of a second sphere a little way away. With every evidence of alarm the bee retreats back into the machine, the poet hastily following.

"The Slithy Toves pursue us." Another pause between worlds. Again they emerge into fragrant summertime, with drifts of pollen tinting the richness of the azure sky. But looking down the Dale where the village should be, there are towering buildings of buff millstone. A savage Byzantium. And beneath them, teams of enslaved humans hauling massive stones for the construction of new edifices, their labours supervised by hovering bees armed with electrical whips.

"Again, my apologies. You should not have seen this. We overshoot yet again, further into bee continuums where, as you see, the relationship between worldlings is less equal. Yet I would suggest that in your own familiar time, humans enslave and steal from bees in just such a ruthless fashion." Within moments of orientating to its oddness the sudden reappearance of the second sphere sets off another leap.

"So we are doomed to roam without control o'er present hours and through futures wide?" says the poet, quoting one of his own works. The portal opens into sweltering tropical heat. They step out into a rainforest raucous with the roaring of unseen monsters. Through its dense vegetal entanglement the poet can barely discern the contours of hill, pathway and vale. The undergrowth has a thick-piled springy texture, and it trembles beneath him, as if from the stomping of monstrous feet, in an unsettling manner.

He is about to turn and speak to his host when there's a gust of snow. And interposed between himself and the sphere is a

Slithy Tove. For the first time he has the opportunity of observing its foul physiognomy. The unblinking lidless yellow slit-eyes. The green-scaled snout, parting to reveal rows of slavering fangs. A crocodile, or lizard. One that wears a uniform of hinged armour, and carries a musket of hideous design. All this glimpsed in less than a moment, for blind panic speeds his feet, and he crashes away though the undergrowth with nothing more than flight in his mind.

The pursuing sphere has outmanoeuvred them. It had arrived here first. They were prepared, and awaiting the bees' arrival. The breathless poet scrambles and slithers up what should have been Penistone hill, suffering a grazed shin and worse. The Slithy Tove in close pursuit. Reaching the crest of the hill he careens down the slope at the far side, each panicky step taking him further from the sanctuary of the bee's sphere. Here it should be possible to circle around the base of the incline, and reconnect with where the footpath should be. And so return to the machine. But this is so confusingly strange he can no longer be certain in which direction his frantic steps are taking him.

The stench of decay is intoxicating. The sun glimpsed above the tropical treetops is more vast than it has any right to be. Dull red, and extending halfway across the sky. Even the air he's inhaling has a toxicity as strong as gin. Logic fails him. Is he lost in a vision of primeval Earth, or in its far future senility? His legs are weakening. Bursting through a barrier of tall reeds he's shocked to immobility. His forward escape barred by a herd of monstrous reptiles cropping the treetops. The nearest of them turning giant heads slowly in his direction. Involuntarily he steps backwards, and turns. The Slithy Tove raises its bizarre musket. Aims it at his head. And pulls the trigger.

Death. Or something very like death.

The sign above his head, moving imperceptibly in the slightest of breezes, is the familiar Black Bull. He sits beside the wooden bench, a pint of ale in his hand. For a long moment he sits perfectly still, allowing the pounding of his heart to steady, the rasping of his breath to return to something like normal. From where he sits he can see down the slope of the main street. The people are people, nothing more. So it has all been delirium tremens, nothing more? His dream of being summoned by skeletal death, only infinitely stranger. Or perhaps not. The

15

reptile pursuer was not killing him, but returning him, resetting the infinite layers of worlds back to their correct configuration? If there is poetry here it is of a kind far more exotic than Samuel Taylor Coleridge. Dare he write it? Are there rhymes sufficient to tell such a dream?

He lifts his glass. Glancing down he sees a drowning bee scudding in the dark alcoholic tide. He extends his finger into the beer, feels the bee's soft touch as it crawls onto his skin. He lifts it clear of its impending doom. Holds his finger up close to the end of his prominent nose, squinting at the bee through his thick spectacles.

Its gauzy wings dry. It prepares to take flight. The poet whispers to it. "You. Yes, you. I know your secret…!"

LONDON BRIDGE IS FALLING DOWN, FALLING DOWN, FALLING DOWN

Professor Moriarty's last, and strangest adventure.

The rat emerges onto the mudflats beneath Blackfriars Bridge. It pauses, lifts its whiskered nose and samples the foul air.

The mudlark sees it. Squints his eyes at it. A big brute, as big as a cat, or a Jack Russell. And black as coal. It also has six legs. He squelches up to his knees in foul sludge, hunting salvage. Now he searches out a smooth stone embedded in mud, balances it in his hand, like the fast-bowler in a test match, and lobs it. The stone explodes in long gloopy strands of filth as it impacts close to the rat. It doesn't scuttle away. Just shifts its rodent attention around, towards the bratty boy. A second rat appears behind it, from out of the dark mouth of the subterranean River Fleet. Then a third and fourth.

The boy sniffs, wipes his nose with his snot-encrusted sleeve. The sky is dirty with smog. Looking downriver, he can scarce see the dome of St Paul's. Something makes him feel uneasy. When he pulls his leg up out of the mud it makes a vile sucking noise. With long stilting gait he intends making for the firmer shore. But the rats are skittering out of the dark river sewer, as though coordinated, to cut him off. He alters direction slightly, increasing speed despite the deep pull of cloying mud hampering him. Then he stops.

He can hear their chattering. See the implacable hatred in their gleaming gem-eyes. He fumbles down, swishing his hand through scummy water, searching out another stone. He pulls out a dripping gold fob-watch on a gold-link chain, the kind of thingummy that would buy him food for a month. But this time, it's not what he wants. The first rat leaps and tears razor-teeth glinting into the bare flesh of his forearm. He yells and hurls it away. He's bleeding. Through eyes misting with tears he can see the others. A feral wave of them, pouring in to engulf him. He screams, falls backwards in his haste, as the ripping biting scampering six-legged rodent tide overruns him, teeth like a shrapnel of shattered glass puncturing his eyes, gnawing, cutting into him, tunneling into him, furred and bloodied wriggling and rising up his throat and windpipe…

*

He's falling. Loose. Gone. Breath devolving to a glutinous choke. The roar of the Reichenbach Falls sucking at his ears, before it vanishes forever. He's wet as a propped-up corpse in the rain. Tortured membranes hum and vibrate like tympani. Feeling already dead inside him. Whatever they've done to him has fuzzed his brain and tamed his muscles.

"So you're him, Professor James Moriarty, the Napoleon of Crime…?" The speaker would have passed for a respectable company director. He wears his frock coat as it should be worn. A tall, lean, elegant gentleman, his prematurely greying hair lending an air of distinction. He could have posed for a whiskey advertisement in a popular magazine.

"The Corsican himself wasn't physically prepossessing. In the final analysis, it's the strength of will that counts. The will to power that elevates us." Moriarty is also dressed in funeral black, accentuating the facial pallor and high domed forehead. Yet although the laboratory-room is sparsely furnished, his presence fills it.

To ask questions is to cede control. Never let the opponent get the conversational upper hand. An old habit, reasserting itself, even in these strange circumstances. So he turns it into a statement. "You rescued me, from the brink of death."

"Not quite. You died 4 May 1891. You were revitalised from a point just after your death. Neither was the surgery mine. You will address me as Sir Frederick Thomas Trouton, merely the instrument of government responsible for making it happen."

"So I am dead? Yet as good as new?"

"Of course not. Don't be ridiculous. Reanimation is not a pleasant word. But yes, you were ignited by an implanted electro-magnetic heart. For which we have the control. We live in an age of science and reason. Anything is possible."

He was simultaneously aware of the hard metal shell implanted into the flesh of his chest, the sharp wires puncturing the skin spidered around it through puckered white createrlets. And he recognized the truth of the words. He stood there, dripping onto the floor. Dripping onto tiles as parallel as ruled lines. Dripping perfect tears of water from the Reichenbach Falls. But no... not water. His nostrils detect the faint trace of formaldehyde. Not water, but methanol, embalming fluid...

*

Theodore Hadley Hermitage glanced warily at the seething twilight. Dark oppressive clouds are gathering in the slats of sky between the eaves of grotesquely high buildings, and he still has a way to go. Through a storm of vendors yelling and jostling their wares. When the rain begins, it is black. Smoke? Industrial filth? Long dark tears stream down the curve of his umbrella with a steady rhythmic drumming.

Then a plop. And another plop.

The gutters are overflowing with filthy water. He steps off the curb expecting to splash through shallow surface tides of rain swirling around gutters, but his foot submerges ankle-deep. A confounded nuisance. Hermitage curses. Stands on one leg like an ungainly flamingo, and shakes his sodden foot. It's at that moment he notices the golden frog, as big as a navvie's fist, its eyes bulging up above the murky surface of the pool. Their eyes meet. They stare at each other.

His umbrella dips with the sudden weight, and another golden frog slips from its rim, bendy splayed feet flailing, to nose-dive into the scummy water. Then another.

He edges the umbrella back, black rainwater spattering his face, so he can squint upwards. The sky is filled with falling golden frogs. And all around him people are screaming and scattering in fear. Hermitage is a rational man. He's not given to superstition. There must be a reasonable explanation, even for this most implausible of occurrences. He will not run in panic like the foolish herd-mentality of the common disease-ridden mob.

The golden frog flops onto his face. Its mouth open. Its long

19

barbed tongue flick-flickering like a lash. The sting is a bolt of electricity shocking through his face, instantly paralysing facial muscles. Now it's his turn to scream, except the scream freezes in his throat before it can be uttered. He drops his umbrella – a gift from Mrs Hermitage – as he stumbles. Lurching splash-splash-spashity-splash across the waterlogged street, squelching frogs beneath his heels, they explode yellow-green bile that streaks up his trouser legs. His face is on fire. He falls to his knees into the water. A frog on his head. Another falls and bounces off his nose, spinning away like a golden Catherine wheel.

He lies face-down in the street. The street is filled with fallen men, women and horses. Golden frogs hop and flop from corpse to corpse, barbed tongues flicking batrachotoxin venom, blocking their victim's nerve impulses, contracting the muscles, inducing heart failure.

*

The sealed train transports a manacled Professor James Moriarty across Europe. From Interlaken, through the endless-ness of France, to Calais. He watches the fields and the farms spoke past to the clattering rhythm of the carriages. He uses the time to learn more from his impassive host, Sir Frederick Thomas Trouton, whose manner relaxes a little as their hours of close proximity extend. Although not versed in matters scientific, he spoke of the principles of wireless telegraphy in relation to a Scottish mathematical physicist called James Clerk Maxwell. How it was proved possible that electromagnetic waves could be propagated through free space. That was enough for Moriarty to base some speculation about the workings and control of his new heart. While all the while sensing his body healing, his energies returning.

From the train they were escorted onto a Royal Sovereign class naval vessel, and hence across the channel. Conclusive proof that whatever he was being subjected to, was happening under official auspices. That adds little to what he already knows. He'd been snatched from the grave for a purpose. What that purpose was he has nothing to base guesses upon. So he waits. This time is a gift. An opportunity.

There was a time when he'd been too quick with the blade.

That was his trouble. Yet the firm grasp of a knife in the hand can be as reassuring as a good cigar. When the circumstances are right, he will take advantage of them, and turn situations back towards those of his own choosing. In the meantime, he was allowed to stroll the deck, with vigilant seamen observing his movements. At first, too much physical exertion was taxing, leaving him weak and breathless. But he establishes a discipline, forcing his body to strengthen. Then pausing at the rail to watch gulls riding the wake. The glimpsed coast of England stirred no response in his electro-magnetic heart. Soon it became obvious that they were entering the Thames estuary, towards London.

He knows London. Where is Colonel Moran, his long-time colleague, can he be located? What are the statistical chances of scheming escape? Surely prison cannot be his destination? If that were to be his fate they might as well have left him dead. No, there's more, something he is as yet unable to guess at. If it were possible to contact Moran, to get a message to him? He was constantly watched. But everyone is corruptible. Everyone can be used. It's simply a matter of mathematics, of appraisal and calculation.

Westminster at dusk. He was escorted down to a rowboat and sculled across to the landing stage beneath the gleaming bronze effigy of Boadicea, queen of the Iceni. There he was handed over to a civilian guard with cold civility. Four discretely armed men, accompanied by Sir Frederick Thomas Trouton, and an air of slight distaste. He's placed a top hat on his head, and wears a greatcoat against the November chill. The amber glow from evenly spaced gas standards creating a receding series of luminous spheres along the embankment. The guard were insistent, but more through curiosity than fear; he allowed himself to be led into the place of government. The very seat of this ridiculously pompous Empire that had plundered the world in the name of civilization. Along corridors gaudy with the soft light of chandeliers, hung with oil paintings of the great and the noble.

Now, he was so close. He could taste it in the stale air of repressed vice. They halt. Trouton knocked at a heavy door, and waited, in a long and sticky silence. At a barely imperceptible voice they were admitted. Two armed men first. Then Moriarty, with Trouton. Then two other armed men.

21

"Ah, Professor Moriarty I presume. I'm so pleased to make your acquaintance," said the elderly gentleman, rising from behind his desk to extend his hand.

*

Alice Carpenter kicked away the rotten woodwork of the door. It swung on rusted hinges. She glanced nervously up and down the night alley. No-one. No-one there to see her. No-one to stop her. People say there are new strangenesses in the grimy air. Surely nothing stranger than the night-visions that gin brings her. She's not been living well.

She stepped over the threshold into the vast emptiness of the derelict warehouse beyond. She scrunched the door up closed behind her. She'd earned a shiny shilling. The lecherous old man she'd picked up in the tavern hadn't lasted long, trembling and grunting with an asthmatic wheezing at each excited thrust, with so little effort on her part. That shilling would have paid her overnight lodgings. But she's spent it on third-rate gin instead. So yes, this will have to do. At least for tonight, perhaps longer, if she's furtive, if she doesn't draw unwelcome attention to herself. Be patient, control those despicable urges that bring reprimand and disgust.

She shuffles across the floor. There are mounds of dusty crates, cobwebbed together into ghostly structures, the phantom landscape that has become her domain. By right of trespass. There's a flight of narrow steps up to the first floor, which has regularly spaced windows looking out over London rooftops. She should be able to see as far as the dome of St Paul's. Oh fiddle, she should be able to see the Palace of Westminster somewhere over... there. Were it not for the foul veil of grime and smoke.

A sound behind her. A scrattling. She half-turns. Surely no-one else has got in here before her? Damn. She mouthed six obscenities in a row. Her eyes strain and adjust at the mildewed twilight. Something crawling at the nape of her neck. A scary unease. Something is not right. She must be framed against the window. She moves a stealthy pace aside, so as not to make herself a target.

The sound again. Not a human sound. An animal. She quests

around for a weapon. She can see eyes, gleaming yellow eyes, and a low snarling growl. She calculates rapidly, she has time to reach the stairwell, if she moves quickly. Not too quickly as to draw attention, to incite the beast instinct of the hunt. She sidles as unobtrusively as she can. Then halts abruptly, hung in mid-step. Stopped by a second pair of gleaming eyes emerging from the stairs.

She gawps as they're closing in on her between light and dark, between the quick and the sharp-edged stillness. Two of them... no three. Maybe more, coming at her. At first they seem to be dogs, driven predatory by ravenous hunger. They're as big as large dogs. They snarl with carnivorous intent. She backs away. Her expression skewed in horrified terror, but commingled with a deep sense of poignant resignation. Every good thing in her life turns sour. She feels a consummate sadness at having missed the solace of at least one night's dry shelter. At having her usual bad luck to run afoul of these vile abominations of nature. They are not dogs. She stumbles up against the whitewashed wall, cobwebs enveloping her. The foxes have gaping sabre-tooth jaws bristling with needle-sharp fangs. They close in for the kill. Alice is about to die in excruciating pain, but that's always been the inevitability of her fate.

*

"There is evil abroad in this city, Professor Moriarty." Faced with the Minister's penetrating stare, guilty men would have nervously confessed on the spot. And innocent men confessed to crimes they'd never committed.

"Why should this be a concern of mine? This is a city that has attempted to break and imprison me. It has treated me with nothing but implacable hatred. You have brought me back from death to inform me of this? Better you cast me into Bedlam."

"If we could find a jury to convict you, and a prison capable of holding you. No-one alive – even temporarily so – knows the London criminal underworld better than you, Professor. And, although I feel it indelicate, I must point out that you really have no choice. We reactivated your heart. We can deactivate it just as easily."

"You offer inducements other than threats?"

"You have your life. I'm empowered to grant you even more in recognition of your compliance. What would you have of Her Majesty's government?" He spoke as though discussing the weather. Nothing of greater import than that.

"Death has a tendency to clarify thoughts. Everything yields to its logic. Naturally I'd expect immunity from all charges. That goes without saying. Beyond that, I need time. Indulge me a moment. Mathematics was my first passion. Applied to the celestial movement of the heavens, through astronomy. A science cleanly elevated above the squalid vileness around and within us. Given time, I'd voyage to the roots of the principles which govern it all, to the Aegean isles to live out my remaining days in humble scholarly pursuits."

"Granted. But first you provide the services we require of you."

*

The Thieves Guild meet in a vaulted cellar beneath a tavern in Frith Street, a notorious place of ill-repute. Moriarty was a man of method. He required freedom of movement to carry out his enquiries through the various cells of the criminal underworld. Although always aware his life now depends upon the invisible cord tethering him to those who hold every beat of his heart in balance. He resents that control. But there are yet things to learn that can be turned to his advantage. Colonel Moran had dropped off the map. He was nowhere to be contacted. So once he found himself discharged onto the familiar streets of London, he made Frith Street his first port of call. Moriarty retrieved a foaming tankard of stout from the barmaid, who smiled a lewd invitation that offered more corporeal promise, and retired to a corner alcove to observe proceedings. This is a place where pickpockets and embezzlers meet, the high and low. He didn't have long to wait. He was greeted with some hostility.

"Moriarty, they told me you were dead." A blunt and unsubtle stubble-bearded thug, Grimes chops the ends off his words as if about to use them as handspikes.

"As though even the grave could hold me." He could not resist the jibe.

"Nevertheless, you can't expect to return as though nothing

has happened. Things have changed." He wrinkled his long nose and shook his head in a warning gesture. A hidden element of cruelty about him, something not quite defined, but associated with his eyes and mouth. "And you needn't look so righteous. I grant I don't look the part. It's been said I resemble a boxer, and they meant the breed of dog, not the pugilist ring artist. But you pay respect to me; things have changed in your absence."

Moriarty gloated over the fellow's ludicrous impudence. If, in his absence, they were fighting to establish a new hierarchy in the network of crime, and Grimes was the best of them, he has little to fear. "I seek nothing, my friend. You are welcome to your empire of dust. All I require is information from this band of unruly brothers. Nothing more."

"So be it," grumbled Grimes.

The brooding tension was shattered by the shambling gait of a tatterdemalion on crutches, who greets them both cordially, raising his darkened glasses in a conspiratorial manner. Although known as Blind Pugh, his were little more than afflictions of convenience.

"I hear rumours of strangeness bedevilling this great city of ours," prompts Moriarty, while enduring the beggar's over-familiarity.

"You could say that, yes," admits Grimes. "You refer, no doubt, to the plague of six-legged rats as big as cats. I've heard tell they've called the military in; they're burning and demolishing buildings in a pitched war against them. Then there's them cockroaches as big as yer fist invading Spitalfields. Yes, we know of these things."

"I hear there are fanged bats that descend upon unfortunate travellers," burbled Pugh gleefully, his fingers going rum-ti-tum on his crutch. "That they assume human form and drain the blood from their victims. But that could be hearsay."

"Shut your foolish grumble-hole," barked Grimes. "Yet there are shining phantom wolves in Kensington."

"What can you tell me of these phenomena?" pressed Moriarty.

Grimes shrugged, and looked down snarling pleasantly. "What concern is it of ours? Don't we have enough to occupy our time, what with our duty to the redistribution of wealth?"

"Of course, you are absolutely correct. Nevertheless, indulge my idle curiosity about such arcane matters…"

Pugh snorted phlegm, and spat onto the floor.

The information he needed emerged only gradually, immersed in sidetrack reminiscences and irrelevant details. It amounted to what Pugh could have said in a single name. Bedlam.

*

"You must incarcerate me in Bedlam," demanded Professor James Moriarty.

"I will countenance nothing of the kind," retorted Sir Frederick Thomas Trouton.

"You have legitimate reason to do so. Am I not a danger to the state? Has not the sanity of my criminal endeavours been called into question? You have every moral right to cast me to the tender mercies of Bethlem Hospital. In fact, I insist you do so. With certain precautions, which I will outline."

He was conveyed in a sealed carriage with high barred window-slats through the streets to St George's Fields in Southwark, south of the Thames, to the walled sanatorium, a forbidding neoclassical structure that ran along a substantial portion of Lambeth Road. Escorted inside, Moriarty was placed within the building's east wing, devoted to individual cells occupied by the criminally insane. For the first time, his resolve faltered. Madness moved around him with its many voices, whispering of odd distractions, stirring his fears with taunting ghost fingers. The wailing of tormented souls mingled with the stink of human filth and open drains. A melancholy dirge played on a penny-flute by the unseen inmate of the adjoining cell. Already his head throbbed with its endless din, as though malevolent demons were wielding sledge-hammers within his skull. If any place could be said to be the incarnation of evil, this is the place. A place to test the most extreme limits of reason. He sat cross-legged in his cell, attempting to ignore every distraction out of existence. To stay resolute. Focused on what he's here to do.

He did not have to wait long. A key in the lock. The stout door swung inwards. A runty little newcomer, standing arms akimbo, between two thuggish asylum-keepers.

He recognized the intruder. "Doctor Conrad Von Herder. Academe is a small world. If I recall alright, you were struck off, disgraced for malpractice."

"Professor James Moriarty. Your reputation precedes you. You're correct, I was Von Herder. I was that person. Here I am known under another identity, 'Robin Lafayette Lord'. You and I, we share an academic past, we must discuss your work on the Binomial Theorum, a work which ascends to such rarefied heights of pure calculus few can appreciate it. It is something of a privilege for me to entertain so abstruse a mathematical scholar, a fellow man of esoteric sciences. You, alone among the inmates here, perhaps unique in the city itself, will have some appreciation of the great venture upon which I'm embarked."

He beckoned. Moriarty was led through poorly-lit corridors, ascended spiralling stairs towards the asylum's central dome. An abattoir smell. "We have surgeries and operating theatres where we strive to interpret and cut deviant behaviour from the brains of the mentally afflicted. This is valuable clinical work we expedite here for the benefit of all men. It allows me to continue the earlier work for which I was vilified, but under the mantle of the law."

An operating table fitted with straps and restraints. A rack of knives, clamps, saws, scalpels cleavers and drills. Some ominously murky bell-jars containing organic samples suspended within, sections of coiled human brain-matter.

"But there is more." The adjacent room into which he was led was lined with cages. Each cage contained experimental creatures, each abomination more monstrously malformed than the last. Some of the cruel and hideous species miscegenation were mewling and whimpering piteously. He recognized the familiar odour of methanol, used to disinfect and cauterise surgery. Tension crackled around the room like destiny sparking up out of a telegram.

"Vivisection. You are splicing and restructuring these unfortunate creatures? But surely they're unable to breed true?"

"You underestimate me. I'm grafting my chimera within the very seeds of life," the man who had been Von Herder said, wispy locks of white hair plastered to his forehead with perspiration. The domed ceiling contained his voice, its arches carrying it to the highest point and amplifying it, giving it overtones of authority.

He opened the shutters looking out over the endless roofs of London. "See here, over the polluted stench of the city. We live in desperate times, Professor. If we don't change our profligate ways we face terrible retribution. Before the coming of the Romans, before the time of the Anglo-Saxons, this river-valley was a verdant place of forests, bountifully thronged with a wealth of wildlife. The air was clean. The very waters of the ancient Thames were as clear as crystal, and swarming with fish more numberless than you could count. What have we done? What terrible crimes have we inflicted on this good earth? We have sinned against nature itself."

"These are elegant sentiments indeed, sir." Moriarty attempted to arrange his reactions coherently. This man's mind is a pit of horrors. He must go deeper. To argue might be wrong, but too hasty compliance would also be suspect. "Yet I fear you speak of crime as though an exact science, when it is nothing of the kind."

"The idea of right and wrong is inherent in every living soul."

"You think so? You really consider it such a simple matter? As a rational man, it leaves me bewildered that the world even functions as it does. We are a pimple of reason riding a primeval mass of terrible instinct, fears and terrors. Life cares not a tinker's cuss for who lives it. Those who attempt to impose some kind of moral order are deluded in their endeavours. No, there are no rules. We invent them for our convenience, and can just as easily extricate ourselves from them as we so choose. Are not the greatest criminal minds those of whom we know nothing? Those who scorn so-called natural justice entirely? Those who see beyond the limited view to the reality that underlies it? I'll wager many of them sit comfortably robed in ermine in the House of Lords."

"I believe in simple truth and justice. Those who trespass against eternal rules must stand accused, condemned and punished by cosmic law, if not by man's institutions. I seek merely to adjust the balance of nature. Evil is eating this city alive. So I induce and anticipate changes that natural selection must inevitably introduce, if only time allowed. I accelerate the process. Arm nature in ways that allow it to retaliate. To reclaim what it has lost. Yours is a monstrous philosophy. A blasphemy against all that is decent."

"No, that is my gift. To have the clarity to see where others are blinkered. Why else would you need me now?"

"I need you because you are a scientist. Because only the man capable of deciphering *The Dynamics of an Asteroid* is capable of understanding what I am doing here. My creations are going to bring the very bridges of London crashing down. And you have the abilities I need to assist me in my work, and to succeed."

The man who had been Von Herder summoned the two thuggish asylum-keepers. "Kindly return Professor Moriarty to his cell. We will give him time to consider, until he decides to join me in my crusade."

*

With slow deliberation, he recalled every detail of what had happened with as much clarity as he could summon. After all, it had been his qualities as a methodical analyser that gained him his chair at Durham, before purely academic pursuits proved too limiting. Before he found horizons constrained by the loop in the river Wear to be too narrow, and his cool appraisal that a playful application of his great intellect to the conundrums of crime could yield greater rewards. And he would have succeeded. Were it not for the intervention of a certain Great Detective. A worthy adversary in this, the most dangerous game of all.

Yet an editing and reviewing process is essential. A criminal enterprise must be more than an instinctive lashing out of rage. It should be a calculation offering tangible gain. Even if one shares something of Von Herder's disgust, there must be more than mere revenge. There must be quantifiable advantage, otherwise the equation is devoid of logic. So the greater personal reward lay in putting a stop to his madness. The experiments had to be terminated. An accident had to be organized. And the plans he'd meticulously devised had brought about that end.

Pugh was not only a man who resembled a length of boiled string, he also had the fortunate attribute of invisibility. He could hobble to and fro virtually unnoticed, as he pleased. He entered Bedlam in pursuit of his beggar's trade, slept there when no alternative accommodation presented itself, and left as and when he chose to leave. No-one notices a blind cripple. For a financial consideration he could be induced to serve as a useful conduit for inmates coherent enough to require lines of communication to the outside world. To bring books or food, to carry messages to family, or colleagues. Even from Moriarty, to Trouton. Hence the syringe that was concealed in his cripple's crutch.

When the attendants discover Moriarty apparently dead, his body was removed to the chill mortuary basement. Once the self-administered drug that stilled his electro-magnetic heart lost its potency he awoke on the twilight slab, covered by the crisp white folds of the shroud. It was the early hours of darkness. Night magnified every small sound a hundredfold in the rank air, acting to increase the intensity of his awareness. The howls and shrieks of agonized madness that always haunt the corridors distracted night staff sufficient to allow him to move with a degree of freedom, so that he was able to retrace his earlier path towards the laboratory. The firm grasp of a knife in the hand, even a cadaver's dissection blade, can be as reassuring as a good cigar. He'd lost none of his efficiency at wielding it. The human body has pressure-points that result in swift silent death when administered by those versed in anatomy. He usefully employed those skills as required.

The minor inconsistencies in the plan he'd formulated did little to adversely affect its essential contours. Of course, formaldehyde and methanol are highly flammable. An incendiary device merely awaiting his spark. The confrontation with Von Herder, armed with an air-pistol, was unanticipated. With the laboratory wrecked and in flames, crawling with vile unleashed chimera, his furious appearance was vexatious. And could have been problematic. Moriarty was facing death… yet again, he should have become immune to its threat by now, but he was not. He was fear-frozen at the prospect. It was at that moment that Von Herder was seized from behind by the nearer of two huge mutant eagles. The startled expression on his face as he was raked by the enormous talons was not without its comical aspect. Moriarty felt his lips draw back in a fierce grin of relief.

The obstacle that the armed man had presented was lifted, as he himself was physically lifted by slow degrees by the beat of the horned bird's mighty wings, so powerfully the acrid flames flared away on all sides. Von Herder was screaming commands.

Then he was just screaming as he was levitated high through the ruptured ceiling and out into the toxic night beyond. The two savage razor-beaks tearing at each other as they squabbled over their twitching dangling human morsel. Higher they soared. What a panorama of London such heights must have gifted him, if only he was in a situation to appreciate it. Moriarty tarried no longer than he could safely do so, which was adequate to see the insane vivisectionist ripped apart into two bloody segments, the eagles flapping lazily towards the silver moon with one half of him apiece.

The screams of Bedlam were even more intense that night. Nightmares to test even the wildest derangement. Moriarty watched from a safe distance outside the encircling walls as the explosions ripped through the dome and the guttering flames incinerated all evidence of the vile experiment. He could feel each detonation deep in his bones. And if there were witnesses within this fortress of madness, who would believe testimony from Bedlam itself? The secret was safe. Nevertheless, the night breeze moved around him with its many voices, whispering of odd distractions, stirring his hair with taunting ghost fingers.

Sir Frederick Thomas Trouton was as good as his word. Professor James Moriarty, the Napoleon of Crime, was allowed to leave London without a backward glance, all evidence of his previous misdeeds expunged from the records. Thus freed from the past, the future had also been kicked away from beneath him. There was nothing left for him to cling to. The world had never understood him, and it would never understand him. Humanity was on the skids. To get the smell of it out of his nostrils for a while would be a relief. He travelled by train to Venice, and from there to the seething stench of Istanbul. He stood gazing out over the Bosphorus towards endless Asia, the golden dome of Hagia Sophia rising behind him. Such a magnificent city of culture and classical legend, befouled by the obscene squalor of the unclean masses. He stayed only long enough to release a breeding pair of giant six-legged rats into the Basilica Cistern beneath the city. To redress the balance.

He boarded a Greek ferry which took him to the port of Argostoli on Cephalonia, and from there to Vathy on Ithaca. This was the perfect location, the final destination of Odysseus after his mythic trials. Moriarty felt a sense of kinship with the ancient mariner, they were fellow adventurers who had gambled with the gods, and outsmarted them. He leased a substantial property known as the Captain's House, overlooking the bay, and furnished it as best he could to his taste. He installed a writing desk and purchased a number of hardback journals. He would write his philosophy and personal history. Explain himself to the intellectual community of the world.

He sat in the shade of a time-warped olive tree in the courtyard, sipping a cool drink, mentally rehearsing his forthcoming literary work.

In answer to a pulse from London, his electro-magnetic heart stopped.

THUESDAY TO FRYDAY

When two make three, there are repercussions that persist for a life-time...

I could never marry Lucia, because she was Catholic. And we are not. I made that decision aged ten. Hardened my heart against her. And live to regret it. Some people are only attracted to each other because their demons know each other.

They said Jingle had been run over. They said she was hit by a car on a feline mission when she was crossing Beverly high road at night. An unfortunate accident. No-one was to blame. But I know better. I saw her, a mess of smeared fur and spewed-out guts. A car had not done that. She had exploded from the inside. I never told anyone else that. But I'm telling you, now.

The village lane is fraught with terrors. Lines it is hazardous to cross. Mr Sizer is a misshapen misanthrope who lurks in his musty cottage, emerging to target verbal abuse at any child unfortunate enough to be in range. And crows. Crows are even more scary, because they don't keep to the lines. They alight unexpectedly. Black as death. And further up the lane, there is the posh house where Lucia and her sister Loretta live.

Lucia always had that witchy quality that mesmerizes me. The day we ran away together she said, and I quote:

> *"Me and you*
> *make more than two*
> *together, we make three*
> *me, you and we."*

It's maybe half-seven or eight, daylight paling. She'd been crying, I could tell. A dusting of freckles across her ten-year-old nose. She said, "I'm never going home. Never again," with an intimidating defiance. "We can go away and they'll never find us. We'll be alright, won't we...?" As always, I'm out of my depth. Struggling to do what's right. Afraid to appear weak in her eyes. "Tell me we will always be together." Less an appeal. More a statement of fact. "Me, you and we, we will never be apart..."

There's a stupid song from the 1950s, "arm and arm over meadow and farm, walking my baby back home..."

It's as we were being torn apart that Jingle exploded. After the uproar over my 'abducting' her had subsided without the disruptive invoking of legal proceedings – "did I touch her? did I make her do things?" – Lucia and sister Loretta are switched away to a convent school in Hull, while I fail eleven-plus and go up to the local secondary modern. Around the same fimefix we were rehoused to a council prefab in Cottingham, some miles away. There was always a sneaking suspicion in the back of my head that strings had been deliberately tweaked, to force us apart, to keep Lucia distanced from the negative pull of my baleful delinquent gravity. Is that really likely? Did her father's influence have that reach? Maybe. It's not impossible.

It never comes with a smooth Papa-Oom-Mow-Mow easy-flowing consistency. More a series of hard indigestible chunks. Difficult to swallow, impossible to digest. An episodic life. A poorly-plotted mini-series that never got past the first test-screening, then got quickly sidelined and axed. Incidents happen constrained by their own dimensions. They don't necessarily link into a narrative flow, which annoys the hell out of the methodical part of me. One thing doesn't logically lead into the next, odd bits of time are left loose and hanging. Abrasions that don't heal. Wounds that still ache across years. Splinters of time impaled in your brain.

But worsty-worse was incoming. By then I was working in the accounts department at a print works, and Thursday to Fryday, weak-knightly, she was temping. Said she was at Uni. She'd dyed her auburn hair black. Wore black blouses with long black sleeves to her wrists. And she has a boyfriend. Marty is a big solid Leader of the Pack guy with a revved-up BSA motorcycle. She straddles his pillion, as he accelerates away. And I'm the nervous indecisive kid with bad acne and a stammer. How can I compete? I can never compete. So I just talk to her, whenever there's the opportunity.

I even manage to get her to go for a coffee. The very air shimmers. There's no-one else alive from here to the great spiral galaxy of Andromeda. I'm dumb and clumsy. Just me, and her, with that same kind of spell that bewitched me. All the things I should have said. All the things I should tell her.

Instead, "There is no god, is there?" she tells me.

"No. There is no god. Just us lost little humans."

She smiles, as though I've made the correct response. "My life was always odd." Her eyes gleam with secrets she does not intend to share. "I always lie. I can't stop. I get bored telling the same story twice. But I want to tell you this. All those years ago, when we were kids, I envied you…"

"You, envied us? But you were the posh kids up the lane."

"Maybe. You always seemed so snug, so happy in your little bungalow. You never saw what we saw."

It was then she told me she'd left home, that she was in some kind of squat. There'd been a family falling-out. An acrimonious split. People didn't talk about abuse back then. Of course, it happened. People knew it happened. But it's not done to mention that sort of thing. Was it physical or sexual abuse, or both? I don't know. She never says. There are just hints and suggestions.

"I didn't grow up bad. I had to learn it."

"We all have scars. We get used to it."

"Oh smart-arsed one, what do you think you are? Some kind of analyst?"

Later, I watch Lucia with Marty. I watch in a bitter rage of suppressed jealousy as Marty throttles down. See his swagger, his big lopsided grin. And my hatred rises, into a physical thing. I watch that delightful way girls have of fanning out their hair as she slips her jacket on, and just for a moment the blouse sleeve button at her wrist snags and comes away, and I lie awake that night ripped at what I've seen. Seeing her. I see the razor-scars up her arm. Some glistening fresh. I close my eyes so tight the world blacks out. She's in pain. I see her drawing the blade across a softness of skin, dazzling-bright blood seeping up along its track, biting her lip to stifle the pain-inhalation. The good pain that anaesthetizes the bad things in her life. Concentrates it down to the cleansing needle-point singularity. The dance of light. The sharp sting of incision. The pulsing numbness that lingers.

I strain to reach out. To touch her damaged spirit.

She phones in. Marty's come off his bike, cornering too fast. When he's discharged he walks that same swagger, but with a John Wayne limp. She's back at Uni, or someplace. A memory trapped inside a hollow space.

And I've met Abigail. Safer, more stable by far. A stupid song from the 1950s, "I can't get away to marry you today, my wife won't let me…" With Abigail it was solid, if passion-free. She was solid when I ran the car off the A64 and they breathalysed me and I was way over-limit and lost both license and job. We pull through. She was solid when I had that stupid fling with Patricia. She cried, and yelled at me. But she stayed. At the end, when she found the breast-lump, we were more affectionate friends than lovers.

And despite everything there were drifting might-have-beens about Lucia. We'd have torn each other to bloody fragments. She'd have devoured me. And yet I can't help wondering. What is she doing now, at this precise moment? Is she in a relationship, is she happy, do her thoughts ever drift in my direction…? I hold onto her memory tightly. Because she's dead to me, and might fly away.

*

I'm the world's last human. The last person alive.

As I weave down the Headrow, turn right into Briggate, phantoms flicker at the edge of vision, the shadows cheat my eyes, making movement where there is none. The stores fill with ghosts, half-figures on the edge of being. They form and shift around me, pacing me on the precinct, skittering alongside me, then rearing into the upper floors, mounding up into crowds, swelling, billowing, peering down, grinning like the walking dead. Animated corpses.

I dare not pause, or stare too closely. Cowards dare not look. I shuffle in stony silence. The silence of stones. A stoned silence. As if I'm stoned on something Papa-Oom-Mow-Mow toxic. A shadow in a shadow world. Semi-detached from the world. On a parallel path, but one step out of proper synch. Trapped in the twilight zone. It's weird being the world's last human. In a silence made up of a thousand hushing sounds from the surrounding street. The spectral conversations of the dead, spoken with dead tongues from dead mouths. Stirring dead air into echoes.

Leeds at world's end is a place of sensory deprivation. My life in lethal stasis. I squat down at the corner, outside Harvey

Nicks. A man-shaped thing, but a quivering see-through jellyfish-form of a man shimmers by, half-smiling. A family with a small dark girl, maybe seven, maybe ten. She looks directly at me with sharply bright eyes. Almost as though she sees me. She has beads in corn-row braids, and a red top.

Abigail is dead. And since my wife took the endless sleep, nothing is real, and everything meaningless. It's like my own death. Everything fractures. The world has stopped turning around me. I never even mastered the art of ironing my own shirts, because she does it.

What stupid deity designed a biology where the cells attack the host body beyond repair? Riddling that soft caring organism with black. The priest wore black too. I spend time in Aegina, for no other reason than that we came here together many years ago. Mythos and ouzo pleasingly blur memories of bougainvillea and pistachio, but a fatigue that all the drugs in the galaxy couldn't kill. I stroll around the curve of scrubby headland. There's a shingle cove where you can lounge and immerse naked. Two primal salt-fluids, one suspended within the other, blood and seawater. Placental warm.

I might swim out to the point where it's no longer possible to swim back. Join the mouldering seabed bones. Hellenic warriors who'd faced the Persian fleet here in antiquity – in those beautiful triremes at Salamis. Now rotting together in the lap of tides. Pecked by crabs. Starfish eyes. Kelp hair. Seahorses darting in and through an open ribcage warted with barnacles and periwinkles...

The pouting sail of a passing yacht snaps me back. I was close. So close it terrifies me.

My rage could rip the roof off the world. Smash cities. Leave a Cursed Earth of endless desolation to mirror the numb deadness inside.

Alighting back in Yorkshire, once more alive in the living world, things are getting nastier. Saxton's England First-ers marching and chanting, with motives black as death. Scary, because they don't keep to accepted lines. The government panicked into sliding out of the European Union. Enforcing ethnic expulsions.

Our daughter, she'd met a French-Canadian at Uni. Now she's a Canuck. We iChat, which is... how do they phrase it? –

Oh yes, a comfort. A comfort, that's what it is.

I once imagined that at the precise moment of death we get a chance to speed-edit our lives, go back and amend or fine-tune incidents, kiss those girls we were too nervous to kiss. Say those last words to your mother you never got to say. Kiss your wife for the last time. Then I imagine that what if this is the speed-edit, and I'm already dead? This is where I get to correct the things I did wrong, do the things I never got to do – now, before it all goes black.

Lucia isn't on Facebook, although I tweak and twiddle. Women shapeshift across the years. They marry and change their names, or some do. But quite by chance I stumble upon her sister, Loretta. She's found Jesus in a big way. Her timeline is littered with bland homilies about the gift of joy, salvation and lurve. Beatific visages radiating cosmic light. Angelic conversations. She responds to my messaging with polite formality. Yes, she remembers me. She's pleased to make contact and hopes I'm happy. I persist for information about Lucia. Not wanting to appear a creepy stalker, selecting my words carefully. Delay the messages, one day, two days, then send. The world won't end any sooner for having to wait. Lucia was in Ireland for some years. Now she's returned and lives near York. Nothing more. Despite patient well-spaced follow-ups, anxious not to appear over-eager or troll-obsessive. Sometimes you make haste slowly. Wait. But there's nothing more.

I go into her 'friends' file. Lucia is not there, although there are what could be kids, even grandbrats, extended family. I check out each in turn. PM a few, to no response whatsoever. I delve into Loretta's photos. A wedding. Smiling holiday groups. Faces I don't recognize. Scrolling back there's just one that has me reeling, a scanned-in black-&-white family shot from the 1950s. Maybe snapped at Butlins? Mum and Dad, little Lucia and smaller Loretta. Both girls sit close beside Mum. Dad sits slightly apart, in a loose-fitting suit, a comb-over of hair. A smug smile, maybe even a leer? I study the photo, deciphering body-language. Two and two make seventeen in my head.

Why no other, more recent, sisterly photos or links? Has there been a row, a falling-out? About religion? Or dark family secrets?

Then, totally unexpected. An email. From Lucia. Obviously

there's been some soundings-out, some responses ignited by my probes.

I sit and stare. Scarcely daring to click. There's that thing about the kick inside. I feel that kick inside, and it leaves me breathless. Papa-Oom-Mow-Mow, merry meet and merry part and merry meet again.

*

A bistro by the Ouse Bridge. There are barricades and diversions. Police with visors down and riot-shields, just in case. Marauding tribes of shaven-head men with beer-guts and flag of St George tattoos. Why's she have to choose today of all days? Posters and rolling-TV news document the visit. If Saxton gets in – and the pundits predict he will, things are going to get a whole lot grimmer for racial minorities.

She chooses latté, a walnut scone with strawberry jam. I watch her. Lost in the same wonderment, sinking in the same quicksand. Her hair. Her eyes. The motion of her breathing. The softness of her skin. She's none of the clichés I'd half prepared myself for. Not the witchy New Age goddess with healing crystals, herbal teas and tarot cards, the hanged man, tower struck by lightning. Not the Goth eccentric in blackness and tattoos. The mad cat-woman who scares the neighbourhood kids. Just very sensible patterned print top and faded cargo-pants. Only the anti-fascist badge pinning her loose scarf to indicate such a normalcy is in itself as much a game as a Magritte image. We are both aware of the layered deception. After all, the word 'lucia' means light.

She says, "I knew you'd come."

"You couldn't have known. I didn't know it myself."

"And yet you're here. Together, we are three.

Me and you
make more than two
together, we make three
me, you and we."

"Wait a minuet, I never really understood that rhyme. Well – yes, I know the top-wise word-game. But there's more to it, isn't there…?" My body refuses to respond to normal signals from my nervous system. She sucks the real from my cortex, and fills up

39

the emptiness with mush. The fear is in my bones, like a ghost. Frozen for a heartbeat. Falling out of control.

"You're so smart, I swear that if you had half a brain you'd be almost dangerous. Of course there's more to it. The dark side of my soul is drawn to the dark side of yours. Together, they form a whole, a separate discrete entity neither of us can control."

"I don't believe in souls."

She shrugs. "So call it the psyche, the subconscious. Call it thanatos, the will to darkness. And it only works with us, me and you. I've tried it with others but – whad'ya know, it's down to us, just me and you, no-one else."

"We were never a couple. It's not as though we were ever a couple."

"It could never have happened that way. We'd have killed each other."

I laugh nervously. As though it's a joke. Although I know it's not. "We never even had sex."

"Only in my imagination." A rare flirtation lights her eyes. "We fucked each other in the head. Sometimes we still do. Time and place are only something your mind creates, only boundaries your mind makes."

She still has it. She still has that ability to unsettle. She's a sigh inside my head.

As an evasion strategy I indicate her badge. "You're politically involved?"

"That's why I need you. Times are bad." A pause as I consider that 'need'. "After the Romans left and things fell apart, this was part of the kingdom of Elmet, you know that? Then it was invaded by the Northumbrians, who in turn were conquered by the Norsemen who establish Danelaw, which existed until the Normans. You see what I'm getting at…?"

"Frankly, no."

An irritable gesture, as though she's speaking to a halfwit. "Change. You can't resist change. Stability is sterility. What they're doing now, the isolationists, the purges and expulsions, they can't go on. They must be stopped. England First means people last. Humanity loses out."

"It's not as simple as that. Anyway, I don't see what we can do about it."

"You're wrong. It is simple. That's what makes it magical. So simple it's sweet on the tongue."

Yes, I get it. Even when you reject Catholicism, its habits remain. She's traded spiritual commitment for political commitment.

"You using your sugar?" When I shake my head, she picks up the two sachets quite nonchalantly, and shoves them into her shoulder-bag, for use later. Then, "Do you remember when we ran away from home?" Another dizzying shift, into the teasing intimacy of shared back-story.

"Of course I remember. I remember every detail."

"Do you remember it now? Close your eyes, do it, do it for me now."

Feeling self-conscious, I do as she says. As I always did, as I always do. No will to resist.

"Are you there?"

"Yes..." It's maybe half-seven or eight, daylight paling. A shivering strangeness. It's then the pressure drops. As though I've stepped over a precipice edge, Papa-Oom-Mow-Mow. Sorting out what I'm seeing from the bursts of light ripping my brain. The sky moves sideways in an abrupt wash of riding shadow. As though my own head's no longer mine, in a claustrophobia that's also placentally warm. Smothering into the dark. It's like she's passing her hand clear through my head, again. She can slice me to pieces. She has that ability...

The motorcade enters Ousegate. Three long black cars. Crowds heckle and jeer behind police barricades on the left. Across the strip more crowds chant and jeer.

I re-run the clip over and over.

The lead security car. Then Saxton's car. Then the back-up car. A couple of motorcycle outrider cops. Digital numbers flicker, sports updates and Stock Market figures ribbon across the screen-footer. A 'coptor overhead. Some network or other.

The chill drops abruptly. A creepy-crawly feeling. Barely noticeable. A mere fluctuation of colour contrast. The time-code slows as I adjust remote. This is the exact time. A little way away, at this precise moment, we are together in that bistro. My eyes closed. Lost in recall.

A faint darkening around the centre of the three cars. Breeze-blown exhaust maybe? Then the detonation. Sharp and vivid.

The explosion that lifts the rear of the car up off the asphalt with such force it's flipped clear over. A napalm-bright eruption of hellfire, like in the movies, only more so. The motorcycle outrider skids and keels over. The other one throttles to a halt, and goggles mouth-agape. The third car veers across the central aisle, demolishing a bollard.

A viral clip that's ricocheted around the world. More hits than the Reality Star secretly filmed smoking crack.

Perspective-shift to another feed. Aerial, from the 'copter. A moving blur pixilated to protect sensitivities. Saxton killed outright. His personal secretary a human torch, staggering from the wreck. Now wired-up in intensive care with 60% burns.

I get up to percolate myself a coffee, marvelling at the ordinariness of doing it, every action so normal. Then slouch down and back-up the clip, to re-run it more carefully, freeze by freeze as close as possible. Focusing on the faint darkening around the centre of the three cars. Back-forward. Back-freeze. The enigmatic shadow refuses to clarify, but I recognize the outline of its dark figure, a tortured caricature that shifts like a magician's dissolve. A haunting resemblance that teases the back of my mind. Then, yes, a stupid song from the 1960s, "it's a little bit me, and it's a little bit you, too." I spill my coffee. It explodes across the floor between my feet. And yet I'm more surprised to find that floor still firm beneath me.

Crime Scene Investigation discount terrorism, Jihadi, or concealed assassination weapon. No group claims responsibility. Saxton was a controversial figure. He had enemies. They're working on a sequence of possibilities, a number of lines of enquiry.

But I know. I never told anyone else that. But I'm telling you, now.

We are three.

Jingle was an unfortunate victim of an undirected lashing-out of mental anguish.

Marty was my jealous envy, amplified unwittingly through her prism.

Now she's learned how to target us. Me, you and we.

I watch the clip again.

Yearning for her to contact me again. Dreading the moment she does.

THE DOOR TO ANYWHERE

Look at what the cat dragged in…!
A small alien Rat-thing. How to get it home again…?

This is how it started. This is the way it happened.

Next door's cat has caught something. Jingle, a mean moggy with tiger-stripes and bad attitude. It's in the back-yard space, and it's killing something. Derek watches. He watches from the kitchen window as his transistor radio plays. The something is trying to get away from the killer talons. Jingle allows it the brief illusion of escape. Then pounces again, toying with taunting paws.

The song on the radio finishes. It acts like a signal. And once he's arrived at the decision, Derek moves fast. To the kitchen door. Out into the yard. Jingle sees him coming. Grabs his prey and makes for the gate with it. Derek cuts him off. Jingle darts behind a row of potted plants. He's quick. Derek is quicker. His hand reaches and grabs scrawny feline neck. Jingles writhes and wriggles. Derek grasps tighter. The prey is seized in vicious cat jaws. Derek closes his fists in tight around the windpipe. Jingle is kicking and squirming. Claws slash lines of blood across the back of Derek's podgy hand. He curses, and hangs on. Shaking the cat now.

Drop it. Drop it. Release it.

Coughing and spitting, Jingle drops it. Derek holds the cat to him, firmly, but more reassuring now, stroking the short fur as the retching cat recovers. He opens the gate, throws Jingle out. He lands on all fours and shakes himself, as Derek closes and latches the gate. Locking the predator outside.

Then he returns to the victim. It's injured. Derek turns it over where it lies on the paving. There are puncture marks. It's breathing in short jerky-sharp gasps. But what the hell is it? Derek is not sure. A kind of rat maybe. A bald hairless rat. A bald hairless rat with a lizard's tail. But strangest of all, it's wearing clothes. Or what looks like clothes…

To an adult, the steps would seem ridiculously small. Little

43

more than a descending heel, or an ascending toe's purchase. But this size makes them personal to twelve-year-old Derek. A domain designed and exactly suited to his requirements. A place to sit, listening to the discordant music of the house. A place to sit, looking out over the receding grid of backyards, and the terraces beyond the dividing wall. A place uniquely his own, in which to exercise complete control.

Derek Edge. A rather strange solitary moonfaced boy, who plays silent games of eyes and ears.

There's a tall window climbing the turn of stairs up from the entrance hall. A lead-mapped window made up of differently tinted floral art-nouveau sections, each stained glass insert centring on a round white Yorkshire Rose. So that as you mount the steps one by one, the panes shift into focus, blurring the vista of rooftops, backyards and outside toilets into magical single-colour patterns...

From the landing the narrow creaking steps climb further upwards to the hunch-backed attic, a steep ascent that unleashes a whole mythology of weird fantasies. Brush-stroke ripples in fade-patched emulsion form caricatures that breed two-dimensional odysseys acted out across imaginary plains and oceans. A triangular sail of peeling wallpaper hangs away from the wall, showing an intricate network of fissures in the shaded damp-patterns on the plaster beneath. In its shadows he sees landscapes of infinite mystery and invention complete with bridges and deep chasms, forests and craters. Continents navigated only by spider's rigging. The arc of light cast by the ever gently swaying bulb defines the limits of the legendary dark wastes that spawn mutant barbarian hordes, that sweep across the half-night towards the lands of light – only to confront the forces of long-sunken Atlantis. And over there John Carter battles the great jaws of carnivores across the dying deserts of aged Mars. And the pyramids of Quetzalcoatl squat in hidden folds untouched by Cortez. Silverfish swim through the window's spongy wood surrounds, and woodlice, prehistoric in their hard shells, scuttle from the light as you bend a section of linoleum back from where it abuts the wall.

Dreams are good. Reality is tougher. Occasionally the rise and fall of phantom empires gets disturbed by the reality of the frequently nameless faces who take up temporary residence in the attic room above. Their creaking footfall destroying proud towers, stranding the voyaging longships beached beyond the reach of heaving waves, stilling the plunderers heading sword-in-hand for Ultima Thule. The descending or ascending figures – alternately blushing, puking, flushing anger or jealousy as they pass through the light of the 'mosaic' window, until they move, pass over the stairs, and disappear to attic or street. Temporary boarders who stay for a weekend, a month, never longer than three months. Some are truck drivers. Some are salesmen. Labourers on short-term contracts.

Some grunt greetings, or curses. A few even pause to pass the time of day.

Twice, invitations are offered of tea – or perhaps more? – if he'll only ascend to the attic, is that possible? Each invitation ignites new scenarios, but nothing more, once the stairs are again solely occupied. Carefully considered variations on a set of themes – international Diamond Smuggler, a furtive wife-murderer on the run from the CID, a serial-killer selecting his next victim...

Derek scoops up the ratoid. It is warm. Its jerky movements a little unsettling. There's blood on his hands. He's not sure if the blood comes from the creature, or if it's his own from where Jingle opened up his hand, from where it stings with faint thrills of pain. He carries the thing inside. Mam and Auntie Jean are out. They'd probably yell at him. Tell him to get that disgusting object out of the house. But it's hurt. It's hurt bad. He carries it up the stairs onto the landing, then into his bedroom. He lays it gently on the carpet then scavenges around for something, he's not sure what.

His glasses have run down his nose. He pokes them back up again. There's a shoebox under his bed. Some old plastic toy soldiers in it. He tips them out. He scrunches up some pages from *The Beano* and sculpts them across the bottom of the shoebox. Then carefully lifts the creature inside, and lays it into the warm nest. There's not a lot more he can do. He's done the same thing with injured birds before. Sometimes they live. More often they don't. Life is cruel. It's the shock, more than the injury that kills them. He places the lid over the shoebox. He's done that with injured birds too. The darkness is soothing for them. It's their instinct to sleep in darkness. Perhaps it'll work on this thing too.

He slides the box beneath his bed. Then he sits on the bed. Perhaps he should give it some water? What does it eat? Maybe a piece of bread? Or cheese? Instead he picks up what's left of the comic. He'd scrunched up the inner pages. The outer four pages are still there. He begins reading them again. Soon there's the sound of movement from downstairs. Mam's home. It'll be time for tea soon. He drops the comic onto the coverlets and sets off downstairs to meet her. He's hungry.

Derek sits on the sofa eating a hunk of toast with cheese melted over it. Mam sits at the table with the latest boarder from the attic-room. Mr Zill, or something like that. She's done him bacon and eggs, mushrooms, tomatoes with bubble 'n' squeak. And a mug of Yorkshire tea. Why 'Yorkshire' tea? If there are tea plantations on the Pennine slopes out beyond Huddersfield they never get mentioned in Geography at school. He's Irish, or Polish. His hair receding, and what's left of it close-cropped, so his thick bull-neck runs sheer from collar all the way up. Like he's from some heavy-gravity planet. His shirt is dusted grey with cigarette ash. His trousers are worn pinstripe, fastened at the waist with a broad belt. Derek can't always understand what he says. He supposes it's Polish, but doesn't really know what Polish sounds like anyway. It could equally be Russian. Or Martian. Anyway, the conversation that goes on behind him is boring. He can't follow the details. It sounds like the man's voice is shot. While her voice is a scratchy but cogent drone that goes on and on without ever actually reaching anywhere.

Derek concentrates on his fully-illustrated colour reference-book of British wildlife. Field-mice, Pine Martens, weasels, Natterjack toads, water voles. But he can't find anything that even remotely resembles the creature. Perhaps it's not a native species? He puts the book aside, it's no use. What if someone's brought it in from... say, Ethiopia, to keep it in a special temperature-controlled tank as an exotic pet? Only it got away? But why did they dress it up in clothes, in a tight little red jacket with belt and gold studs? Unless they're training it for a show. It could have escaped from a circus. But there are no circuses here at the moment, none that he knows of in the area.

Which leaves few other options. What if it's a miniature alien from the far side of the Moon? In which case it must have a miniature spaceship. Where would it land? In the park? On the brambly slopes of Barmston Drain? Maybe it accidentally crash-landed on a surveillance mission and its ship is damaged somewhere, awaiting repair? Are there other survivors, or only him?

Mam is still talking to the Russian. He can't seem to get a word in edgewise. He just grunts or nods every now and then. Just to keep her happy. Derek sneaks the crisp corner of toast with a warm ebb of pale melted cheese covering, and folds it into his hankie. Without saying a word he stands up and leaves the room. They hardly notice. From the entrance hall he goes up the stairs to the landing. The next flight of steps continue up to the attic-room. But he turns right, into his bedroom. Once inside he raises the lid carefully and peeps into the box. It's lying still. As though it's dead. But no, there's a tearing snapping sound from deep inside its throat. A disgusting choking sound. He slips the piece of toast in, besides its head, then puts the lid back.

In the morning he gets up and puts the transistor radio on. It's Saturday. He sits on the bed, scratching his groin. After several long moments of nothing in particular he remembers the rat-lizard. He pulls the shoebox out from under the bed and hefts it up onto the bed counterpane. He's wary about looking in, unsure what he'll find. It might be dead. But if it's not, and it's recovered, it might jump out at him. Trapped rats attack you, and rip out your throat with their sharp white teeth. Everyone knows that. He lifts the lid cautiously. And it's gazing back at him with bright little sapphire eyes. Startled he slams the lid back. Waits a moment, then lifts it again.

They regard each other with an equal curiosity. It's obviously still hurt, the scrunched-up paper snugly around its body is discoloured with spots of blood. But it's conscious and alert. Derek smiles at it. "Hello, I'm Derek" he says. "This is my bedroom. You're safe here. I won't hurt you."

The radio is playing. But something is wrong. He only becomes conscious of it slowly. The record they're playing is sticking. It keeps repeating the same phrase over and over. He grins at it. This is good. The record is by Hank Locklin. The phrase it keeps repeating is "please help me, please help me, please help me..." It hits Derek a moment later. He switches back to the rat, his mouth wide.

47

"You? You're doing that. How are you doing it?" He looks at the radio. He looks at the creature. He looks back at the radio. The music has resumed again as though nothing is amiss. And maybe it isn't. It's just here. This rat-creature has done it. "Yes, I get it. Please help me. I understand. But I don't know how. I don't know what to do that will help you. Hank. Maybe I should call you Hank? What do you think about that, eh, Hank?"

He gets up nervously and opens his bedroom door. There's noise coming from downstairs. Mam and Auntie Jean. They're up and moving around. Doing things. He closes the door again and sits on the bed beside the box. The creature is watching him, Hank, its eyes follow his every movement. Another record on the radio. Neil Sedaka. "Climb up, way up high. Climb up, way up high. Climb up, way up high."

"Climb up? Climb up what? The stairs you mean, you want me to take you up the stairs? I can't do that. No way. Sorry pal." It looks back at him. Its stare is unsettling, intense.

Some time later he hears noises on the stairs. Mr Zill is going down, clump clump clump. Then the muted sound of conversation downstairs. He can't hear what's being said. But he can imagine. Mam will be brewing a pot of tea. He will sit at the kitchen table, drawing on a cigarette. Him and his thick heavy-gravity bull-neck. Wait.

"Derek, are you up?" Her voice shouting up the stairwell. "We're going out to the shops. Half an hour, you'll be alright won't you? See you soon." The door slams. The radio is playing, but there's no other sound. Derek waits for a moment, just to be sure. Then gets up, opens his bedroom door, and listens. No, the house is empty. He looks across the landing to where the steps lead up towards the attic room. Climb up, way up high. Why should it want to go up there? Perhaps he's got it wrong. Perhaps he's misunderstood the message. He looks back into the box. It meets his gaze, and holds it, unwavering.

"No Hank" he tells it, "no, sorry, I can't. I'm not allowed to." He picks the box up carefully and carries it across the landing. He walks with measured tread, up the first step, then the next one, climbing one at a time. At the top of the flight of steps the door is closed. He tries the knob. It's locked. He places the box on the top step, makes sure it's in a safe position, then stumbles back down to the landing. And further, down the stairs past the mosaic window into the kitchen. Mam has a key she can use if she needs access to dust and clean. He knows where it's hidden. The bottom draw beside the sink, beneath the tea-towels. Yes, he's got the key. He pauses. The house is empty. The clock ticks loudly. He can hear the faint burr of traffic from the main road. But the house is empty. Half an hour she'd said. Probably it would be longer. Once she and Auntie Jean get to the shops and they get to rummaging around, it tends to take them longer than intended. But can't take chances. Mr Zill has gone out too. Perhaps he's only gone as far as the off-license. Or maybe to work, whatever it is he does. He always carries a large case whenever he goes out. No way of telling how long he will be. But he's frequently away for a long time.

Holding the key tight he hares back up the steps, back to where he'd left the box with the rat-creature in it. Why is he doing this? He knows he shouldn't. It's as though something is overriding his better judgment. As though Hank is influencing him. He slots the key into the lock. His breath caught in the back of his throat. He's been in the attic-room before, with Mam, when she's been cleaning. After one boarder had left, but before the next had arrived. He'd been in there, it's got a sloping ceiling, but it's just a room. Nothing special about it. Why does Hank want to go in there? "Climb up, way up high. Climb up, way up high. Climb up, way up high." It doesn't make sense.

The key turns. The door opens inwards. He picks up the box with Hank inside it, and steps over the threshold. That's when things get seriously odd. The first thing he sees is the door. There's the bed, which has been left unmade. But in the space beyond there's a door which definitely shouldn't be there, and wasn't there before. He places the box on the untidy contours of the bed and crosses to the door. The doorjamb is free-standing. The door is closed. Derek walks all the way around it. He pushes it, but it's solidly fixed and doesn't move. As he circles it and comes around the other side, looking back at the way he'd come in, he sees more. The waste bin beside the bed is full of tissues, and also bones. Delicate white bones picked clean. As though he's been sitting on the bed eating, a bogey-man sucking morsels of meat from small limbs, leaving only the bones. Wiping his fingers on the tissues, or maybe holding the small animal-limbs with the tissues so he doesn't mess grease on his fingers. Even worse, resting on a crumpled newspaper centre-spread there's a bloodied meat cleaver.

There's a scrattling sound. Hank is getting agitated. He's raised himself, obviously straining hard to do so. His little hands grip the edge of the box to pull himself up. Derek watches, half inclined to go and help, but a little scared. Hank is indicating, waving to him. Derek doesn't understand. But the little creature is smarter than a whip. There's a sideboard with a vanity mirror. It's always been there, alongside the chair and the tall wardrobe. But on the sideboard, beside a pile of well-thumbed girlie mags, there's a box-shaped something covered over with a towel. Derek glances around. There's no sound from the rooms below. He's still alright. He paces across, and lifts the towel. There's glass beneath it, like a fish-tank. An aquarium. He lifts the towel higher, and steps back in alarm. The tank is occupied. Six of them. Ratoid creatures just like Hank, trapped inside. They're moving around, prowling on two legs, upright, walking like people, but their lizard-tails circling and curling. They are pale grey like Hank, but one of them has a greenish tinge, another slightly aquamarine blue. Their clothes are different too. He just gets a blurred impression of colours, one wears a peaked hat, another baggy-pants, like bloomers.

But already things are clicking into place in his head. And it's horrible. The creatures. The small white bones. Mr Zill has been catching them. Storing them here. And eating them. Somehow Hank had managed to escape, only to fall foul of Jingle, the mean moggy with tiger-stripes and bad attitude. Derek tests the tank. It's heavy, but not too heavy. He teeters it down onto the floor. The creatures inside are chittering in an agitated way. He sets it down on the floor, then slowly tips it over onto its side. The creatures inside brace, and move across as it settles.

There's a moment of panic as they tumble out of the tank and begin skittering around him, chattering in high-pitched squeaks. He lifts the shoebox with Hank inside down beside them. They gather around in obvious concern. Derek stands back and watches in fascinated amazement. They've helped Hank out of the box, supporting him. He's walking a little, experimentally, as though he's unsure. He winces and stops. Then walks again. They're heading towards the free-standing door. Hank turns and beckons to Derek. Obviously, he can't reach the doorknob.

50

Almost without thinking Derek steps across to the door. There's a kind of coded security-lock with symbols, like a miniature fruit-machine. He can't make head or tail of it. So he stoops and holds the palm of his hand out. Hank steps up onto his hand. The touch of the little feet is warm. He can feel the slight dig of sharp claws. He lifts Hank up level with the doorknob. The little creature spins the combination. Derek pushes. The door opens.

They step through into another world. It's bright, but dark at the same time. Two silver luminous moons. But dark ochre sand that scrunches beneath his feet, and sheer cliffs on either side. As if they've emerged into a crevasse, narrow here, but widening further on. The rat-lizards act totally unsurprised, they cascade through the door and across the gritty sand while Derek just stands stunned to immobility. He's about to follow them but pauses, the door is still open behind him. He can see the room framed by the precise square-cut of its jamb. If the door closes he'll be trapped here. Wherever here is. He steps back out of the door, back into the room. Picks up the bin, and uses it to wedge the door open.

Then he returns, crossing a mystic borderline from here, to somewhere else. Leaving the familiar world behind pace by pace, following the bizarre procession beneath the two moons. Is it Mars? He knows Mars has two moons. But Mars also has a thin atmosphere that would be impossible to breathe. And he's breathing fine. The air smells a bit odd, a kind of spicy mustiness to its taste, but it's breathable. It could be ancient Mars? Millions of years ago. The door could be a trans-dimensional portal through time as well as space? He's read of such things in Science Fiction comics. They're rounding the edge of the cliffs, although some of the freed rat-things are scrambling up the cliff-side itself with impressive agility. Then the twilight plain beyond grabs his breath away. A castle, or a sparkling city of blue lights, or a great many-branching tree-dwelling – or a combination of all three, outlined on the horizon beyond the straight-cut canal, dark purple plants growing in profusion along their banks. Lots of little rat-things busily engaged in little groups of frantic activity. Flittering lights in the sky moving between unfamiliar constellations. This is their world. Their planet. It could be billions of light years away across the galaxy.

He's tempted to go further, but he's scared. Not scared of

them, but Mam might come back from the shops any minute. She'll be mad if she knows he's trespassed into the attic-room. It's strictly off-limits when there are boarders. And Mr Zill. What if he comes back? He takes a few further steps, so he can see better. A brilliant pulse of light is rising from the city-castle-tree, climbing ponderously into the sky. He watches it ascend. Maybe this isn't the creature's home-world? A colony that they're carving out of a more arid wasteland on a neighbouring planet?

He looks around. Hank is a step behind him. The little figure is holding its punctured side, but seems otherwise OK. He's indicating back towards the open door. Derek takes a last long lingering look at the magical planetscape, then moves to follow the creature. With a single step they're back in the attic room, the other world standing framed like a three-dimensional slab of strangeness at its centre. Derek scratches his groin in confused amazement.

The sound of voices from below startles him out of inactivity. A man's voice that sounds like it's shot. A woman's voice that's a scratchy but cogent drone that goes on and on without ever actually getting anywhere. Mr Zill. Mam. They're down there now.

Hank is signalling impatiently. Derek stoops to pick him up. He's pointing in a 'hurry-up' fashion with his small-clawed hand. Derek carries him across, shoves the door so it only slightly ajar, so that Hank can reach the security-lock. He begins switching and reconfiguring the settings.

A tread on the steps. Moving up past the coloured glass window. Time to get out. Hank is still busy with the lock tumblers. Derek stands in nervous dread. A stomping on the landing now. Hank waves his hand. Whatever he was doing he's done. Derek lowers him to the floor. He steps off his hand with surprising delicacy. Derek moves across past the bed back towards the door leading onto the stairs. Slips the key into the lock, and turns it. Mr Zill will expect the door to be locked. It'll give him a few moments. But the bogey-man is coming up the steps towards the door. Derek looks around wildly. Gets down and rolls under the bed. There's dust and hairy-fluff, but there's nowhere else.

A sound at the lock. The knob turns. The door opens. From where he lies beneath the bed Derek can see Mr Zill enter. Things

52

happen fast. The big man takes it all in with one glance. The upturned tank, empty of his captured creatures. The dimensional door only slightly ajar, with the single ratoid standing there. With surprising speed he drops his case and takes two mighty leaps. With the first, retrieving the bloodied cleaver he vaults over the bed. Derek watches it happen. Hank is also watching the big man. Timing his next action. At the last moment he ducks through the door and vanishes from sight. Mr Zill's second great leap rips open the door as he hurtles his way through in pursuit. There's a blaze of superheat and a blinding flash of light. Derek cringes beneath the bed, breathing dust and a toxic sulphur-stench. For a second, even with his eyelids clammed shut, he can see a vision of volcanic hell, gushing magma, the exploding surface of a raging supernova sun. He can feel his eyebrows burn. Smell torched fabrics. The barbeque smell of cooking meat. Mr Zill is crisped to nothing. The door slams shut. The light is gone.

Derek lies shocked still. He crawls out gradually. There's a red light pulsing on the security-lock on the dimensional-door. It flashes faster, and faster. The light stops. The door vanishes. Derek watches it shimmer, then implode leaving only a ghost-image on the air. Then not even that. It is gone. There's a strange silence in the room. A melancholy feeling. Hank is gone. He'd reset the door's dialling code tuning it into another galactic destination, set self-destruct, then used himself as bait to draw Mr Zill through it.

Derek stands there with his big mouth moving soundlessly in his round moonface. He thought of the little guy. How he'd shaken him loose from the cat-jaws of death. How he'd laid him in the shoebox. How Hank had altered the radio-sound into messages. Then how he'd sacrificed himself to destroy the predator and protect his own world. And to rescue Derek. Just as Derek had rescued him from Jingle. Perhaps he'd have recovered from his cat-inflicted wounds. Maybe they'd have eventually killed him. Either way, it was a heroic thing to do. Now he was gone. Torched to ash. And Hank wasn't even his real name. It would be something unpronounceable beyond the human tongue. Qwertyuiops or something. It's sad. Life is tough. This is the way it happened. This is how it ended.

What now? He picks up Mr Zill's case. It opens easily.

There's a row of slender pouches inside stitched side-by-side. Traces of blood too. It's not difficult to draw nasty conclusions. The bull-necked bogey-man from the heavy-gravity planet going on safaris through the door hunting and capturing Hank's people, keeping them fresh in the aquarium-tank, and the ones he doesn't eat he butchers and takes them in the case. Takes them where? To a secret dealer? A meat-trader connoisseur of alien delicacies? A network of hunters and consumers spread across the country, across the world…?

Derek sits on the steps; to an adult they'd seem ridiculously small. A mere descending heel, or ascending toe's purchase. But this size makes them exactly suited to his requirements. A place to sit, listening to the discordant music of the house. He can hear Mam talking to Auntie Jean, their voices carrying up from the kitchen.

"Strange about Mr Zill, leaving that way, without giving prior notice," his mother is saying. They'll be sitting across the kitchen table from each other. He can see them in his mind's eye, Man and Auntie Jean. Shoving cig packs from one to the other. Have one of mine. No, have one of mine.

"Yes. But at least he paid a month in advance," she laughs, "so we're brass in pocket."

Then they switch to talk about something else, something more interesting.

Derek had done what he could. Tipped all the little alien bones into the case and hidden it in his bedroom. Then, when it was safe to do so, carried it to the brambly slopes of Barmston Drain. He dug a shallow grave and buried the bones with whatever dignity he could summon up. They were sentient beings who'd been horribly murdered and devoured on a strange planet. They deserved better. It was all he could do. Then he threw the case into the drain, watched it float, gurgle with filling water, then sink from view. The evidence was gone. No-one would ever know. A couple of days later he returned. The grave had been dug up, the muddy soil scattered. The bones were gone. Crunched up by an urban fox? A mangy dog?

The stairs are also a place where damp-stains form caricatures that unleash whole mythologies of fantasy. Now they feature a new hero, a little sword-wielding rat-lizard who leaps through dimensional portals to outwit dull bull-necked hunters

54

from heavy-gravity planets.

BEAST OF THE BASKERVILLES

Arthur Conan Doyle's *The Hound Of The Baskervilles* is a work of fiction. There never was a 'Phantom Hound'. Or was there...?

Waking with thunder in his head and a mouthful of cobwebs. It's happened again. Time Slip. Another lost hour. Brain tumour, it must be. Pressing into the brain tissue.

He's sitting in the Honda Jazz pulled up on the lay-by. This is where it happened. Tatem eases the door open and steps out onto the moist gel of compressed leaves. A faint smell of musky decay in the air. He stomps up and down until feeling returns. Leans up against the curvature of the car to regain his breath. As he's done before. Returning to this same place over and over again. As though through repetition he'll understand. This is where he left Sheena. This is where he saw her for the last time.

A little way beyond the lay-by edge the side road curves lazily away down from the embankment. Not much of a road. Little more than an overgrown track. He trudges with hands thrust deep into his pockets. No whisper of wind to move the dying foliage on the arch of overhanging trees. Halfway down he begins to see the rooftops of the village. The steeple of the church. The roof of the Baskerville Arms pub.

Why would Sheena have come this way? But where else could she have gone? There's nowhere else. He pauses. Had she paced this very spot? Had her sandals squidged onto this muddy verge? Had she been alone? Six months since that last parting. Spring, through to autumn.

*

"Hound? There never was a hound. It's just a story." Holly is emphatic.

"But it was a story before Arthur Conan Doyle wrote it. And

56

it's been a story since."

"I know all this Sherlock stuff. But Conan Doyle is not a reliable witness. He believed in fairies for a start. You know that…? He believed that fairies existed."

Why go on? Bereavement hurts in a unique way that only other bereaved people can understand. Tatem understands. Doyle knew bereavement. If that determined his need to buy into supernatural elements of life, he's not going to deny him that. This is the way it works. Sometimes the desperation to believe is more powerful than analytical procedural logic.

They make unlikely companions. Tatem had flinched at his reflection in the wing-mirror, more scary gaunt than seems right. Like death, not so much warmed up, as microwaved tepid. Mid-life hair already receding at high temples. While Holly is more Watson than Holmes. Nondescript, that's how they'd describe him. The opposite of a description. A little run to seed. So ordinary, he's invisible in a crowd. Nothing to distinguish him. Yet he knows his stuff. Knows the area, its Sherlockian connections. That makes him a useful ally, and when the occasion arises, he can dress that ordinariness up in a coat and a hat and a chosen air. And immediately becomes somebody, whoever he chooses to be. His personality has the same chameleon quality. He can see the bare, meagre facts of a case in hand, relax his own personality and gradually come to see it as they originally appeared to the quarry he was tracking.

On the face of it, a dozen random facts can be spun in any number of ways to create a variant number of situations. But to Holly, those facts can have only one correct arrangement. They've emerged from one situation, and only one. Therefore, if the correct sequence can be found, the original situation can be replicated. So the task is just that, to find the one correct way in which the facts fall into alignment. A twist this way, and that, until the Rubik planes fall into alignment.

It had been a hot Spring day, travelling through Princetown. Sheena reading her Kindle sprawled across the back seat. Tatem wished she wouldn't read that *Shades of Grey* stuff. He finds it a little disturbing. When he mentions a Boyband on the radio, one she likes – surely? She sneers disdainfully. Its Indie guitar-bands now with floppy hair and attitude. Boybands were last year, or the year before. Keep up, Dad, keep up. She's changing. He's losing something of her in the transition. It was then he'd hung a wrong turn, finding them snarled up at the road-works. The lights change, and they only shunt up three car lengths before they change again. Come on! He drums fingers on the steering wheel. The dark hair on the ridge of his knuckles bristling. He spools the window down. The air stinks of exhaust. He spools it back up again. How can you get lost in so small a place? He loses time. Gets increasingly irritable.

By the time they're back on route he's behind schedule. Not that there's any strict schedule to stick with. Carmen will be waiting for the pick-up, but there's built-in flexibility. Nevertheless, punctuality is important. Time is something to be forced into shape. So is this unplanned detour significant? He's been over it times without number. Replayed it in different ways. He should have refuelled. But he hadn't. Instead he hung out for the next filling station. And that's when it all began to go wrong. The fuel-gauge ticking into the red. Nudging zero. Driving on fumes.

According to the map this embankment is a by-pass. At one time the road took a leisurely loop through the village. Now the new road bypasses the village, then it goes on for just over a mile towards a roundabout with a services area. If he'd not taken the wrong turning in Princetown…? But he had taken the wrong turning. Burned gas, burned time. So why stop? Why stop here? Because there's a convenient lay-by. Because he can walk from here to the roundabout and back. It was doable. Sheena stays in the car. Don't get out. He'd warned her not to get out. He's sure he could remember telling her that. He must have done.

It was growing dusk by the time he trudged back with the green plastic can of gas. It cost him a deposit. They'd grinned at him when he explained, like he was stupid. Who runs out of gas? There was a full moon rising. Bone-white light, through the arch of trees, along the embankment. There's the car, where he'd left it. The empty car. Sheena had vanished. This was the moment he kept returning to. She'd been there, sprawled on the back seat. Something about the way she sprawls, the way her skirt rides up, that makes him look away. Hot under the collar. There was even the indentation in the upholstery shaped by her weight. But she was no longer there. And the world opened up to swallow him. She's gone.

"How long were you away?" says Holly.

"A mile there. A transaction. A mile back. How long does that take?"

"But you said it was dusk by the time you got back. Full moon. That implies it took you longer."

He's explained all this before. To the police. To Carmen. But most of all, to himself. Was there anything else? Something he'd missed? He'd tanked the car. He blasted the horn. He'd walked up and down the verge calling her name. Perhaps she's sneaked out to take a piss? Why else would she not stay in the car? At length he'd noticed the side-road sloping down, and followed it until he found her Kindle. She'd come this way. Or been brought here. Dusk thickening. Huge white moon glimpsed through the trees. And something in the stillness.

What exactly was it in the stillness? This is where it gets vague. So much is solid and certain. But the shape moving in the trees is not. Imagination. Something he's conjured or elaborated since. A fox or a badger. But memory says different. It was darker, heavier. And the howling, was that coincidental? A mournful dog in the village? Or something to do with the lurking darkness?

A man. The police had tried to get him to say it was a man, before they lost interest, and filed it 'unsolved'. He wished he'd never mentioned it. It was something so vague that at first it was little more than a shimmer of peripheral vision. But the more he concentrates, the more he tries to force detail onto its shapelessness. Six months of memory replay distorts hints and suggestions out of shape, into monstrous hounds, black dogs, shape-shifter were-beasts teleported through dimensional portals via neolithic Henges and standing stone alignments. Hifalutin words. Symptoms of reality unravelling. Gnawing madness.

"The Baskerville Hound? There never was a hound. It's just a story," Holly insists.

"But it's a persistent story. There are regular cryptozoological sightings of giant-hounds. That's what they call it, the unexplained reports of unknown non-native predators. They've found spoor, droppings. There are photos of the Beast of Bodmin. There were regular sightings of the Black Beast of Ossett. Conan Doyle researched his Sherlock Holmes story into legends of a supernatural cursed hound on these moors. I've googled this. I know."

"Do you believe that's what you saw that night?"

Expressions chase themselves across his face. "Belief is too strong a word. I don't disbelieve."

"Lycanthropy is a metaphor, nothing more. For the dark primal urges within each of us."

"Have another drink. Might make it easier for you to swallow those metaphors."

He allowed time for that to sink in. "Who's your favourite screen Holmes? I'd go for Basil Rathbone every time."

"Peter Cushing can do no wrong. He did a very respectable *The Hound of the Baskervilles* for Hammer in 1959."

"What about Bandersnatch Cummerbund?"

He wigwags his hand. Signing give him time. We'll see.

The two men enter the village. The village feels sick. A single twist of road lined with decaying houses. A church at midpoint, its graveyard lost beneath wild brambles and nettles, across the road from the pub, The Baskerville Arms. "Traffic used to come through here. Travellers would call off at the village store for a newspaper or a sandwich. Or get a drink at the pub. Until they built the by-pass. Now the cars all speed past along the embankment without sparing a second glance at the turn-off sign."

They keep walking as far as they can go, following the road until it peters out into nothing. A few derelict cottages collapsing into the encroaching mire resembling the bows of doomed ships sinking beneath the slime, which shimmers away in dark corrugations of mud and reeds, slurred by mists of dancing midges that turn like iron filings in a magnetic field. They backtrack a little way towards the pub. There's nowhere else to go. The door creaks as they stoop through the low entrance into the bar. A couple of locals in a conspiratorial huddle beside a big old fireplace. Low dark beams with horse-brasses.

"Bottled only," grunts the landlord. "No cellar. Not anymore. No-one's got a cellar anymore. It just floods with water. So we got bottled, alright?"

"Budweiser. That'll do fine, thanks."

If anyone can convey a shrug without moving a muscle, the landlord does it.

They retire to a corner table. "No cellars. What's that in the

Shades of Grey book about the demon lover with the S&M torture-dungeon. No such luck for the poor pervert here. The embankment did that for him too. Blocked off natural drainage so the trapped water-table just keeps rising. The village is slowly drowning. Most people moved out. Only the most tenacious or peculiar are left now as it all submerges into fen-water."

"Grimpen Mire."

"No. There never was a Grimpen Mire either. That was Doyle's invention. When Holmes' adventures happened in London he stuck pretty close to the A-to-Z, or whatever they used back then, because readers would winkle out any inaccuracy. They still do. In that TV-episode with the terrorist tube-train primed to detonate beneath Westminster they specified Holmes and Watson got on at the wrong station, and were never allowed to forget it. But the further out of town Holmes went the less he bothered with detail. Who cares? Nobody. Nevertheless, Doyle based Grimpen Mire on Fox Tor Mire. So yes, maybe."

"Ever see that film *Deliverance*?" says Tatem. "Check out the few locals left here. Inbreeding's got a lot to answer for. Bet they've got webbed feet too as a result of all that swampy semi-aquatic ooze."

"When did your black-outs begin?"

"What about my black-outs? They've got nothing to do with it."

"So when did they start?"

"Soon after Sheena went missing."

"Not before? Not around the same time?"

"Could be. Things get confused. Carmen couldn't deal with it. Not with Sheena's disappearance. Not with my behaviour. I wasn't sleeping. I was obsessing. This stuff didn't help." He swills lager around his glass. Trying to swish the thoughts to the back of his mind. "Time got twisted, bits kept coming loose, lost weekends blur and merge into one another. I was impossible to live with. She went back to her parents. She's still there."

"Are you two past reconciliation?"

A long pause. "Nothing can ever be the same. This is the end. My black-outs are a symptom. I've got a brain tumour, it must be that. My own body attacking me, my own cells devouring me. Pressing into the brain-tissue. It's not diagnosed, but I know it's there. So I'm on a short time-fuse. And I need closure first. I need to know the truth before I die. You understand what I'm saying?" He doesn't raise his eyes from the table-top, his hands trembling. Slightly self-conscious about allowing passion to run away with his tongue.

Holly nods. Swallows a big mouthful of lager and wipes his mouth with the back of his hand. "You want to stay here overnight? Give us chance to take a more leisurely look-around?"

"Sure. Why not?"

Holly fixed it up with the landlord. Then they step outside into the gathering gloom. Misty moistness hangs in the night air so rich it splashes over their faces. They retrace their steps up the slope, in a slow erratic plodding gait, back up towards where the lay-by waits. The moon half-glimpsed behind roiling clouds, through sparse overhanging foliage.

"Where was it you found her Kindle?"

"A little further." About halfway between the embankment turn-off and the village itself, he stops and turns around slowly. "Here." He kicks at the grass verge. "It was here I found it."

Holly allows his eyes to crawl slowly over the dip beneath which half-conceals the village. The misty church spire. The pub roof. A row of phantom cottages in the process of being consumed by tendrils of limp weed. Sinking like slow-motion wrecks into relentless tide, into quicksand. Somewhere here, a girl went missing. Somewhere she's submerging into memory.

"You saw this dark figure?"

He feels uncertain. Logic is deceptive. Reason ties you up in knots. Go with it. Follow your intuition. "Yes."

Behind them, the verge slopes steeply upwards. Dandelion clocks, celandines and trash. Then scrubby bushes give way to trees, all the way up to the by-pass road at the very top of the embankment. The wedge of trees tapers the higher the side-road gets, until it intersects the larger road. Conversely, it broadens as it descends down towards the village. A dark wood neglected since the village died.

"Where, exactly?"

Tatem hesitates. The moon breaks through the clouds. This is the way it was. Ivory white. An ice-white field that freezes his nerves to bare wires. He can smell the dampness in the air. Smell the musk of moist soil and rotting leaves. He climbs the verge, slippery with dew. Hauls himself up. Worms writhe away flexing. Snails draw back into their shells. He grabs the nearest bush for support, to pull himself up. Thorns rip his fingers in bright icicles of stimulating pain. His feet slip-slithering for purchase. From the bush he can reach out and grab the rotting trunk of the nearest tree. It is spongy-soft beneath its crust of breaking bark. There's a warped shelving of wide white fungus running down its spine like a goblin staircase. Standing with his back braced against the tree he can look down at where Holly stands, looking up at him. As though Holly is himself, on that first terrible night. And he's the beast.

The trees grow denser here, their tops fingering the sky, the ground underfoot undulating in boggy shoulders and ancient ribs of mossy rock and fallen branches, gradually climbing yet higher. But there's something that almost resembles a path weaving in and around exposed fingers of arthritic roots. It might be a water channel. When it rains and deluges on the road above, gathering pools of surface-water must sluice through gutters and force a surging course down between the trees, leaving a path of exposed shingle. Or it could be an animal trail. He stumbles higher, struggling on all fours. His hands are bleeding. Spasms of tortured transformation. The moonlight cascades and shivers. He breathes hard. As he grasps from tree to tree the dark hair on the ridge of his knuckles is bristling. Black shapes move ahead of him, flitting through peripheral shadows.

"Sheena! Sheena! It's Dad!" His voice bites in his throat. It comes out in an animal roar. His face is streaked with tears. "Sheena. I'm sorry. Please forgive me. I couldn't help myself." He stumbles. His ankle explodes in pain. He curls down into the mud. Choked breath cutting his throat. Heart rattling loose. The black beast circles behind his eyes. His muzzle. His curve of needle-sharp claws. His pelt. He howls with a long animal howl dragged from the depths of his soul...

*

Waking with sirens in his head and a mouthful of cobwebs. It's happened again. Time Slip. The sheets are clean and white. The bed is luxuriously soft. He sinks deep into it. His ankle throbs, but he's strangely calm. At first he doesn't understand. Then it grows gradually. He's stayed overnight at The Baskerville Arms, as they'd planned. He turns over and drowses.

Eventually he gets up, washes and shaves. Then goes down the stairs to where Holly is tucking into a full English. He takes the veggie option, with mushrooms, potato croquettes, and coffee.

"I heard sirens. When she was little, Sheena called them Nee-Naws."

"I've got news. Don't know quite how to tell you. How to break it to you. I'm sorry Tatem. Last night, after you'd passed out and I brought you back here, I got to thinking. What the landlord had said about there being no cellars here in the village."

They go outside into the hazy morning. Two police cars are pulled in like chevrons at one of the dilapidated cottages along the road. Yellow-and-black crime-scene tapes strung across its drive-entrance.

"I don't understand."

"We joked about the local pervert here not having an S&M torture-dungeon. So I got to wondering, what does he do? He builds an S&M torture-attic. Looking out from my room in the pub I could see it, that cottage over there has bars across its loft-window. I called the cops. I was right. Your search for what happened to Sheena is over. I'm truly sorry, Tatem."

He gulps in a huge lungful of air. Unable to meet Holly's eyes for a long long moment. "You know, last night in the woods, I was certain that…"

"I know. You don't have to say it. But it's over now. I guarantee you'll get no more black-outs either. No tumour. You're free, Tatem, you're free."

DEREK EDGE AND THE SAUCERFUL OF SECRETS

It begins with a coffee-stop at a Motorway Service Station.
It ends half-way across the Galaxy...

THE STAR SEEKERS...

Halfway up the slip-road the radio blips out. There's a blank
pause. Derek thumps with the heel of his hand. It stays dead.

Seconds later, tyres crackle to a halt on gravel. 'The Merry
Muncher'. A satellite, hung on the South Orbital. Stepping out,
the parking area has the still calm ambience of deep space. Over
the slow hill of neatly clipped lawns, beyond the shaggy-domed
willows, they can see Nissans and Fiestas shuttle dumbly like
silent coloured beads up and down the M-way threads. Motes of
smouldering blue windscreens glinting.

They scrunch away through a silence so clear you can hear it.
Where only crows strut and croak, feuding over gritty entrails of
a smashed hedgehog. Derek lopes as if he's in free fall. Lopes as
if he's lighter than air. As weightless as a pinpoint of light. Lopes
as if he's attached to gravity by the slenderest umbilical of
physical necessity.

They pass the Traffic Control van with the radar-dish on its
roof, go across between the lawns, and into the halls. From
gravel and grass, to concrete and glass...

Sometimes things connect. Sometimes they don't. As Derek
and Gordon slouch into the reception hexagon, half-noticed off
this way, between the video machine cave and the travel-shop, a
tall man with jet hair has his head impaled up a phone hood. As
they pass, he starts by thrumming sharply and repeatedly on the
phone cradle. Then he hits the unit itself sharply, once, twice.
Giving up, he pauses, stares intently at the dead unit, and
smashes the receiver hard into it, leaving the splintered curve
penduluming beneath it as he steps irritably away.

Derek turns. Watches him for less than a moment. Like the Intercity 125, his train of thought seldom arrives precisely on time. He jogs his memory the way you shake a clock, to see if it still works. It works. Only just. Something has just happened. He's not sure exactly what it is. Yet.

But Gordon doesn't notice, he's already watching the girl…

FIRST STEPS INTO OBLIVION…

Echo and concrete, a food-court with blue plastic seating…

Derek swings back from the table, and comes down onto the chair with the grace and inevitability of a building collapsing under its own weight in slow-motion. Gordon watches him critically. The white moon-face, cratered with acne. The black oil-slick of hair. A bad cartoon. Eyes that swim like bloated jellyfish behind thick lenses. A chalk and charcoal sketch, of a loser. But then, why choose a low self-esteem inadequate like him? Why 'borrow' the company Transit van – without their knowledge – for a weekend in Blackpool, yet choose him for a companion? Why – because what he betrays on the outside, is what you feel inwards. If he is the moon, you must be its unseen night side. Socially dysfunctional. Ill at ease. And yes, because Derek is the only person you know lower down the social food-chain than you are. There's a thought…

"I sometimes imagine that I'm going blind. Have you ever thought that? A disease of the retina. With no cure." Derek clams his eyes shut and runs his finger across the table-top, drawing battle-lines with spilt coffee through a burst of silence. Adding, "I think somebody put something in my drink, this coffee is as addictive as heroin."

"I know what you mean. Even its smell is hallucinatory. Just inhale it, and you come over all olfactory. I'm prickly with it already."

"Another thing. Contact lenses often retain the imprint of sights they've seen. Have you heard about that? Apparently it's true. So when you put them in, you catch bits of things you did yesterday. And the day before." Gordon imagines he can see the caffeine beneath the glaze of his eyes. They share something. They must share something. Dissatisfaction. That's what it is

"So what happens if you put someone else's lenses in by

mistake, eh? What happens then? Or if you trade them, like 'You look at what I did if I can see yours'?" He glances away. The people at the far table are photos in negative, but slowly developing in mid-air. Figures evolving out of darkness, like creatures spun from night.

"Yeh, I know what you mean." Derek, reading his expression, even as he thinks it. "It's creepy here. So what about driving some more, you up for it?"

He glances across, yes, the girl is still sitting there. Is she looking away a little too quickly? Like she doesn't want you to know she's been looking across at you? Stay, on the off-chance of what will never happed? You'll blow it. You know you will. Stuttering and st-st-stammering it away. You always do. Go – why not? "Sure, I'm not so much Turbo. More UFO. But trust me. I'm a *really* safe driver. Trust me."

The space outside is large and cool, leaves are rustling. They cut a diagonal back over the lawn towards the van, heavy-gravity now, as though their bones are sheathed in lead. Out across the neat grass verge of the car-park. In the van he thumbs the key in the ignition. Nothing. He tries again. "Shit. It's dead."

"That's stupid. It was..." his voice drifts off. "What's happening down there?"

He follows the indication. A little way down the slip-road back towards the Orbital, there are two cars. Radiator steam clouding from the first one. A Honda Civic. People arguing angrily. For no real reason they leave the dead Transit where it is and climb the embankment to see better. "A shunt?"

"Looks to be. But then again, it's the car out front that's been mashed – from the front. See?" Gordon pauses, punching his outstretched fist up against something he's collided with. Something he can't see. "We've run into something too. There's a sort of invisible thingy here."

Derek's thoughts move on a sluggish wheel, even as he notices something that baffles him even more. "That's odd. Even the trees are growing in a curve."

Gordon stabs a stick unsteadily up into the branching foliage. "There's a barrier there. Some kind of invisible wall going all the way up. Must be bowl-shaped, inverted. So these trees are growing up against it. And we're trapped inside it. Inside some kind of force-field dome."

As wind sweeps in like tide over a dark field, he pokes the stick at Derek. "You realise what this means. We're imprisoned under an invisible force dome. We're trapped inside it. And I get the impression there's no way out."

"So how come there's wind in here…?" As a shudder quivers through the ground, trembling the trees, and grumbling away in low undercurrents of soft pulsations.

"And something else. The South Orbital. Haven't you noticed? Doesn't it look as though it's further away than it was before…?"

SLAVES OF SUPER-SCIENCE…

Day whispers to a close. Night envelopes like a panic attack, so nervy, so wiry, it has you constantly glancing over your shoulder. Derek's eyelids are already fighting a losing battle with gravity. They sit together in silence, watching dusk creep in across the floor. Across a vast void, a door opens, and a phone stops ringing. The more they watch it, the more the food-court takes on a mystical appearance. Islands of intriguing silences. Half-a-dozen people all afraid to admit that anything is wrong. A strange acropolis of crouching tubular steel and blue contoured plastic. Peninsulas of steamed Perspex serveries, haunted by the dark odour of percolating coffee, lines curving out edged with slides for trays, and indents for cutlery, sugar sachets and serviettes. They watch a fly circling in lazy orbits, from their space in the silent citadel, their heartbeats the ticking of bombs, 'which will detonate, and throw the shrapnel of our bodies across the world.' Wow – weird fancy, or what? The mind is a strange mechanism.

"Did you ever get that idea? 'Cos I do" says Derek. "When you're on the bus, going somewhere. What if the bus is suddenly snatched through time? Into the far distant future long after the human race has ended, and the world is a red desert of dead cities, like Mars? Or into prehistory, before there are humans? Or another planet under alien moons? An alternate dimension? There's just you, and the other bus-passengers sat around you. You look at them. Size them up. You're marooned together in another world. How would things begin to organise? Over days, weeks, months. A community must develop. Which woman would you choose? Which would choose you? Her? Or her over there? Which one would you wind up with...?"

"Her. I'd wind up with her." Yes, she's still there. Tall. Dark-haired. Asian perhaps? "That could never happen anyway. Because the Time Police would intervene. The Temporal Guardians." A pause. "You think that's what's happening here?"

"No. No, it's watching too much TV that's to blame for the way I am. It's just a thought. Just something I think, sometimes, on bus journeys."

"So what *is* happening here? Something odd. I think we should take a look round. Not just sit here talking stupid shit."

One door leading off says 'Manager's Office'. The other, concealing a short staircase going down, says 'Staff Only'. So they go down. Down through where faulty strip-lights strobe, office furniture slumbers under dust-sheets, and a murmuring echo of unseen machines hum in sinister unison. Further along, ahead of them, there's a big bluff woman in an orange company uniform. She's coming out of the Caretaker's room in the maintenance quarters here below ground level. For some reason they can't explain – at her approach, they yank themselves back into concealment. And watch. She passes so close they can hear her breathing.

"A guy at work told me that in the sixties they said you could tell a girl's personality by which Beatle she most favoured. Paul was for dreamy romantics. John for intellectuals. Ringo the comic. George the mystical."

"In that case, she must have favoured Yoko."

Then, as they snigger as they watch, she pauses. Looks down. They'd not noticed, but she has. A coin on the floor. Fifty pence. She looks around, almost furtively. Then bends down. But it's what she does as she bends down that makes their skin crawl. She uses her left hand to roll back the yellow Marigold glove from her right hand, and as she goes in to scoop the coin they can see it. Three claws. Like one of those shiny grabs in the arcade game which you winch out over the prizes and try to lift them into the hopper. Only it's not shiny alloy. It's furred, like an animal claw. And she uses it to precisely spear the coin along its edges, swiftly lifting it. She glances at it covetously, then stuffs it deep into her uniform pocket, before carefully replacing the glove. Again she furtively looks around. Good. No-one saw.

Except – of course, they did.

Derek's brain hangs upside-down, working overtime. "That clinches it. The Caretaker's from Outer Space."

"Not necessarily. Could be the genetically mutated results of in-breeding. There must be isolated incestuous farming communities around here, like in *Deliverance*. But what I'd like to know is what the hell she's doing here. Let's go take a peek." Once the coast is clear they prowl further towards the Caretaker's Room she's just vacated. At first they're disappointed. Mops and buckets. On a shelf, a bottle that says 'Toilet water'. "What's that – water from a toilet that's been pissed in?" snigger-snigger. Some lockers, locked. "Nothing here. Nothing but the usual stuff. Let's get the hell back out of here."

"Er, pardonisation... and go where? The van won't start. We couldn't drive it out of here if it did, because there's a wall all around us. You can't 'phone out. Radio waves don't pass through. And there's that creepy caretaker. It's way too weird here." Until at length Gordon shifts some toilet-paper cartons aside and his persistence is rewarded. "Hey, there's a trapdoor here. Let's see what they've got stashed away down there."

Together they lever the trapdoor up and open. There's a rung-ladder leading away beneath it. Gordon crouches, gaping swiftly down. "This place is crammed with stuff. And it's not scrap iron."

"It's machinery. But what's it doing here? What does a motorway services need stuff like this for?"

"Let's get out of here. I've got some kind of stupid idea. I've seen something like that equipment before. Not in real life. But in a comic-book. There's only one explanation. I know it sounds loopy, but this equipment looks like the Gravity Neutralising generators they use to levitate the cloud-cities of Mongo in the Flash Gordon serials."

"So what are you saying? That this entire building is some kind of Spaceship!"

Derek glances down as they walk back into the reception hexagon. His watch is going backwards. By now the floor has begun vibrating, the walls shaking, and there are customers deluging from the dining area in panic, jostling past them. Leaving voices as they go. 'What's happening? Is it Al-Qaeda?' 'Have they dropped the H-Bomb?' 'The place is gonna collapse –

70

must be an earthquake? Let's get out of here.' A din pierced by a shriek from a man coming in from outside. "It's no good – no-one can get out. We're all trapped."

By the time they step back out into the food-court the whole building is echoing to the oscillation of strange engines. And out of the panoramic window, far beneath them now, the miniature South Orbital glitters into the near urban sprawl, picked out by moving lights. How many people are there down there looking up? he thinks. How many of us are up here, looking down? Artificial landscapes of cloud drift over the distant city in weather patterns. Moonlight makes white the clouds they're ascending through, the shine of towns and hills glimpsed in fragments between them, roads in long spools of spilt tape.

"We've got to raise the alarm. We've got to alert people what's going on. We've got to find some way to get out of this place fast."

He's aware of a lowering hum coming from the generators in the cellar. But Gordon still has to speak a little more loudly to make himself heard. "It's already too late. We're in deep deep muck."

DEREK EDGE
AND THE SPECTRES OF THE BLACK STAR

There's a transparent dome centred on the Merry Muncher, enclosing its car-park, and a spacious bite of the undulating slopes around, including a short section of slip-road. But it takes less than twelve-and-a-half minutes to walk right around its periphery. Because Derek and Gordon walk it. The eatery itself is also constructed in a circle, centred around the food-court. It has a green spiral roof with its conical point slightly off-set in a supposedly jaunty way. There's a huge illuminated burger over the main entrance. It has two eyes and two spindly cartoon-legs, its spindly cartoon-arms point invitingly downwards at the main entrance. Its smiling mouth is formed by the curve of the burger itself between its two layers of white bread. Around the back of the building is a small delivery yard with two large green skips that smell sour, and a pile of pallets. From the yard you can look into the kitchen where two girls in bright smock-uniforms attempt to prepare food although there is now no power, and two waitresses sit motionless, as if catatonic. Following the circle around, there are clean, regularly-serviced toilets, although the cisterns no longer flush and there is obscene graffiti in one of the men's cubicle that has yet to be erased. Then there's an administration office, adjacent to the stairs going down into the 'no-entry' maintenance basement.

The dome enclosing it all is also spherical so that everything within has been reduced to minute toys in a huge drifting bubble. At first it seems as clear as glass. But – the more you concentrate, the more you detect its faint yellowish hue, so that high overhead the night sky has an oddly skewed taint, but shimmering, strengthening, and moving so it's difficult for the eye to focus on it. Listen, you hear its faint, almost inaudible hum. But there's no longer any sense of acceleration. Nor the murmur that drifts along the hills as the golden sphere ascends higher. Far below, is the visible curve of Earth, a hemisphere shelving away into forever. Lancashire shrinking away into England. Into Europe...

Across from where Derek and Gordon conspire – a woman sits, scratching her head as though unconcerned, the artificial light bleaching her features. Her bored melancholy is measured by the exact tilt of her head. Her husband should be arriving home around... now. Finding her not there. Not that he'll care. Not that he'll even notice, probably. Until he finds the dinner-table not laid. The food not prepared. Then a tall man with jet hair, his eyes narrowed, as though internally judging, but keeping his own counsel, arms tightly folded around his girth. Aware of the curious state of having an expanding waistline, and having to coexist with that expansion. His briefcase is sceptically angled. It is full of identical leaflets describing, with line-drawn illustrations, the benefits of cavity-wall insulation. He hopes against hope that the present strangeness will not result in anyone discovering the copy of *Knave* secreted in there between them. And a bored girl of eleven, hands on hips, eager to be off. Her head haloed by the bright wash of light. Her stomach feels queasy. As time meandered and her parents sit without speaking she'd wandered out past the 'Travel Shop'. It was empty. The staff had drifted off leaving the till untended. So she begins on a giant tube of Smarties, then moves on to half a Mars bar and several Kinder Surprises. Now her fingers feel chocolate-sticky, her stomach feels odd, and she's impatient to go. Then there are two men in blue uniforms who sit facing each other in silence across a table. The yellow flash above the padded pockets of their flack-jackets says 'Traffic Control'. Beyond them, a huddle of other marooned travellers, their limbs and bodies becoming tangled, abstracted, as though they're melting together into extrusions from a single organic mass, into one horrid fusion of body-parts…

It's then that Callisto walks ten paces directly across the food-court, to sit across the table from them. Tall. Dark-haired. Asian. Her large dark eyes look unwaveringly into Gordon's evasion. "I'm Callisto, and I'm in on this too," she says. "What's happening here? Where are we?"

"We are nowhere. A very good place to start." While talking, he's all the time looking resolutely away, out of the window at a patch of the increasingly tenuous tar-coloured sky, anywhere. He imagines he can see the first stars.

"Yeah. The Temple of Death." Derek bites back a fierce retort. "This is a comic-book story. Like *Amazon Slave's of Pluto's Moon* or *War-Gods of the Golden Planetoid*. Only this time, we happen to be part of its stupid plot-line."

"And this story concerns a Motorway Service station, a Merry Muncher that gets abducted by Space Aliens? As Galactic Zoo exhibits," she says. "No-one would buy that."

Gordon clasps his hands on the table-edge, squeezing until his fingers are pressed dry of blood. "Or we're being taken for some kind of experimental breeding programme." Glancing at Callisto. "Sorry. Piss-Ball Ricochet." He swallows coffee and stares at the table-top. There are thin scratch-lines running through its lamination that look like intersecting highways. All of them lead nowhere.

"I've been living through a lot of negativity," she offers. "I've been pressurised into situations I resented. I've been forced into places I didn't want to be, for pretty much most of my life. You, you're different. I've been observing. Watching you. You seem to be in tune on some intuitive – if abstract, way. I've not yet got the hang of it…"

"It's moron-speak, the only level we're capable of operating on. But it's by no means exclusive. You're free to join in."

She laughs indulgently. Then switches her tone, using the

one you use to soothe a fractious child. "Everyone else here, my parents included, are too shell-shocked to move, too terrified to do anything. So we're in this together. The three of us."

"As in, you think we're *not* terrified? If you think that, I've got news for you. But yes, we must find out what *is* happening here. It's something odd, we know that much. I think we should take a look round. Not just sit here talking stupid shit."

"Didn't you just say that? A moment ago," as their three chairs scrape back.

Adjacent to the 'Manager's Office' is a door that says 'Staff Only'. The three of them go down. Down through where faulty strip-lights strobe and the unseen machines of the power-grid hum in sinister unison. They go further down, towards the end door, which is marked 'Caretaker's Room'. It gives access to a single long space. Only this time, it's empty. An oddly deliberate emptiness. As though it might once have been a store-room. Yet there's no air of disuse. Instead, the floor is polished, as are the walls and ceiling. Look closer and it's apparent that every surface is coated with a resilient, brilliantly smooth brown substance. But there are no windows, and the only break is at the door itself, through which reflected light leaks in, making it glow dully. For Derek, the cold seizes him. He's already hanging on the stalk-end of his nerves. This is less a room, more a cavity. A strange insulated cavity. A high-frequency insulated cavity? No other word seems quite right. As though whoever had adapted it for the unknown purpose which it now fulfils seems to have always intended it should be empty. And that its function lies in that emptiness. For now.

But wait. A single fly circles in annoying spirals. Gordon watches its lazy orbits. "Wait." A fly. A fly with a tiny human head? Gordon ventures a few steps into the room. Follows its meandering path, until it settles at a precise point on the floor. "Look, the room is not *exactly* empty, there's a trapdoor here."

"Don't you think we should find out what they've got stashed away?" from Callisto.

"No. Not unless you're looking for trouble."

"You think trouble hasn't already found us, without our looking? This is important."

"I'm sure you feel it is." The tension lies strong on them, together, as they lever the trapdoor up. A cascade of flies tumble up out of the opened aperture. They all have tiny human heads. There's a rung-ladder falling away beneath them, and a faint distant light. Gordon crouches, but Callisto is first to squeeze her way swiftly down. He expels inheld breath, disturbingly conscious of the sinuous body-ripple of movement beneath her clothes. The scent of her. "This place is full of stuff," over her shoulder as she passes. Gordon follows, his eyes darting everywhere. It's dark down here, darker than dark – but no machinery, just a hazy square visible directly beneath the hatch, and an answering glow at some further distance away. It smells of earth. And fungal things. Fear cramps his stomach. He's got spooks in his brain. Panic syndromes. "We're beneath the building now, beneath even its foundations, how far do we have to walk to prove there's nothing down here to find…?" It's about then that he walks into the spider's web.

Derek is last down. He squishes bulkily into slime. The floor must be raw clay. With walls of dug earth. He sees vague creatures in the shadows twitching towards him, then retreating into the frame of his eye. Strange insect-anthropoids with emaciated limbs and big hair. Their facial pallor the colour of the moon. Things move on violent wings in the shadows. Sudden death with bells on. He turns too quickly, his foot slithering sharp-right in a shock that quivers the length of his body, twitching through every cell. Nerves jump. Muscles knot, and he's slip-sliding forward onto something unpleasant. Only to be brought up sharply – *skutch!*, propped against the damp wall, grinding his teeth. There are ridges of hardness within the yielding wet-softness. Even without trying he can determine their contours. As though he knows already. Here, a rib-cage. There, a pelvic bone. Lower down the smooth-dome skull-curve.

"I've seen this before," straining hard to keep control. "It's a bad movie. When they built this place, this service station, they didn't know it, but this was the site of a Neolithic bronze-age cemetery. They're all down here. Layers of the ancient dead, entombed in druidic ceremonies by priests with antlers on their heads and skull-masks. And they placed druidic curses on the sacred dead that should they ever be disturbed… and now, the bulldozers and JCB's, the bricklayers and construction workers, they've done it. They've disturbed their eternal death-slumber. And they're out for revenge, reaching out beyond the grave, from before the mists of time..."

"Shit. You're wrong. I rented that on DVD. It was an Apache burial ground."

"Same difference." Derek steps back, towards where he remembers the ladder going up. But his feet skid away from under him. He collapses under his own weight. Hits his head hard on something that might once have been alive. And the red exploding impact is like stepping into the red hell of Jupiter. Falling. Soft clay dog-turds in his hair. Worms working their way down through the roots, planting their eggs, burrowing into his eyes. The eggs swelling and throbbing with pupae. Green caterpillars writhing their way out in quick ejections of dark liquid, viscous glairy fluids. As he grovels in the wet muck a creature swizzes blob-eyes round to him, its secondary eyelids flicking across, vertically. Its breath reeking of putrefaction, like it's already been chomping a corpse in its multiple mouths. But there are bits of humanness about it too, arms – only too many of them – a multitude of ears in odd juxtaposition, genitalia of different sexes mixed up and duplicated, as though bits of all these corpses entombed in the walls have liquefied and melted together into one horrid fusion of body-parts. Its combined abnormalities suggesting occult dimensions way beyond those of any creature of this world, ever...

"Shit," yells Callisto above the sound of trapped breathing. "It's enough to turn your face inside-out." She has a thigh-bone brandished in both hands, using it to lash out at one of its strange pendulous formations, its attenuated dewlaps or wattles, each of them ending in cup-like mouths. Her impact is dull and squelchy, the pseudo-limbs erupting in showers of green ichor while simultaneously bulging and expanding aggressively in abrupt interminable stretchings, bifurcating into long, lithe proboscades lined with throated suckers, various abnormal mouths and members.

Gordon has him by the scruff of the neck, hauling him back and up, an ungainly weight, as she's pelting the growing monstrosity with rocks, mud, bones, whatever comes to hand, and its tentacular extensions retract inwards to cover its multiple constellation of eyes.

Lurching back up into the empty room. Slamming the trapdoor hard down. It stays shut as they retreat back towards the food-court in stunned silence.

Derek is the first to speak. "I think I pissed myself down there. Either that, or its mud on my pants. What in hell were we doing in that bad movie anyway? What was it down there, a portal leading all the way down to Hades? Or a way out?"

"I shudder to ask. How can it lead to hell, or anywhere else, when we're up here suspended in mid-air?"

"It's a metaphysical thing. You've heard of that, right? There doesn't *have* to be a physical connection to get there."

"I have another, much more logical explanation," Callisto's voice. "We're not here. Not in any real sense. There was an accident on the South Orbital. We were going east. You were going west. We didn't meet here, in the food-court. We met there, in a head-on collision. We were all totalled. There were no survivors. Even now, if our eyes could penetrate that far, we'd be able to see the police cars clearing away the mess of tangled metal impacted into each other, hosing away the traces of our blood and brain-matter from the carriageway. Other cars slowing past to gawp..."

"But I'm glad you're here with us," from Gordon. "You were amazing down there."

Derek strives to decipher the look that passes between them. "I don't remember seeing a sign saying 'Danger: Ghosts On Highway Next 33-and-a-third miles'. Do you?"

A beat later, stepping back into the central court... the Earth has gone. Then... the solar system itself is dropping away in their wake...

DA CAPO...

Echo and concrete, a food-court with blue plastic seating. A geography of steamed Perspex serveries, haunted by silver mists of percolating coffee, a curving shoreline edged with promontories for trays, and bays for cutlery, sugar sachets and serviettes. By now chickweed is growing from the open mouths of slot-machines. And for an hour they sit watching the flickering reflections on the ceiling from their space in the silent citadel.

"We're heading into some kind of nebula. Its immensity kinda makes you feel insignificant, doesn't it?" says Gordon.

"I always feel insignificant. Always." Derek. 'Sometimes, I

look inside me, and I don't like what I see. But I can't stop my brain running wild..." There are great star-clouds glittering fiercely as far as vision extends – and well beyond, swarming constellations of suns combining into a macabre brightness. Igniting reflections trapped within the table-top laminations, spattering their faces into animated planetariums of moving pinpoints. And a looming vastness of nebulosity, even more luminously silver than a full-moon night, dwarfing stars to sparks. Interstellar drifts of dust light-years across, mountainously vast, incandesced by the wealth of suns caught up in its invisibly churning electro-magnetic choreographies.

"All we were doing was going to visit my Aunt and Uncles, in Withington," offers Callisto simply. "I didn't even want to go. We stopped-off here for a toilet-break. I had an iced doughnut. My father had a bilberry muffin. We were going back to rejoin the carriageway when our car hit the barrier. The radiator smashed. It began steaming. And the man in the car behind, the tall one over there with the briefcase, the one talking to that group of people, he starts into hassling us, as though we've done it on purpose..."

Their three sets of eyes follow the contoured archipelagos of iridescence from their drifting bubbled mote. As those same inconceivable vastnesses tremble across the brief spaces in their eyes. It's a slo-mo explosion spun out across parsecs of space, thinks Derek. As though we are entering the original Big Bang itself, the primal detonation at the beginning of all things. Yet this is only a nova-ghost. A common enough galactic phenomenon, despite those glowing eddies big enough to swallow the solar system whole.

"I don't think Withington's in there. What's the post-code of limbo? And will it hurt when we hit?" Curtains of nebular haze are already closing in around them through partings in the fiery wall. Stars winking out, one by one, drowning in refractions of vagueness. With writhing light all around them as they float on tides of flickering radiation.

"I want you to know," says Gordon hesitantly, "I don't regret whatever is going to happen to us in there, because it brought us together. That makes it worth all the badness." She smiles, reaches across the table-top to trap his hand in hers. At precisely the same moment a delegation approaches. The tall man with jet hair and an expanding waistline shoulders his way grimly to the fore. The cavity-wall insulation salesman, his briefcase tight under his arm. Behind him, Callisto's father. Behind them, an undifferentiated line of people. Still further, two men in 'Traffic Control' uniforms.

"You with us?" he demands. "It's time. We've got to act now, before it's too late. What's wrong with that fool of a manager? Why isn't he doing something? We've armed ourselves from the kitchen. Laser-knives. Skewers…"

"They do kebabs here?" She notices one of the Traffic Control uniforms is smudged with brown paint.

"You with us or not?" Ignoring the interruption. "The manager's office. It must be."

Derek looks at him goggle-eyed. "Why not? Sure." Even as he has a numbing thought that turns the blood in his veins to ice: 'It's no good. We'll get no help from the manager. Don't you realise? He must be one of them!' They tag onto the milling group, moving across the food-court together. Derek's eyes swimming like bloated jellyfish behind his thick lenses. The reflection of strange chemistry and even stranger physics beyond the window is more than a little hypnotic. An endless barrier of weird opalescence tricked by refraction, its iridescence deepening as their strange craft is absorbed into its continual flux.

Into the reception hexagon, past the video machine cave, the looted travel-shop, and a phone hood with its splintered receiver slow-penduluming beneath it. In front of them now there's a door concealing a short staircase going down into the 'no-entry' maintenance basement. It says 'Staff Only'. Another, leading off from that, says 'Manager's Office'. The man with the briefcase is about to knock, then decides against it, and kicks the door open instead. As they surge into the office, a heavy-set man in a pinstripe suit sits behind a curved desk-unit. A wood-effect sign between the Rolodex and the Tipex says 'Manager'. Beside him, a big bluff woman. The sinister Caretaker, her evil eyes glittering.

"Where are you taking us?" demands the salesman. The tremulous tone to his voice saying he is less confident than he seems. "What are you going to do with us?"

Wordlessly, the manager turns around to face them. At first he turns his head from left to right, as if chasing glimpsed shadows, while refusing to meet their eyes. Something about his distraction suggests he's gazing into space. Perhaps so far into space he's watching snowfall on Syrtis Major. He's got internal malfunctions, thinks Derek. He's an insect. With psychic antennae. He's the kind of person who wears a colander on his head to prevent people reading his mind. But at the same time he's reaching up to remove his face. As the Caretaker does the same. Faces coming off. Grotesque ape-faces beneath. While calmly and deliberately the alien creature presses a button with a talon-like claw. In response wall panels begin gull-winging open silently.

"This isn't just an office," gasps Gordon, stating the now-obvious. "It's some kind of navigational control room."

The Caretaker is delving into the concealed depths of her orange company uniform. No yellow gloves. Her claw emerging with a murderous pistol of alien design clutched in her three-fingered grasp. "So, you've learned the secret of this place. How unfortunate for you. Now I must request that you all to return to the Food Court. Or do I have to make an example of one of you first?"

But Callisto moves faster. With a reckless speed and agility that amazes them all, she flings herself into action, hurdling the desk, vaulting over it to catch the woman feet-first, squarely on the orange-uniformed chest. Both of them falling back in a confused heap. The Caretaker tumbles senseless to the floor. Simultaneously, other things happen. The man with the brief-case hurls a laser-knife. The knife impales the manager's face, which splits open like a smashed over-ripe melon. While the Caretaker's gun detonates. A blue electric charge scorches over Callisto's shoulder, and burns the man's face off. His briefcase spins loose, sceptically angled. As it hits the edge of the desk it cracks open, erupting a spray of identical leaflets describing, with line-drawn illustrations, the benefits of cavity-wall insulation. The copy of *Knave* which was secreted in there between them billows lurid open-legged nude-spreads. At the exact same moment the decapitated manager's body falls hard-down across the desk – and the entire travelling world tilts as he does so, lurches out of balance, hurling people off their feet and across the floor, until it spins away on a new trajectory.

Oddly, Derek is one of the first up. He steps cautiously

towards the desk, bright flecks of brain-matter on his sleeve. "Ugh, it's ketchup-a-gogo time!" A dislodged eyeball lies on the floor like a glaucous slug. He almost steps on it. "If this thing's not dead – it ought to be!" The manager's thick-set body and what's left of its head is sprawled heavily across a complex control-board. Red studs, pressure-pads and winker-lights pulsing wildly beneath the uneven distribution of its sudden weight.

Callisto stands, brushing herself down. Gordon draws her close. "Are you OK?" 'Sure,' in her head. 'Just that my face is wet and numb, and it feels as if I'm wearing a mask. Apart from that, sure, I'm fine.' But she allows him to curl her into his protective embrace. As others stand, to crane over the stunned Caretaker, staring down in glassy-eyed revulsion. "Ugh, even the face isn't real, just some kind of latex prosthetic. These things were never born on Earth."

And all the while the oscillation of machines grows worse until it becomes hideously painful...

SET THE CONTROLS FOR THE HEART OF THE SUN...

The heat levels intensify, becoming unbearable. There is a sun, within the nebula. A glitterball of incandescence. Slow drifts of nebular particles silting in permanent curtains of drizzle to mottle its unstable surface in constellations of continual micro-impacts. And, unguided now, they're drifting in towards it, trapped just as surely as those dust-tides.

"Great. We're lost on a Magical Mystery Tour in the Seventh Galaxy, and you've murdered the driver. The only man who knows the way home," says the woman. Long overdue for dinner.

"He wasn't a man. He was a thing. A fiendish thing. And he wasn't about to take us home." From Gordon.

"At least he was taking us *somewhere*. Not plunging us into the heart of a sun."

"Perhaps we can help?" For the first time, the two blue-uniformed Traffic Control men stand forward. The ceiling above them is creaking audibly. Soft plumes of grit spiralling down.

"We saw your van. Yes. So why don't you put some traffic cones around that?" Derek points out at the blazing sun.

"You misunderstand. We monitor the flow of temporal traffic caught up in the time-stream."

"Ha. The Temporal Guardians," leers Gordon. "I told you. I said the Time Police would save us."

"And it's you that's been working in that empty room, am I right? You've been deliberately preparing that cavity, painting it an insulating brown," demands Callisto. "So why haven't you intervened on our behalf until now?" She has removed her track-top to tie it loosely around her waist. Gordon approvingly notices the way her T-shirt now attractively contours her glistening skin.

"Space, and time – are roughly constant. That's the base-line. What varies is only your outlook to them. Time waits for no-one. That's usually an altogether satisfactory arrangement. So it was necessary to formulate which alternative course of action would disturb it least – by intervention, or by not acting. After all, your abduction may form an acceptable variant within the mainstream historical-flow. Unwittingly using those aliens as interplanetary gardeners, the transplanters of civilisation, of species, of spores, seeding worlds with special cultural genes. That's entirely possible. But your deaths, which now seem imminent, will probably not be so historically accountable."

The whole room is shaking. Gordon looks wildly over his shoulder. "That makes admirable – if disconcerting – logic. However, it doesn't alter our predicament. So we need... what ? Time Pills?" The whine of dissonance is growing deafening so he has to yell to make himself heard… then the ceiling implodes with a roar. A deluge of sections cascading down into the centre of the Food Court smashing and burying tables and formations of chairs. In instant response a sprinkler system fizzes into life, hazing down across them – before it abruptly cuts off. No mains water supply anymore, only sporadic coughing plumes of scalding steam. The eleven-year old girl with the queasy stomach, standing close between her parents, begins to sob.

"The Guardians' duty is to monitor the integral cohesion of time. To keep places like this from falling into the hands of chancers intent on altering the normal course of time. So we could be justified in setting you all back..." The other blue-uniform nods thoughtfully. "But only by returning you to the exact moment at which all of this began. To do otherwise would be to invoke certain disqualifying paradoxes, so it will mean you entering a moment you have already lived through, but on an altered trajectory…"

"Yes, yes, we've done that temporal conundrum bit. We've read the Sci-Fi, we've seen *The Twilight Zone*."

"So, follow me." For the last time they go down, all of them in a milling group, carrying the body of the cavity-wall insulation salesman between them (the copy of *Knave* discretely returned to the briefcase now resting on his stomach-paunch), splashing through pools of gritty water which steams into evaporation as the floor heats. Outside the panoramic window they can see the willows igniting into tall fireworks beneath a sky-huge sun. Across the reception hexagon, carefully skirting past the door that says 'Manager's Office', the collapsed Merry Muncher sign lies on its side bent out of shape, its burger-smile turned upside down, and down the short staircase that says 'Staff Only'. Further, where faulty strip-lights strobe across office furniture slumbering under dust-sheets, through the murmuring groan of the tormented power-grid straining in its uneven conflict with overwhelming solar gravitation. Until, at last, they reach the end door, which is marked 'Caretaker's Room', the slight clearance-break around its rim leaking light, making it glow supernaturally. Opening into a single polished space with no end. Empty. An infinitely deliberate emptiness, filled with light. Its function now focussed on that emptiness.

"The dish on our van focuses temporal dislocation into the room. All you must do is enter, and pass through it. We'll do the rest, the reports, the paper-work. For you, it happens like this, you are uplifted from here – back into then, where everything that's happened since will cease to exist."

"What of the creature-saurus we saw in the passage beneath the room?" says Derek.

"And what happens on the other side, will we remember any of this?" Gordon glances nervously across at Callisto, a note of desperation trembling in his voice.

"The tachyon exhaust-stream sucks odd side-effects out of past, future, and possible-time. That's probably what you saw in the passage. And no, naturally you will have no memory of this, because it will not have happened."

"There are odd mutational side-effects, and you expect us to step through it…?"

"So none of this will have happened to you or me," says Callisto carefully, as people begin filing into the light. "You will never have known me, Gordon. And I will never have known you. That must make this the strangest, saddest of goodbyes. We've only just met. Only just got to know each other. And a little more than just know. With so much more to come. So much more to discover in each other. Yet once we step through, we will never even have met."

"We will know. Something of this will survive. What I feel now is too strong…"

Derek glances away. "The alternatives aren't up to much." As he steps into the emptiness of light, the cold seizes him. He's hanging on the stalk-end of his nerves. His plate-round face bleaching to uniform whiteness by glare. The lenses of his glasses opaqued to perfect white. For a moment he turns back, to see Gordon and Callisto kissing in a feverishly desperate embrace, before they follow him, embracing, walking hand-in-hand…

The father picks up his eleven-year old daughter. It's the first time he's held her in a long while. She clings tight as they step into the light.

Ten-thousand light years away, a dog barks.

ANDMOREAGAIN…

The sign says Merry Muncher. Halfway towards the slip-road the radio blips out. There's a blank pause. Derek thumps with the heel of his hand. It bursts back into life again. Citroens and Fiestas shuttle dumbly like silent coloured beads up and down the M-way threads. "Services ahead. You want to stop, for a coffee?"

Coming in the other direction, towards them, a cavity-wall insulation salesman, a wife mentally planning the meal she will soon be preparing for her husband (not that he'll even appreciate it), and a silver Honda Civic. A girl's face glinting behind its smouldering blue windscreen. Tall. Dark-haired. Asian perhaps? For a moment their eyes meet. A strange expression. A strange frisson. An odd sense of disorientating loss. For less than a moment there's a feeling that… then the speeding vehicles have passed each other, and they're gone…

"Naw, let's keep moving. That way we can be in Blackpool before its dark. I'm not so much Turbo. More UFO. But trust me. I'm a *really* safe driver. Trust me..."

Dedicated to the inspiring legacy of Frank S. Pepper, David R. Motton, and Sydney Jordan

REFUGE

Migration lies in people's souls.
Until there's nowhere else to go,
and no possibility of ever leaving…

A thin line of flame burns along his forearm. No, a crawl of white-hot ants are shivering up beneath the skin-surface, up as far as the tourniquet. His arm is no longer part of him. It's a separate thing. An incandescent thing of pain.

"I am Cesare, I pull lobsters from the sea. You, my friend, are the strangest lobster I ever hauled up into my boat," a voice talking above the pain. "I am 175-years. My Maria is older, although she'll never admit it."

"Hush signore, lie still." A smiling woman wipes his forehead with a soothing white cloth.

Then the fever takes him again. And a series of nightmares clamour through his head. Memories blow like dust in the wind. Not all of them his own.

There was something like thirty people on the coach as it pulled out of the village of white buildings. Jounced up and down with every revolution of the wheel, the bag containing his property knock-knocking constantly against the overhead luggage-rack. That was his advantage. He travelled light. Nothing to hold him down. Idris leaned back against the worn seat upholstery, eyed destination signs as they spin past. The kays piling up behind him. Further. He drowsed, the steady rhythm of the coach lulling him. Half-asleep with half-dreams. He remembered everything. Running through memories like an old movie, a print that never fades. He's forgotten nothing. It's all there. Every detail. Every pain and humiliation.

It's a lunar landscape to the north. The bus rolling through dust into a grimy Asmara interchange thronged with jostling people. There are bored men with guns. Some are local militias. They can stop you, demand ID, check your luggage, confiscate whatever they take a fancy to. Others are just men with guns. He sleeps in the alley that night, to conserve what money he has. It has to last. It has to eke out. Shadows scamper. Voices ebb and filter away. He wraps his arms around his chest for warmth. Here, he lies exposed and defenceless. And if a predator lurks at the door, all it has to do is sh-o-ve. And there's not even a door. But he sleeps, as hard as falling off the edge of the world.

With morning Idris starts walking towards the west, the direction he's facing. He looks half-heartedly for work. There is no work. He'd known that already. But he enquires anyway. Most times they just wave him away irritably with tight hard scowls. He knew when he was beaten. Should've known better after twenty-eight years. It was time to move on. He got a lift in the back of a truck. There are two other people with him. An older man with a face like leather, and a boy who might have been his son. They watch him warily and don't speak. The next town is Omhajer, fifty-minutes from the Sudan border. He walks through the night, wary of armed Rashaida who hunt and abduct migrants, slaving or organ-trafficking. With first dawn he can properly see the great dreary circle of the horizon, punctuated by dry scrub.

Idris was smart. He knew he was smart. He was strong. He had a good back. He could lift. He could make a living. If only he could get the breaks. He had some names. He had some addresses written down in a blue pocketbook. He'd learned some phrases in Italian. He turns them over in his head. Memorizing them. Trying to pronounce them out this way, then that way, shifting the accent. Tasting the words.

Memories blow like dust in the wind. Not all of them are his own. Sometimes he recognizes memories he'd shared with his grandfather. How they had sat together on the hill overlooking the village, while goats crop at unhealthy vegetation. They'd sit a silence. Each knowing that the other was sharing the same memory. Savouring details of the same past event. They'd smile at each other in a wordless conspiracy that said so much. It had always been this way. Down the centuries. Their past a common property. Every now and then, for no reason, he would catch the essence of past family lives.

Crossing the Atbarah River in Sudan by antiquated ferry under cover of night, crammed in with other refugees. Four months in a Khartoum camp beneath tarpaulin sheeting, a lean-to against a dry wall, before hooking up with a people-smuggling network, in a truck across the Nile. Long parched days on a road little more than a red sandy track. Libya is no different. But there's the shimmer of sea out across the dunes to the right. He arrives in a small port on a moonless night three months later. He can live here anonymously. In a grey rooming house, eating sorghum bread. He's sick, vomiting and wracked with diarrhoea. Ground floor, just as well, because he's too weak to climb the stairs. He's drunk-giddy and weak, shivering and miserable.

There are transients, there are always transients, maladjusted and rootless, escaping the fighting or the drought. Fleeing either the militants on one side or the drones on the other. It must be one of them who took his bag. His money is gone. What is not exhorted, was stolen by dealers and corrupt officials. With three others he jemmies open the back of a truck parked in an overnight lot. The route an ever-changing pattern, the maps all tangled up. From Tripoli, to the shadow of the Al-Zaytuna Mosque in Tunis.

The next day there's a huge cruise ship. A floating city. He watches them monitoring as they come and go along the quayside. At dusk, along the harbour-side from Green Square where the sky is filled with starlings, a late middle-aged American tourist, furtive of manner, strikes up a hesitant conversation outside a cafe. Buys him a mint tea, invites him back to his hotel room. He feels grimy, awkward, uneasy. Once there the American makes it obvious he wants what god forbade. Others had taken money this way. He'd thought he could too. Until the last moment, and he'd recoiled from the man's touch. But when Idris reaches out in rage to push him away, the American's hair comes off in his hand. He stands absurdly holding a limp hairpiece, like a dead animal, laughing out loud. He leaves the cowering tourist, covering his embarrassed baldness, but takes his Apple laptop, his Leica camera, his iPhone. He's not proud of what he's done, but it was necessary. It grudgingly raises enough.

Crouched at the foot of the stairwell, he checks out addresses. Down the corridor he makes enquiries.

*

Impressions blow like dust in the wind. This time, they are largely his own.

"You should not have brought him here."

"What else could I do? I couldn't leave him to die."

They're speaking a highly accented Italian dialect. Yet he can follow it reasonably well.

"The arm is infected and badly inflamed. He needs to go to the mainland for treatment."

"You know we can't do that."

The village doctor, with a bush of white hair and thick-lens glasses presides over the debate. "Ours is a small commune. I will not allow it to be destroyed. The outside world must stay outside..."

Other voices are raised in violent disagreement.

After that, thinking stops. Replaced by psychic echoes from the past, in the faintest of whispers.

He'd known it was a mistake. But he'd crossed the street anyway. Led in single file down into the dark waters. Two shadow vessels cut from the night. A tug. And a decommissioned ferry, lying low in the water. The vehicle ramp lowered into the tide, a column of people carrying bags and bestrewn with gloomy children scrambling up the steep wash, herded onto the already crowded car deck. An ancient rust-bucket already heaving with people. He manages to fight his way through, clambers up the companionway to the narrow balcony-deck above the vehicle-well already crammed with people. A steel mesh affixed to the gunwale extends out over the lower darkness enclosing them. He rams his place clear, backs up against the outer plating, and waits.

First there's a two-and-a-half-hour delay. Lost time frittered somewhere beyond the curve of the harbour where people doze or eat out of silver foil parcels. The ferry is obviously unpowered. It is towed behind the tug, its thrum vibrating across the churning wake between them. In the tang of diesel oil. Then twelve hours towards Lampedusa. Once there, the Italian coastguards will intercept them, take them on to a refugee camp. Towards a new chapter.

He drowses. Time unhooked and drifting. Until below, something slammed. A confused rustling began, a red crackling that dances its reflected glow from faces and bulkhead. A fire spreading across the floor, belching up choking dense smoke. Idris felt the first crawl of terror. Coughing, eyes smarting, he backs up against the mesh. He tugs at the netting, but it was stronger than it appears, clamped securely at its base-points. He moves along the catwalk. He got four paces before the pain became unbearable. The oily smoke already unendurable, but the flames below show there's no easy escape, vent-spaces only as wide as a man's fist.

The hulk lurches, the floor shifts abruptly away beneath him, he crumpled and fell forward on his face into the dark, feeling the iron-hard floor against his nose. He struggled to get up, memories vomiting into his brain of all the pains of his life, the beatings and cruelties. Then the pain of his father's life, and death. His grandfather. A hundred years of pain. An accumulate-ed weight of memory so intense he was ground down close to blanking out.

Flames roar through the companionway opening like a blast-furnace chimney. He can feel the residual heat crisping his skin. He ran for the opening, breath held, and jumped, landing heavily. The covers fall with a crash, sparks and flames leaping high. A series of explosions add more fury, the night lit by red, fitful colour. "I can't stay here. I've got to get out." People are running, figures of living flame. A corroded iron escape stairway is level with the end of the balcony-deck. Towards what had been crew-space. Bolted from inside and rusted shut. He glances around, trying to get directive bearing. Keep it together, keep control. One lower square glass-pane is shattered. He reaches through stars of glass, fumbling down to the sliding mechanism on the other side. It won't move. He braces and exerts more force. Suddenly, there's a grating from the bolt, it slams away, he lurches as it clangs forward, ripping the flesh of his arm wide open on the rectangle of dirty glass. The door swings in, carrying him with it, beyond the knives of pain.

He paces onto the smashed bridge. All instruments ripped away and scattered. It smells of mould and stale piss. The outer glass gone. Open to the night. He can see across a narrow space of night to the tug. It had cast the ferry adrift. As it turned away it had rammed the ferry, either accidentally or deliberately, cracking open the ancient plating. Tide burbling in like a series of ruptured hydrants. It was the resulting panic that had kicked off the fire, spilled fuel acting as accelerant. He heard the loud flat retort of gunfire too. Others were following his lead, forcing their way in behind him. The scraping sound of their stealthy movement growing louder. No way forward, no way back.

His arm is wet and warm, throbbing oozing pulses of blood. He forces himself to stay upright, trying to shake off the sudden pain that drills through him in a dozen places. This is a death ship. It's going down. He climbs through where the windshield should have been. Braced on railings that betray the granular texture of corrosion. Teeth clenched tense, it seems he's seeing everything that happens in slow motion, so rapidly are his thoughts and sensations racing. He teeters, and jumps into nothing. The sea hits him like a solid black wall, and he goes down, submerged beneath its roaring surface…

From a distance he can see the first fury of flames is now spent, but fitful startles of fire crackle intermittently, bursting the blackness. Eruptions of steam geysering up into the sky. At first there were screams. Then there are no screams. Everything is dying to a steady red glow. The smouldering hulk is listing, inducing a vertigo sense of unnatural perspective. Small dark figures squat on its up-tilted curve. Others float unmoving around it.

Then he's too far away to see, there's no ship. Just empty sea. Scaly fingers of ancient aquatic creatures reach up through the undertow of tides, seizing at his leaden limbs, pulling him down beneath the surface. A terrible lethargy eats away at him. So easy to let go, to submerge with them. His mind freezing over by slow degrees, unconsciousness enfolding it like the lull of deep chill water. Fogging away memory, hopes, thought, everything.

His grandfather is still out there. Helping him. He can sense his presence. An ability genetically transmitted down the chromosome line. Past and present time drift and fray, coming temporarily out of phase and overlapping. Incidents transposed from past into the present by an inexplicable freak of genetics. There have always been people-migrations, shifting populations seeking better lives. As far back as memories go, stragglers shuffling stumbling across that next hill, to the other side of the river, beyond the mountains, to a new life in some other place. A tribal exodus of ten, or thirty, or a hundred. Stopping at night. Moving on at dawn. The old, the weak, the lame left to perish.

Out of the heart of Africa itself. Out of the rift-valleys of Ethiopia. In flimsy papyrus-rafts, dugout canoes, reed-boats, and dhows across hazardous stretches of stormy sea.

Yet the friendly interchange of minds, once annihilating distance, is fading, the faint beacon of his grandfather's mind grows dimmer. Until his grandfather's voice is gone. Severed away for the first time in his life, as devoid of feeling as the deadness of his arm. But he's momentarily brushed by another's consciousness. The deep pit of another's memories. It gleams at him in the night like an owl's eye. Leaving nothing but that luring pulse of light. He follows it…

*

The new voice is flooding him. The one that had drawn him here. A voice of long cold emptinesses. His head is thronging with its chopped-off memories. Old when the Venetians were here. Old when the Carthaginians were here. Minutes drift. His perception too dim to keep count of time. He's lying beneath a single cover on a narrow bed, his right arm is dead. A limp thing that hangs lead-heavy from his shoulder. Gingerly, he feels his way down his left side, rib by rib. Nothing broken, but it hurts. That in itself is a desperate distorted triumph. He lies back, perplexed. A question not framed in words. More an unsettling uncertainty. He drowses again.

"We are secretive folk here" Cesare is saying to him. "I have no words for it, but – the oracle keeps us hidden. Shields us from the world. Except for you, it seems. You are different. It likes you."

"We have a good life here," says the woman, Maria, who changes his soiled bed-linen and bathes the fever-sweat from his body. "You are very sick, but you can be fixed. So I say to you, you either lose the arm, understand? We amputate, and you leave here. Or we help you, you let us help you, and then you must stay…"

The giddy roaring in his head makes the words indistinct.

Then they're helping him up. Two men. Cesare, the lobster-fisherman, is one. The other is one of the voices he'd heard in his delirium. Maybe the Doctor himself. He catches the aroma of their sweat. As he rests his weight on their support a thin line of flame burns along his forearm, up as far as the tourniquet. The arm is a deflated thing, chorded like string. He'd been confined only a short time, but already the notion of movement seems unfamiliar.

And agoraphobia hits him the moment he steps outside; it's scary to have the world returning around him. Everything dominated by the single mountain rising steeply ahead. Volcanic in origin. Then the tumble of white, cream and lemon houses straggling down through the greenery of fir trees and dark groves of ancient olives gnarled into ghoul-faces, spider-webbed with nets to catch falling fruit. And pink and white houses that seemingly grow out of the rock to face the sea, scattered as though carelessly flung among a profusion of vineyards, as if they're one element with the land and sky. Further down the steep descent, divided into terraces enforced by rings of dry-stone escarpments, lies the crescent-sprawl of the town itself, cafes and bars hunched around the sparkling sea-rim deluged in oleanders and bougainvilleas. Women in headscarves do their laundry along the edge of the river that empties into the harbour.

But they're not taking him there. With Maria leading the way they're carrying him, strong arms supporting his weight, a little distance along the stony path. Lurching some way towards a weather-beaten sun-baked church. Joined by the Priest, who insists on being complicit with everything that goes on within his island parish. The Priest hums tunelessly. There were Christians in Ethiopia. He knew Christians. They respected each other. But no, they're not taking him there either.

Instead, they guide him through an arched space behind the church. The twelfth-century edifice guards and conceals a cave-mouth, a dark passage opening that leads into pools of shade, with the coolness settling around them like a familiar garment. Into dripping blackness. The world darkens, and solidifies. Their figures already corpse-white against ash black. It must surely be possible to claw tension from the air, weigh and test it? Along with the taint of sulphur, the ancient staleness, and the sourness of unformulated fear that lies thick on them. How far…? How much further…? No strength to resist.

There are obsidian structures that are semi-organic in curves and towers that vanish into the darkness far above. And the murmur of tortured water, to where a shimmering pool of jet stretches away, twinkling with ripples. And the slither of something breathing beneath the surface. A cold intelligence as old as the world, as old as stars, as slow as the spiralling of galactic clusters.

They slump him down onto damp stone. It crawls up the contours of his body on a web of wormy tentacles. It smothers his face. A thousand fibrillated barbs drill through the skin of his forehead, micro-filaments that ripple through his skull, a mass of cilia penetrating into the coils of his brain. Breathing is impossible. His mouth is filled, his throat choked so densely that he's incapable of screaming. His body twitches in violent spasms. Searing pain, blinding in its brilliance, in vivid sun-flashes ripped as raw nerves are barbed. He's sinking into a pool of infinite depth, finding wells of great understanding and even greater knowing, ageless pain haunting and terrible. Sharp strobe-blinks of its own migration across the stars, only to be stalled and trapped here, forced by the necessity of survival into a kind of symbiosis with these primitives.

Then the madness left him. His mind is cool and clear. His arm healed.

"I am 175-years," says Cesare. "My Maria is older, although she'll never admit it. It's the oracle, you see. It cares for us. We have a good life here. So long as we never go outside its influence. So long as we never leave."

Islanders drink fragrant espressos, enjoying the warm evening shade of the small cobbled quayside piazza, grizzled bewhiskered men sucking pipes, white-haired women in black confiding in endless conversations. Few young people. No children. Peaches ripen against the dark tumbling wall behind them, heavy with the strong scent of blossom. While ahead of them a line of five linguine-bound octopus hang suspended like descending aliens above fishing-boats that sleep in the setting sun, barely rocking on the lap of tide. Their names in indecipherable blocky script that hints at, but never quite gives up their secrets. They suggest a leisurely activity that barely disturbs the old town's basking serenity.

"Migration lies in people's souls. In future centuries maybe we migrate out beyond the stars? Who can say?" He's shocked by the sound of his own voice. It has lost its power, emerging thin and hoarse. "Me, all I needed was to reach Europe."

"No more. You are one of us now," with a big white-toothed smile, and – for one who claims such longevity, a complete lack of physical deterioration beyond a slight stoop and a crown of white hair.

Sunset is a spectacle of colour-gleaming clouds that turn the sea a rippling carpet of reflection. A pebble track slopes gently down to the undisturbed expanse of beach. The low-ebb tide has left mud-smooth wet sand that stretches away along the sea's constantly moving rim where gulls ride the lazy swell. Wavelets advance, slop and recede. So far, until it can go no further. The beach cast desolate in the grey light as warming breeze turns chill. This is some magical out-of-the-world off-trails near-forgotten island... and it's breathtaking. He hadn't meant to come to this place. This isn't quite Europe. The mainland is still a hundred kays away. Yet this is journey's end. All migrations stop here.

Idris smiles. "Yes. I know..."

THE NON-EXPANDING UNIVERSE

A little lost girl in the big bad Blott.
What will she find there…?
And who will rescue her?

That's the moment the sideboard tipped over. She hadn't intended it to fall. That was not part of the game. She'd begun on the leather arm of the big chair. From there she climbed up onto the sideboard. Tiptoe step by step, from this side towards the far side… beyond that was the stool onto which she could drop, so crossing the width of the front room without once touching the floor. But that's not how it works out. Instead, her slight weight unbalances the sideboard; it sways unsteadily, lurches, and then falls in a loud landslide of crockery, ceramic ornaments and lace doilies. Crunched into the wooden chair which rams forward into the table.

Ayesha fell to the floor and cried out. The threatening furniture overhung, about to lurch again, smash down and crush her. Her hands come up around her head in terror. She's biting her fingertips until they hurt. The sideboard groans. The chair creaks in protest. But they fall no further…

Haha, that's good, but there's worse. Riding home on the bus. And the dosser sits next to her. She cringes away, as tight into the seat-corner as she can. He sits perfectly still for two stops until he looks down at her, and whispers in a low growl, "Do you want to see Uncle Wiggly, my pet caterpillar?" No, no, go away, leave me alone. His breath as rank as the gutter with the stench of sour beer. She knows that smell too well. It means bad things. But then she feels her mouth drop open. She knows it makes her foolish-looking, but she can't help it. Never so relieved in her short life to see a huge creepy caterpillar uncoil on someone's shoulder.

Some people call it the Blott, others just say the shit-hole.

Some claim 'Chernobyl-on-Tyne' extends ten miles from end to end. Others say it's no more than two, and the add-on is just feral wasteland. It's the dangerous place, a place the grown-ups warn you about with scare-stories. Don't go in there. There are jetties poking out over glistening mudflats into the Tyne where they used to dock to offload, before the accident. Before the toxic spill. The incident. Before they switch radioactive-waste import operations coast-to-coast to Barrow-in-Furness. They say, at its core, the air still fizzes with Strontium 90. They say you feel the rads frying your skin. There are acres of filtration units, a corroding spaghetti of pipes, each one torso-thick and torso-round. And empty buildings resembling concrete blockhouses where rough-sleepers, pervs and winos seek temporary refuge. A junkies' shooting gallery by night. A forbidden adventure playground for daytime kids. An empty place with hidden warrens and secret dens to hide out and play taboo games.

A place for Ayesha to hide. She is ten years old, and a little overweight. She's confused when they call her Paki or Patel. Those taunting words mean nothing. She knows she's neither, so why do they say it? She was born in that terraced house, over there. Her mother is Punjabi, but she was born here too. Better not to understand, just avoid the hurters. Go places they don't go. Further into the Blott than they dare go. Which means it's also a safe place to go to escape nosey, intrusive and violent adults.

They wouldn't allow this place to exist down south. But no-one gives a damn about up here. They even try to shove planning permission through to bulldoze it and erect neat little chintzy developments with names like Sycamore Drive and Bluebell Meadows for folks who never ever heard of the Blott. They keep getting knocked back. A business park. An out-of-town mall after a token detox. It's bound to happen eventually. But not yet.

Ayesha was suddenly shivering, an ice-wind gusting out of memory. Terror at what she's done haunts the rest of her day. She daren't go home when she should go home, at twilight. Instead she cowers alone in the bus shelter, shivering uncontrollably and sometimes giving way to dry-eyed sobs. Buses going to the town centre draw in and stop. People get on. People get off. People with things to do, places to go.

But there's just one coherent thought sprinting through her mind with the slow-passing hours. She didn't reach the decision consciously, but rather by meandering intuition. She can't stay to endure Daddy's revenge, whatever form it takes. If he catches up with her, he'll hit her. Or resort to subtler and crueller indirect attack. Petty snipes and irritations that'll go on for days, intolerable as they accumulate. There's no-one she can turn to. So she'll stay away for as long as it takes. Forever if necessary, taking her chance of dying of thirst and hunger. Then they'll remember her, and feel remorse.

Rackham's in the security cabin. Small frames of white light carved into it. Which means yes, he's there. With all the screens covering all of the perimeter rim. But it's going to be a long night. He'll be in there watching porn on his laptop with the 'private browsing' turned on. Chances are he won't notice anything. Too cold for him to come out and investigate even if he does. On what he's paid, c'mon! He's there all night, isn't that enough, without investigating stuff as well? To hell with it.

The darkness beyond the electrofence isn't so bad once she's wriggled through and dived into it. The sky ice-sharp clear overhead. They always twinkle reassuringly here, brighter than in the world outside its enclosure. Not really of course. It's just that the streetlights and house lights and shop lights are more distant, and getting further, so the darkness gets correspondingly darker. She knows that. But it's still creepy. She knows this place. Knows to circle the coils of dog-crap. Not to crush the buckled energy-drink bottles tangled in the briar like heat-melted junk-sculpture. Further, there are foxes with luminous eyes that glare out of hollows and vague corners of old masonry that project from briars and nettle-patches.

And other things, spooky things that have no name.

*

"What do you want?" he demands.

As he opens the door they can see his arm is bandaged. Amrik and Rakesh turn towards David, like two sections of the same unit. Amrik shorter, stockier, with a thin moustache. His brother is taller, skinnier. "You need help."

"Like you've ever cared before. Why now? Are you

admitting you were wrong?"

"That was a long time ago. We're just saying we know you need help. Maybe it's time."

Priya stands behind him. She manages a threadbare smile. "It's a sad story." Then the smile oozes away. She sets her chin defiantly, to meet her brother's gaze fair and square. "Let's talk about why you're here now, not about what happened before."

"Ayesha is lost in the Blott. It falls to us all to find her. We wish her, and you, no ill."

She holds David back before he can say more. They stand still, watching each other, waiting to see who will make the first move. Amrik and Rakesh indicate towards the street. There are two cars idling. David nods truculently.

A little way across the opposite verge is the perimeter wire. The closer you live to the Blott, the lower the rent. She works at the Call Centre. The minibus comes round the estate and picks her up at eight. He doesn't work. Not from want of trying. No matter what he undertakes, there's always something stood in his way. The resentment gnaws away inside his guts. "It's like, whatever I do is not good enough."

*

The big sluice-pipe that empties onto the mudflats is always warm. The pool that gathers beneath its warm flow is warm. A clear pool with a gravel of small stones visible beneath its surface. When it's really cold little ghosts condense up from its surface. The kids come here to paddle their bare feet. She sits and watches it drip. The slope around the pipe mouth is a good place to find four-leaf clovers. She's thought about this before. Why is the water warm? Because it comes from a warm place. Follow the pipe back, and it will lead to the warm place.

She scrabbles up to the top of the slope. From here she can look out over the glistening mud to the dark swirls of the Tyne. Gulls circle and glide. She can feel the faint warmth coming up through the soles of her feet. She paces back along the trail it makes, slipping on ruts. Steps over a pile of sodden pizza take-away ad leaflets. The pathway has become choked with vegetation, some of the overhang droops as though caving in, with poisonous thorns and grasping plant-tendrils like tentacles.

Into the deep dark wood where the Big Bad Wolf prowls. The odour of death and decay permeates everything. Somewhere close by a dog is barking. It sounds big and vicious. Dim white shapes flit and glitter like fallen stars in the gloom. Shadows have lives of their own. Things that have no natural right to exist.

That's the moment the sideboard tipped over. She hadn't intended it to fall. Ayesha fell to the floor and cried out. The threatening furniture overhung, about to lurch again. Daddy David had come at her, his arm outstretched like a grab. Mummy Priya was screaming at him to stop. Mummy reached out and seized Daddy by the shoulder, pulling him back. He turned. His face was a monster's face. He hit Mummy. He hit her. He HIT her. Ayesha wriggles out from under the suspended cliff of collapsed furniture. Mum was crying. Ayesha was in the kitchen. She was scared and desperate. Her brain clogged with screaming voices. Her fingers close in around the laser-knife. Unsheathing it from the block on the draining board. It feels firm and solid. The handle is red plastic. She comes at him from behind and plunges the serrated blade into him before he can hit Mum again. The blade sinks into him. Through the jumper. Through the shirt. His whole body judders. There's blood on the blade when it comes free in her hand. She looked at it. She dropped it. And she fled...

Put-put-put-put. It goes put-put-put-put. And it's the sound that sets her on edge. She likes Saturday night because Daddy goes out. She and Mum sit together on the settee and watch *X-Factor* or maybe a lavish Bollywood DVD musical. It's warm and snuggly. Then, later, she hears the sound of his scooter approaching, as he turns it into the ginnel. It goes put-put-put-put, she knows that sound too well. It means bad things, and it sets her nerves on edge. It's time for her to scurry upstairs. His breath will be rank as the gutter with the stench of sour beer. From her room she will hear their raised voices. Not always the words. But his voice is loud. And Mum is crying. The arguments go on even though she buries her head in the pillow. She can hear hectoring voices going on and on and on...

*

"A question," says Amrik, leaning across from the car towards the guard kiosk. "Shut me up if it's none of my business, but I'm curious. Just what is it you're acting as security for here?"

"Can't say," grunts Rackham. "Not that I'm not at liberty to say. Just that I can't. Some time back – before I was recruited – security was out-sourced. Then the agency that took it over out-sourced again to a further group. So now, I don't honestly know. I just come and sit here."

"But you must be aware that the fence is more porous than gruyere cheese. Kids get through. People get through."

"None of my business, pal. You know how far that perimeter-wire extends? No, neither do I, but it's a hell of a long way. Another sub-contractor is responsible for its maintenance. And anyway, there's inner containment personnel. We've been subject to staff downsizing and economies of scale. So we do the gates. That's enough."

"It's just that we had a bad unfortunate scene. A domestic spat. And our daughter's gone missing. We think she's hiding out in there, and she's scared to come home."

David winces when he hitches his thumb in the direction of the gates, Rackham notices his bandage. "You've been injured?"

"It looks worse that it is."

He operates the barrier. It lifts to allow the two cars through. "I'll escort you as far as inner quarantine, and leave you to their tender mercies. There's a man name of Dern there. No promises. It's all I can do."

"Cheers. I appreciate this. We owe you one."

Rackham clambers in beside David, and directs them forward. The cars move along a ragged blacktop that curves through weed, the headlights washing the darkness back.

"Don't you go worrying about Judge Dredd's Cursed Earth, you best believe the rad-badland's already here..." comments Amrik.

In David's head, Ayesha's eyes stare back at him. She can fix you with that special stare that looks right into your soul. "She despises me for what I've done. I didn't realize just how much, not until the laser-knife punched the truth into me. There's no excuse, even though I've got a whingeing data-file full of them. I've not been strong enough. Ever since I met Priya, and we fell in forbidden love, with all that pain so carefully laid out before us. I've failed them. They both despise me and I deserve it. It's like, whatever I do is not good enough. I've been a bad, bad boy."

The drive leads to a complex of concrete bunkers, invisible from the estate, hidden behind overgrown slagheaps and slurry-beds. At their approach, beside a burnt-out auto-shell, a man with a giant caterpillar on his shoulder shields his eyes to greet them. He looks like the kind of old dosser you find rough-sleeping in shop-doorways, but he carries a gun casually in the crook of his arm. Not a normal gun.

"What you got for us here, Rackham? As though we've not got enough shit to deal with here."

"A favour, Dern, nothing more. A lost kid. A girl."

"In here? Strangers are not welcome. You're being delusionally optimistic. But it does get tedious at times, maybe we can do with the distraction."

"That's the possibility I'm basking in."

*

It could be a fox. It could be a bat. Or the wind. Or it could be the Big Bad Wolf.

Put-put-put-put. She can hear it coming for her. A bead of sweat is an insect trickling down her spine. She moans and clutches her temples, blasts of mental imagery overwhelming her, so forceful as though about to burst out through the fine cranial bones of her skull, smearing her with brain-stuff. That's the moment the world tips over. She hadn't anticipated it. This was not part of the plan. The warm-track led her here. She'd thought it would be a safe warm place. An enchanted palace lost in the coils of an enchanted deep dark wood. But the windows are all shattered. With corroded metal folding-doors high enough for a truck to pass through. And a warm dark chamber beyond carpeted in damp blown leaves.

She waits for several heartbeats. This is the place. It was dark. It happened fast. There's light inside. A fallen star trapped in a disc of rippling oily blackness. As she approaches it, the world bends beneath her feet. The universe tilts sideways. Reeling edge-wise on, so it becomes difficult to retain balance. She fights to hold on. All of reality has become paper-thin, a disk a micron-thick with a razor-edge that threatens to slash the grasp of her fingers. Cosmic systems blip and shimmer inside its tilted horizon, they've shrunk to become flaws and scratches on its laminate surface, brief scintillations that glow, dim and flicker out. Trapped fireflies. Then the things are crawling inside of her. Pulsing in vile tides through her body.

Amrik, Rakesh and David shock upwards. Dern and Priya a single step ahead of them. His stomach knots up. It was a bug. But like no woodlouse they've ever seen before. You flush bugs down the toilet. This is Kong-sized. Segmented chitinous shell, nests of flexing legs, two long antenna. And looming as big as a house. Dern hefts his rifle, but bides his time. It's not a normal gun. There are copper-coils wrapped tight around its barrel, and wires to a hunched backpack he wears.

"This is it? This is the secret you're guarding?"

"Not always. They're different each time. Trust me, you don't wanna go near them."

"Mutants, warped by the radioactive residue?"

His laugh is a mocking thing. "Close. First off, way back then, they were out solving the disposal problem, BNF – British Nuclear Fuels, as was. First it was serving Windscale and Calder Hall, then importing rods and spent materials from Japan and elsewhere. It was here they found the infallible solution. A hole to nowhere. They punched it through into a vast nothingness. An empty universe where different physical laws operate. So they began shovelling all that waste shit through. Except it turned out it wasn't quite as empty as they'd assumed. More a kind of reverse mirror-image negativity. A death realm. You following me…?"

"No. Nothing like."

A burst of lightning from Dern's gun. Its halo flickers around the looming monstrosity.

"Why isn't it working?"

"It is working. We're not trying to kill it. We're just driving it back."

"I hope you're right about this."

"Me too," from Dern, thumbing the stud, emitting another electro-burst. The beast lunges forward in pained response. If it was capable of roaring, it would be roaring, not just making this high-pitched nattery chittering

"Let's get the hell out," from Amrik, "time to scramola."

"Ayesha is here. She's lost and scared. You go back. It's my fault, I've got to find her." David steps forward as they step back. And it not so much pounces, more that one moment it's up there, towering into the night sky, then instantaneously it was here, snatching him up in bug-legs as thick as cables. Fourteen jointed limbs crushing him so tight his breathing ceases. So tight he felt he was exploding. A foul stench emitted from its jibbering maxilliped mouth.

The sound of sobbing. A howl of teeth-rasping frequency. It was an ugly itchy-twitchy sound. Ayesha stretches her arms and legs, they feel cramped, a numbness as if she's been squatting too long in the same position. As she flexes, the bug flexes. She can feel its weight all around her. The bone-sharp grip of its shell fused into her. Drop Daddy. I wanted him dead. But I don't want him dead any more. I want him back, like things were before they went bad. Drop him. It drops him. Jerking this way and that, undecided. Chittering and stuttering, then retreating back along the warm-track. She knows the warm-track. It coils down, skitters and scuttles. Back through the big folding iron doors. Into the comforting bug-snuggly dark warmth. She knows the bug is scared. It's lost and far from home. Like her, it only wants to go back to the way things were. Please. She guides it back through the eye of rippling oily blackness. Plop.

Now she's just a girl, cold and frightened. Ten years old, and a little overweight. Her eyes dart from one to the other. Her shattered family. Brought together by this wild adventure. She hopes the bug got home safely too.

She watches Daddy David sprawling where he was thrown. She watches him brace his hands firmly on his knees, push himself warily upright, exercise his neck experimentally by rolling his head this way and that. Then he crouches down and enfolds her in his arms. "Ayesha. I'm sorry. I'm so very sorry."

"Are they all like that big bug?" asks Amrik

Dern spits a stream of saliva into the weed. "Naw. They're all different. And each difference is different. Where the hell do you think I got Uncle Wiggly from?"

They slope off back towards the cars, Rackham nervously shepherding the group. Dern indicates bug-slime on David's jacket, and beckons him through a low doorway. Holding Ayesha's hand, Priya holding the other hand, they step through. Despite its apparent outer dereliction, inside it's strip-lit. A

104

couple of other operatives sit at screen-eyes or lounge back in swivel chairs. They nod, but otherwise ignore the intruder trio. There's a spaghetti of cables, a couple of beds further up the room, and long bookshelves so crammed there's not enough space for one extra volume. On adjacent shelving there are instruments, flasks of chemicals, fluids and jars containing what appear to be murky body-parts.

Dern eases his backpack down and off, heavy with batteries, then offers David a moist cloth sluiced under a hot tap.

"Why not just blow the hole up, or seal it off with tons of ready-mix concrete?" from David as Priya helps sponge ichor from his clothes. Little shivers of unease stinging from the laser-knife wound.

"Doesn't work that way, the other end would still be open and active. Instead, nature's reclaiming it. It will heal. It will take time. Meanwhile, there's half a dozen of us, watching for what comes through. A long-term strategy. But time is all it needs. Not that I'll be here to see it. I'm due for retirement, me and Uncle Wiggly. But, I watched you out there. You and the girl, you make a great team. You were scared, sure you were scared. You had every reason to be. But you dealt with it. You dealt with it once, maybe, with a little tuition, you could deal with it again. What do you say?"

"I've watched a lot of late-night Sci-Fi. I've seen scary stuff. Haha, that's good. You're offering me a position – here, a job?"

"Alright, of course you've got better offers. I should have known. Salary is low here, we don't get much, our lords and masters are not generous employers. But we manage. It's enough to sort out your situation nicely. What do you say? You want in to the quarantine zone?"

He glances around the bunker, glances at Priya, then down at his smiling daughter, and shrugs. "Why not? Sure, when do I begin?"

GENDER-SHOCK

They were gender deviants. How is a lawyer to defend them? Normality is something up for renegotiation in this disturbing tale.

The difficulty in portraying a totally pansexual society is that gender so pervades language it's problematic to eradicate it. This tale is constructed by dispensing with every use of 'he', 'she', 'himself' or 'herself' with every character purposefully gender non-specific – except for the single case of the transgressor, who is on trial specifically for that unforgivable deviation…

The case was not going well, I must admit. As the lawyer responsible, I watch the crowds way below the view-station, surging along the wide radial avenues of the Palais de Justice in the vibrant hues of their chadors and robes. Down there, their talk burns angrily, malevolent and cruel, reaching me only as the muted rise and fall of distant music. But I recognise the tune. It was ancient, primal. That crowd was somehow carnivorous. Descending in their droves to witness the highly ritualised slaying of the unfortunate pervert whose future has been entrusted to me. Yes, they've got a lot of taste… all of it bad. Of course, the argument that the populace is entitled to witness, and participate in the full machinations of the law had always seemed so eminently reasonable. Until now, for the first time in a long eventful career, it seems hollow. Those ghoulish voyeurs were not content with network screen-images. They're not here to see justice done, but to savour each scandalous detail of the case's disturbingly strange sexual aspects.

What can I do? I sigh, then reluctantly return to face my client, detained elsewhere in the complex. This aerial view is merely a tantalising excuse for tarrying. The sound of footsteps from behind me should have alerted me, but they come too late. "Sentrie Renate, reconsidering?"

I turn sharply from the ornate portal. The newcomer, Sheldon Mazoor is a groomed and dazzlingly competent lawyer, robed as

I am. We'd served at law-school together, hence we wear the same long, richly embroidered gowns. The same fringed hair decorated with gold pendants. "No, not reconsidering," I concede, "a little disheartened perhaps."

"You've dropped on an impossible case to fight. Odds were stacked against you from the start. You have my sympathies on that score. As soon as the deviant gender aspects of the thing became public knowledge, prurience ran riot. But then, you can't help but be aware of that."

"I know only too well, of course I do. But aren't there other things at play, weren't we taught not to determine judgement on the grounds of personal prejudice? There are too many aspects of this case clouded by revulsion, I understand these feelings, yet there's something wrong too."

"As disturbing as you may find it, regardless of the right or wrong, you can't argue the facts. What this represents is a grotesque reversion to something more primitive. It's as though some alien being has dropped into our midst, and taken over. And when the vote is cast, that's all they'll need." As I move away, Sheldon takes my place at the view-station. Indicating the crowds. "They've already made up their minds. They know all they need to know. Verella Cade is warped. A sexual extremist. By imposing that perversion on a child… that is unforgivable. I don't see how you can possibly mount a defence. But I'll be intrigued to watch you as you do."

"Yes, they'll sacrifice my client. But not for things Verella Cade did, but for the life-style Verella Cade lived."

"Isn't that the same thing? Society giveth, society taketh away. Society must protect itself. And it protects its interests by punishing dissenters in this long public torment. That's what we are witnessing now. The healthy rejection of the unclean." The words were delivered with an air of finality that allowed no rebuke. "No lawyer is forced into taking a defence case, you know that, Sentrie. You were offered it. You accepted it. If I were you I'd have quit while my reputation was still intact. Mud sticks, no matter what motives attracted the mud-slinging."

I hesitate. Caught in something of a dilemma. "I must go. My client waits. If you'll excuse me?" Sheldon shrugs, a shadow passing over the face, fading along the swirl of inlaid stars arcing from the tail of each eye. A grit of irritation. As though expecting more. I pace swiftly across the mosaic floor to the large double doors. They glide open in admittance, then hiss smoothly closed behind me. Green. Low-level green light softening everything, fusing flesh and bodies into a pleasing uniformity. Brushing through webs of perfume and teasing strands of conversation. Beautiful people among elegant stonework. Crossing the central piazza past the pillared façade from where hidden flights of little steps climb higher and higher through nests of tiered galleries up to the dome. But my relief at escaping Sheldon's artful probing is not long-lived.

Verella Cade sits primly on a low bench, watching the play of a small fountain dancing from the sunken garden in the centre of the room. An obviously assumed concentration intended to exclude everything else. The level of deliberate preoccupation allowed me time to watch unobserved. And yes, despite the necessarily impartial approach of my job, and the moral responsibility it dictated, I felt a little disturbed in my client's presence. That same faint unpleasant unease each time we meet. Cade wears a short tunic that accentuated the obviously female contours of her figure. The face, almost veiled by cascading hair, carried the same blatant, defiant sexuality. There was little evidence of security. Where could the prisoner escape to, dressed like that? Nowhere. Not without getting torn apart by the mob.

Cade made no obvious acknowledgement of my presence as I, too, sat down lightly on the bench. The words were directed at the fine play of water, not at me. "Our case goes badly." I nod dumbly, "I can only suggest, as I have done before, that you make a plea for special consideration."

"Say that I'm insane you mean?"

"You know such terminology is inadmissible."

"You say that, but you also know exactly what is happening to me, don't you? Despite what you say, they are labelling me with their terminology. Inventing an insanity for me. I appreciate your efforts on my behalf, I really do. But what you suggest is that I endorse their decision. Is that really the best you can offer? I'm not trying to make you feel uncomfortable. I'm not trying to make you feel anything at all. It has nothing at all to do with you, and everything to do with me and my son. The world has no right to interfere in that. So don't tell me what to do. It's my choice."

"That's your first mistake. Right there. A child is not a 'possession'. A child is an individual with its own rights. Its own unique potential. It is not something to be moulded according to the whims and prejudices of a biological parent. People see that as a monstrous assumption on your part."

"So I'm a monster? Let me be a monster. That's all I ask. Just let me be..." pretending to watch the fountain.

"Your right to be whatever you wish to be is not at issue. It is perpetrating that life-style on the child that is the crime."

"The child? The child? You're talking about Peter, my son, my son."

Unconsciously I find myself flinching, acutely embarrassed at the blatant vulgarity, the blasphemous bluntness. This is not good. Not good at all.

*

This courtroom is a gilded chamber of horrors. An arena surmounted by the dignified arbitrator. The desks of the opposing counsels face each other across the polished floorspace. Behind them the public galleries form rows of hushed expectant faces. Below them are the busy officials, stoic security, expert witnesses, and the solitary accused. The jury is everywhere in the city, pads ready to enter their verdict. The prosecuting counsel opened in full spate, stating the charges with a briskly emotionless efficiency. "Anthropologically, Verella Cade is a throwback to simpler, less sophisticated times. For the larger portion of history society was divided along strict gender lines by the necessity of hardship. Indeed, there are still tribes out there who persist in living that way, through unreconstructed choice. But think on this. The pre-collapse world was brought to the brink of destruction by such reasoning. When gender is conditioned inflexibly around two poles the natural human tendency to diversity is distorted out of shape. That's what happened. Restricted and repressed desires become twisted into abhorrent behaviour, extreme behaviour, the kind of madness that led to the global conflicts and wars that brought us to the edge of extinction. We survive, we thrive now because we know better. We've evolved beyond that."

A pause for dramatic effect. If this is all about power, then it's unfair. All of this scrupulous morality assembled to crush one unhappy discontent. All this brutal sophistry brought to bear on the weak, by the strong. Yet even in this human disaster story there's a kind of bleak unconsoling humour. A supple movement between laughter and horror in the incessant buzz of speculation. "Although that is not the issue at stake, we should not lose sight of those facts. Gender is not a fixed polarity, but a spectrum of gradual increment. Preference is an individual thing, a chosen orientation, or serial orientations. It is something only the mature adult must decide. Once the age of reason is attained, sure, do what you want, love whomsoever you choose, but let it be your choice. It must be decided by the individual, and not imposed on the young before they're mature enough to deal with it. It's not something to be forced inflexibly on a child, according to a set of social expectations and standards. The offence here is in causing acute traumatising disturbance to the child, resulting in loss of potential identities, stunting its emotional growth. That is the offence. Not the ideas. Not the chosen life-style. But the actions." The counsel bowed with the slightest nod in the general direction of the arbitrator, and sat down.

All the while I was taking it all in. Recording notes. These are the accusations I must answer to at the next session. The facts of the matter were relatively simple. They were not in dispute. The implications were labyrinthine. They were there to be teased out. Would tracing the sperm-sponsor be a worthwhile line of enquiry? Or might the results actually benefit the prosecution more? In fact, they may already have done the traces, and rejected the findings. There is no record of parental collusion, but this is a case riddled with privacy issues and tantalising unknowns. There could yet be new elements to emerge. Better perhaps to chase precedents? There were precedents. None of them offering a viable solution.

Observing. The accused was sitting impassive. If the audience were hoping to detect outward symptoms of guilt, nervousness or fidgeting, they'd be disappointed. The child – Peter, was there too, although barely recognisable from earlier images. More conventionally garbed. There was partitioning to segregate sensibilities. But, at one point, in a moment of intense silence as the session was drawing to a close, with the prosecuting counsels clearing documents from the desk and into voluminous robes, and Verella was being escorted out, their eyes met across the room, and something passed between them. It happened so quickly it was almost as though I'd imagined it. With the court adjourned for the remainder of the day, I replayed the moment in my memory. Later I re-ran court sequences, freezing it. Yes. Momentarily, their eyes met, Verella and Peter, and something else. A signal. A coded message. No-one else intercepted it or even knew it had happened. Caught up in proceedings no-one else realised. But me, I saw it. Something unmistakable.

*

Outside the Palais de Justice I watch skitters circling above the organically rounded contours of the city skyline. I wait impatiently for Sheldon to arrive. We are to share a skitter back to my suite. Watching the scene outside the hall is enough to set the pupils of your eyes dilating. How can so much life be so condensed? Yet my eyes take it in, roving for clues to the drama of the moment, and finding them everywhere in the glittering dramatic possibilities of shock and queasy titillation. A carnival of pity and disgust, not a place concerned with the dispensing of sober justice. What the hell is going on here? You know the reasons – how could you help but know, but not the scale.

Then we glide above the mob, climbing, the city swimming. Facing each other as the beam guides us. For a long space of time we do not speak. As though testing out the air between us. An encouraging hand on my knee, but tactfully no higher, "Are you alright?" It occurs to me that, through all this, Sheldon was hitting on me. "Sure I'm alright." There was an expectation that I'd lose. That I'd be in need of a supportive shoulder, someone to draw strength from, and that there might be exploitable advantage in supplying that comforting friendship. So I play it flirtatiously, "Have you ever been disappointed to discover the gender of a lover?"

"I cherish the mind of the lover, not the physical attributes."

111

"Of course, that's the standard acceptable response. That's the condition to which we all aspire. But come on, we are human too, we have preferences. There must have been moments…?"

"No. I take and give pleasure according to the person I happen to be with."

"And to think otherwise would be wrong?"

"We are what we are. That's the entire point, Sentrie Renate."

In my suite I thumb the dimmer halfway up and decant drinks. We lounge together, but conversation stays focussed. "You want my opinion? You really want to know the way I see it? What Verella Cade is guilty of is hormonal confusion, but writ large. A wild chance, but one allowed enough space to channel instincts into practise."

"I appreciate your advice. I really do." I drank deeply, contemplatively.

"You want my take on it?"

Again I nodded. Hadn't the wish for opinion already been agreed?

"Your client acted according to a kind of warped conscience. Not emotionally in control, but through strange instinct. I imagine Verella was convinced that the actions were for the best – that the fantastical femininity is merely a by-product of the action. Fabricated to justify the action. I make myself clear?"

"You mean that Verella was not consciously committing a sexual indoctrination?"

"Verella devoted time to the child. Conversation, affection, company. Those are acts of love, not necessarily of perversion."

Sheldon is, of course, correct. My failure is the only realistic option. What Verella wants is impossible. It would not happen. The child would be taken and fostered. Cade would be punished. Re-educated. There could not be any other outcome. All I can do is present the argument. Articulate it as well as I can. Appeal for clemency, for a degree of understanding that I find difficult to fathom myself, a leniency. It was cut and dried. So why do I feel this disturbing degree of helpless anger?

Sheldon was preparing to leave. Biding time. "There is such a thing as evil. There is such a thing as perversion. Don't let your sympathies aroused by this case lead you to seriously think otherwise. We look at one person caught up in the system. One… dare I say, victim of the system? Is that the way you intend angling this thing? It's possible, it's certainly possible to construct a case along those lines. I look forward to hearing your argument. Mount your defence, certainly. That is what you are there to do. That is your legal function. But don't ever be seduced by the arguments you're making..."

No, no, of course not. Assurances come easily. We face each other in uncertain silence. A soft embrace, a kiss that is little more than formality. Then I was alone. Smiling to myself. Flattered, amused by the attentions. Aware of the possibilities. Not dismissing them entirely. Instead of relaxing I began skimming screens. Rehearsing and reacquainting, re-familiarising myself with the case. They'd lived unexceptional lives in an old private house by a neglected snake in the river. High walls, a hidden garden that slopes down to the water's edge. A vaguely genteel run-down area, bohemian I suppose, where privacy and a degree of eccentricity easily go unnoticed. It was only as the child – only as 'Peter' grew that their oddness attracted attention, and gossip. The files and reports, few at first, built into a dossier. Their walks together along towpaths skirting the river. The two of them, together. Excluding all others. Until the investigation became official. The child, the boy, Peter, was ten years old. In replayings of snatched dialogue the child comes across remarkably self-contained and confident. And at the same time, a curio. Careful use of vocabulary, but there's no other way. 'His' hair cropped back. 'His' clothing, initially, of another era. Another time. Another world. Verella, by contrast, was initially evasive, defensive. Only becoming more assertive as it became obvious that the interrogators would not be placated. When there was nothing to gain by evasion, and little left to lose.

The images drew me in. Why is this strangeness permeating like lingering ghosts? Why is the idea so disturbing? Why do we fear it? Do we recognise something within its labyrinth of equations that echoes back from some deeper archetype? Surely not. We are rational beings, are we not? I fan out into wider realms. The prosecuting counsel had mentioned tribes 'out there' who still persist in living unreconstructed lives, through choice. I seek out references and possible avenues of defence, rejecting each in turn. Until eventually tiredness overwhelms me. And I sleep.

*

The alarm stabbed through my room, shocking me awake. Coming round blearily. Punching it up. A message from Sheldon. "Verella Cade is gone. So is the child. They disappeared soon after midnight from their respective points of confinement... more details following." Things happened fast, and they also happened gradually. I showered. Drank a tisane, washing thoughts around my head with each sip. How had this happened? Obvious, in a way. Security was light. Because everyone knows what Verella Cade looks like, it would not be difficult to escape notice by altering that appearance. It would only need a chador, and Cade could pass through the Palais de Justice and the wide radial avenues beyond without attracting a second glance. The child, Peter, was in care, not incarceration. Observed. But not impossible to avoid observation... for long enough.

I skitter across to the courtroom. People standing around in groups, talking furtively, glancing at each other. Androgynous people, de-gendered by costume. And beneath the concealing robes, by the snip and reassign, tuck and remould of cosmetic surgical enhancement, implants and depilation into any gender or combination of genders. They must consider me conservative in being quite happy with my body the way it is, thank you. In their eyes, I must seem only a little more removed from Verella Cade, probably. In my chambers there were updates, searches initiated, procedures set in motion, nothing conclusive. Beginnings, not ends. I was too caught up in events to think too much about my own reactions. I thumbed up my files. Skimming through data. There were ideas playing around my head, without any logical connection. Recalling the way their eyes had met across the room. The way something had passed between them. They had planned for this eventuality. They had worked out contingency plans between them. The signal, the coded message, had been the trigger to set it in motion. Then I sat for a long while. Got up and paced the length of the room. Routine was disrupted. Everything on hold. Searches were underway. Until security turned up a result there was not much I could do. I went up to the view-station, looked out over the city. They were out there, somewhere. Where would they go? Did they have some back-up plan? But they'd escaped separately. What would be their first priority? The first move would be to meet up. No words had passed between them. It must have been something they both understood.

I quit the building. Coming outside the Palais de Justice, and into a different kind of tension. The scattering of people knew what had happened. They too were sitting around, awaiting confirmation of some result. I took my skitter gliding above the architectural curves, climbing above them. Unhooked the guide-beam with no particular idea of where I was going. Circling, with the city skyline swimming. The river meanders through the city's west end. I follow it down. It took little over twenty minutes to identify the loop. At first the house was made near-invisible by trees. I took it in lower. There was security at the gates. I set down on the overgrown lawn where it sloped down to the slow-swirling water. There was a guard outside the front door. We talk briefly. The house and grounds had been thoroughly searched, with no results. It was under constant surveillance. If the pervs were unwise enough to return here they'd be seized. No question about it. I nodded my agreement. Strolled sticky-footed down to the edge of the river, trailed my hand in the water. They must have done this many times. In their secretive enclosed world they must have played games across this grass, to this point by the water. This place is riddled with their memories and secret significances, of which I know nothing. Only image-glimpses from files. Where did they go from here?

I took the skitter up. Circled the house. Yes, they used to follow the tow-path. So I followed it too. Not many people take the path. It had become overgrown with briars, tall feathery grass and nettles. They came this way because they didn't want to be noticed. Because they didn't want to attract attention. I came in low, a metre from the swirl of tide. Elsewhere in the city, others would be drawing similar conclusions, splicing together enhanced spyfly footage. They would soon be redirecting their search in this direction. It was imperative I find them first... wasn't it? It dawned on me gradually that this was what I was doing. I wanted to find them. I eased velocity a little, eyes raking the tow-path. I buttoned a connection to Sheldon. No, no developments. They'd turned nothing up yet. Good. Although I didn't admit that to Sheldon. "Will you do me a favour?" the words came spontaneously, "can you cover for me?"

"I'll do anything you want me to, you know that."

Grateful, I just asked to be updated as things happened. And swept the screen clear.

Imagine. Imagine. How far would they have walked? There would be a turn-around point. I was wrenched out of introspection by the sudden low passes of three security skitters above me. Their high-speed passage made ripples in the air that left me gently rocking. They were closing in too. Ahead there's a derelict overgrown former-industrial site. The river disappears under a tunnel-section. They can't have gone further than this. I slow, glide in lower… and yes. As I go in clipping tree-tops they break and run. Two figures. Adult and child. Both in disguising robes, but unmistakably the fugitives. As I glide gradually down, way above me there are shapes cutting across the sky. And below me Cade and Peter are holding hands, running away from me, but they're unaccustomed to wearing robes, the child trips, tangled in briars and flows of material. Verella pauses to help, and I set down a metre ahead of them. With the hood shoved back I beckon, "Hurry, get in."

I can see Verella's face clearly now. There's uncertainty, indecision… fear too. Like a trapped animal. Nowhere to run. Nowhere to hide. A triangulation of skitters scream in low above us. It forces the decision. The fugitives accept my invitation. They clamber in. I lift off in a zig-zag trajectory with the hood not fully resealed. The alert pulsing. Skitters circling above. I hadn't thought this thing through. I hadn't thought ahead. This is working on instinct. And instinct determines concealment. Low over the water. Too low for safety. Lapping and dipping at the wave-tips. In towards the dark tunnel-mouth. The sky cuts out abruptly. The slight hum amplified. Flashes of reflected tiles, bursts of weed and down-hanging slime. Darting creatures, bright yellow eyes, leaping from narrow ledges into black circles of water. I could illuminate, but that might attract attention. Instead I reduce speed to zero and hover in darkness. Looking back there's a small circle of light where we came in. There's a buzz of passage as a security skitter blips past. Then nothing. A cloying sickly smell seeps in, catching my throat like a finger, a deep-stagnant smell, like something died here, and is rotting. After a long pause I ease forward again. The tunnelled section extends further than I'd anticipated, but eventually there's light ahead. We emerge not knowing what to expect. But there's no sign of pursuit. We're well-beyond the outer perimeter of the city. I accelerate, and don't deviate until we're well-clear.

Verella eases her cowl back in a gesture of obvious relief. "Thank you. I'm in your debt. Surprised, and confused as well. But grateful, above all else."

"You shouldn't have done this. You shouldn't have run. My remit is to help you. I was doing everything within my power to do that. Now, if I am going to help you at all, you leave no alternative but subterfuge."

"Who are you attempting to fool? You saw them in court. You saw the faces. The gawping faces, watching as though we're some kind of sideshow freaks. They've decided already. You know damn well what the verdict would be. How many million pads would be pressed all over the city, how many thumbs-down? You know damn well how it would have been. We had no choice. No choice at all."

"I apologise Verella Cade, for my perceived legal inadequacy. I was conducting a very difficult case in the only way I knew. I was doing my best for you under unique conditions that you were hardly helping to normalise. Now you've forced the issue." Following the quivering silver of the river west there's a hundred kilometres of nothing but forest. The waterway overflows, losing its clear definition in vast marshy everglades. The occasional pre-collapse archaeological cluster of ruins, scarcely distinguishable from undulations of landscape. Surprisingly, the plans had been there in my head all the time, even though I hadn't been consciously aware of them. The prosecuting counsel had mentioned tribes 'out there' who still persist in living unreconstructed lives. I'd already sought them, made references and location notes. They lived hard communal lives. But they would not question the life-style Verella and Peter had chosen. And yet, and yet... Verella may have chosen. Peter had not been allowed the choice. His orientation had been decided for him. He was the victim. But the damage was already done, it was too far advanced for correction. Any attempted adjustment now would only do more harm and prove even more traumatic for him. Him? Unconsciously I was now using the same blatant vulgarity, the same blasphemous bluntness she'd used. 'He'. 'She'. No, I had done what I felt I had to do. But I'd be glad once it was over, and I was safely back in the sanity of the city.

We set down outside a small rural community encircled by a stockade. A single cross of streets, a dozen renovated cottages, a few others waiting to be worked into occupancy, a patch-work of agricultural plots hacked out of the wilderness. There might be sporadic trade between here and the city, but there was no extradition treaty with them. They come out to welcome us. Although their lives are run along gender lines, they seem oddly contented with it. I wait long enough to check that the fugitives would be accepted. They would. Then it was time for me to get back. I'm wary of tarrying. Come sundown the skitter will switch to reserve-cell, and although that should be adequate, I'd rather not risk putting it to the test

"Again, thank you. It seems inadequate, but I'm forever in your debt."

"What I did was done as a lawyer to a client. Nothing more."

Cade looked me full in the face. "Despite what you've done for us, you still find me disgusting. Say it."

"My personal prejudices are of no consequence."

"But they are Sentrie Renate, they are."

She paused. The 'she' comes more easily now. It was her choice, after all. There's a playful expression on her face. She leans forward in a conspiratorial way. "Will you tell me one more thing, something I'm curious to know?"

"What is that? Ask away"

"So tell me, serious lawyer-person, when I thank you, to which gender am I giving thanks…?"

I open my mouth on the brink of confiding. But at the last moment, bite it back, "No, it would be impolite of me to be so specific." Maybe I'll save that revelation for Sheldon.

BIG BAD JOHN

In North Yorkshire he paints his masterpiece,
'The Last Neanderthal', from experience.

It was the earthquake that started it all.

They're talking about it over breakfast. "Spent time in Berkeley. They know about tremors there. They're so familiar with them they grade them by different types. The long slow rumble. The short sharp crack. Various ripple-styles. On the San Andreas faultline, waiting for the big one, they know all about earth-tremors."

"And here we get a very minor night-tremble. I believe one vase on a mantelpiece in a house in Cayton teetered, and fell, and smashed on the fireplace beneath, and it's all over everywhere. They're talking about it on the bus, on the local radio and TV." An angular younger man with meat-cleaver nose and undernourished mouse-coloured moustache. His spectacles pushed up onto his forehead, where they perch precariously. "It's an intriguing phenomenon."

"No, it's more than that. It's sinister. You know what it's all about? You really want to know?" the older guest rubs his long chin and grins, a gleam of smug satisfaction in his deep-set eyes. "I'll tell you what it's about. Fracking. In a word, that's what's behind it. They're carrying out test borings on the moors. They don't talk about it, but everyone knows that's what's going on. It happened a couple of years ago around the Fylde area. Remember that quake?"

Danny Fisher's attention isn't really focused. He grunts assent as required, and makes noises of agreement where he feels appropriate. He brings warm white enamel plates of Full English's from the kitchen, along the entrance hall, into the breakfast room. One with mushrooms. He refreshes the toast-wrack with new hot slices. And removes the cereal bowls with the trickle of milk at the bottoms and the crusting of granola.

It's overcast outside the South Wind. The sky heavy over Scarborough's north bay. A kind of shocked stillness left by the

119

tremor aftermath. Back in the kitchen he flips the dishwasher open, removes the clean crockery and restocks the machine.

"Not there," Ginny sighs, as he hefts a pile of clean plates up towards the cupboard. "Will you never learn?"

His teeth grit. "It's a learning curve. I'm getting there," with forced lightness.

"How long? How long? We always put the clean plates in there. We always have. Concentrate, Danny, concentrate." Then a parting shot, "Don't forget that cistern." She has that wonderful way of wrinkling her nose that says so much with so little effort. As though detecting a distasteful odour. Odd to think he'd once found it impishly attractive. Now he sometimes thinks she looks incomplete without her witch's broomstick.

He plods back like a man with feet in glue. Big clumsy fingers. Bitten-down nails. Not artist's fingers. Artist's fingers are long and slim, as sensual as a musician's. His fingers are blunt ungainly things. Like breakfast sausages. His watercolours are hung around the breakfast room. The local views of the harbour and the castle that the visitors prefer. A sketch of Anne Brontë's grave in St Mary's cemetery, he quite likes that one, there are Brontë fans who go for that kind of thing. He adjusts it, straightening it, although it's already straight. But the two guests are so into talking quake conspiracy theories they scarcely glance at his artwork.

Two overnight guests. Hikers with thick boots, cagoule jackets and knitted hats. They've already finished breakfast and have begun moving out, preparing to leave for trudging the Cleveland Way coastal path. He smiles at them as they pass him. "Have a good day."

They return the greeting and disappear up the stairs. Nothing more to do here. Wait, the cistern. He makes a show of retrieving his toolkit from the walk-in beneath the stairs. Selects his shifter-spanner. From the landing he can see out over the town. The Royal Hotel, once owned by Charles Laughton's family. He imagines the actor's ghost loping down the corridors in his Quasimodo guise, and smirks the kind of secret smile that always annoys his wife. He removes the lid of the toilet cistern. Flushes it. Adjusts the locking nut on the ball-cock, and watches as the water flows back in. It stabilises at an acceptable level. He replaces the top and nudges it back into position. That'll do. He's the handy-man. Why is he handy...? Like in the old pier-end joke, because he lives just up the stairs! At least she can't criticise his contribution to the smooth running of the B&B. That's enough.

Once outside he takes the car, checks out a few charity shops for useable frames. There's still plenty of time, so he guns the Fiat Punto out onto the Scalby Road up towards Robin Hood's Bay. The easel and paints on the rear seat. His camera in its case, the strap coiled tightly around it. The day stretches out before him, as wide as the sky. Absurd conversations continue in his head. There'd been that pale couple booked in last month, so insubstantially ghost-white they seem to teeter on the brink of non-existence. He'd mused out loud about how it's as though they're time-tripper fugitives from some oppressive far-future. Ginny looks at him as though he's not quite right.

Now he continues the narrative safely inside his head. Explaining the world of today to the time-travelling visitors because, of course, they won't know. Way back – say the 1950s – all of these B&B's were regularly booked solid through high season. Old monochrome prints show the curving beach and Foreshore Road awash with happy trippers from the West Riding, from Scotland and elsewhere. The Futurist and the Winter Gardens summer bills packed with top star-names, Tommy Cooper, Morecambe & Wise, Ken Dodd. Then the hospitality trade adjusted to the Package Tour boom of the seventies, as punters start taking their main holidays in Benidorm, the Costa-plenty's, and the Tossa this and that's, by catering to the long-weekend market. Then, when folks start taking Barcelona and Amsterdam city-breaks instead, they refocus again, finding ramblers, twitchers and walkers to eke out the budget. You put off redecoration for another year, and you get by.

Turning inland through the national park. He knows these roads, their branching ways into nothingness. No houses now, no minimarts or mobile homes. Just low sheep-cropped moorland hills. The road reduces down to a single lane. He hauls in a few locations he's earmarked earlier. Clumps to the crest of a gorse rise, between clusters of primroses and kingcups, mentally framing its potential. Tourists prefer recognizable views of the high castle ramparts, or fishing boats unloading silver onto the harbour-side. He can do that. It brings in a useful £10, £15 or even £20 to gain even Gilly's grudging approval. But this washed-out watercolour landscape resonates with something primal deep. He squeezes off a couple of photos for future reference. Close-ups of lichen-wheels on part-submerged yellow rock, resembling micro-realms from alien planets. Glacial moraine deposited by receding ice-sheets. Smell that air, it's untainted country air.

From here he can look down on a fenced-off area surrounded by high wire. A formation of portacabins centred on a grid of derrick-structures. He watches the activity in a silence so deep you could write your name on it. This is what deep-set eyes had been talking about in the breakfast room. The fracking test-bores that some blame for the earthquake. And why not apportion blame? There are massive cave-systems beneath here. Pot-holers stay over at South Winds too. They told him of tracking uncharted subterranean rivers down through lost labyrinths, emptying into grottos the size of cathedrals where strange fungus grows and eyeless fish shimmer through bottomless pools. Of course, they could be romancing a tad for effect. But it stands to sense, in a way. You can't disturb and contaminate primeval sedimentary layers without setting up echo reverberations through time.

He watches with a stilled sense of unease for several long moments. Gulls wheel high above. From their gullish elevation they don't differentiate, they see only the interconnectedness of human activity. Watcher and watched. He retreats to the Punto in disgust. His fingers drum on the steering wheel. He watches a fly battering itself against the curved windshield, its drone going zuub, zuub, zuub. He reclines the car seat. From here the Fracking site is hidden, as though it never existed. He closes his eyes and drowses.

He's going nowhere in particular, it's already way-past noon and he's thirsty. The sky is still heavy, with layers of dark cloud. He takes a right-hand fork he's never used before. It narrows even more, down a slow incline between high shoulders of hills. A couple of tumbledown cottages, long abandoned, trees growing out through the bare ribs of once-roofing. At the bottom there's an arch of trees shading a stone bridge over a rapidly-cascading stream. On the far side, the cliffs rear up on both sides, although the track continues. And there's a pub, The Big Bad John. He navigates over the humpback bridge onto the rough ground that constitutes the car-park. An old country pub, in need of care and attention.

He stoops his way in. A couple of seated drinkers look up at the briefly opened door. Locals. Although where they're local to is mysterious, as there seems to be no habitation within miles. The man behind the pumps has bare arms like a pugilist's folded over his chest. Muscles knotted beneath the skin, giving an impression of more muscle than brain. He asks for a pint of Theaksons. And slurps from the glass. "Why's this place called The Big Bad John?" he asks conversationally, wiping beer from his mouth with the back of his hand.

"You wanna know? It's all in there." He nods at a bunch of scrubby leaflets in a display stand. Looks like no-one's investigated them in a generation.

Danny retrieves one of them and retires to an alcove with his pint. He slurps at the beer and relaxes back as best he can into the seat. He glances down at the leaflet, smoothing its curl out across the table. Old letterpress print like Braille, he can feel its indentations on the reverse. Its then he notices the frames hung on the walls. Yellowed newsprint with faded halftone photos. Some kind of local legend, a Yeti figure, a mix of bluff and bunkum obviously contrived in a failed attempt to attract tourism. Sightings dating back to the thirties. Myths from even earlier. The kind of thing mothers whisper to unruly children, 'hush, or Big Bad John will hear you.'

He checks through his camera display, some nicely brooding shots. Gets his pad out and starts sketching. Two pints later and it's twilight when he makes to leave. Stepping outside the chill air meets him dankly. He pauses unsteadily, one hand on the Punto door. Three drinks was unwise. He shouldn't really be driving. Not that there's likely to be police patrols this far out. That's highly unlikely. And sure, he'll have sobered up a little by the time he's back in Scarborough, sufficiently. There's no alternative. He's late already. Ginny will be displeased. Already she could be out there cruising the sky on her broomstick, seeking the smell of his blood. He smirks the kind of smile that always annoys her, and gets in. The engine turns over easily, the headlights punching the night away.

He reverses, with exaggerated care, over-concentrating, fighting the canting nausea in his gut. Slews the car around towards the humpback bridge, away from the pub, and hits the accelerator. The front tyres bite, and climb the abrupt rise…

Then shock bludgeons across the windscreen, splash-lurches heavy, solid, an impact jouncing him back in the seat. He yells, the wheel spinning away between his fingers. Out of control. He slams down hard on the brake. The tyres scream in response, spraying grit. The car lunges away to the right. The stone-built wall of the bridge leaps at him. The crunch is terrifying, exploding the headlight into furious blackness, crumpling away the wing in a metallic screech. A juddering forward lurch, over the rim edge, the wheel spinning on nothing, but motion has ceased. A chunk of masonry has cascaded away down the dark drop into the surging water far below. He's hanging one wheel over the edge of the ruptured bridge. Without thinking he slams into reverse and releases the clutch. The engine screams with a sudden stench of rubber. He strains back into the seat, willing the car back. It moves, gains purchase. Grip and lurch, grip and lurch. Slithering sideways and back, away from that terrifying plunging void.

He's cold with sweat, shivering with aftershock, bent in over the wheel as the engine dies into weird silence. He shoves at the Punto door and explodes out into the chill night. Whatever the hell was it he'd hit? Whatever the hell had hit him? There's a sprawled shape on the grit, close by the first rise towards the humpback bridge. Oh shit, oh shit, oh shit. He's killed someone. He stoops down over the body. It's a man. A naked man. Beast-weird from the hunched attitude of his body to the disarray of his black hair, to the savage frown. Eyes that glint like splinters of anthracite. But no, not dead. Bleeding, but still breathing. As Danny straightens up there's blood on his stubby sausage-fingers.

What to do? Load him into the car and head out for Scarborough General? It's too far, and they'll ask questions. There'll be a breathalyser and blood tests to establish alcohol levels. He's over-limit. No two ways about that. He glances back at the pub, ragged nerves sick with fear. No alternative.

Shoving back in through the door the bar-room is empty. Surely there were two other drinkers? The landlord looks to be readying to close. He glances up.

"Help me, I've had an accident. Someone's hurt, hurt bad."

Brawn-for-brains reaches down beneath the bar and produces a shot-gun. For a terrifying moment Danny Wilson cringes back in new terror, anticipating cartridges ripping his flesh. But the landlord simply hefts the weapon under his arm. "Show me."

Back out into the gathering night. Across to the Punto. Danny looks around in jittery desperation. "He was there, right there, I swear it." The fact that he's got up and lurched off somewhere is obviously good, isn't it? At least it shows he's revived and his injuries are less than life-threatening. The landlord is down on one knee checking indentations in the grit, like a hunter, sniffing the air like an Apache tracker in a western movie.

"I don't understand. He just came out of nowhere. I swear I couldn't avoid hitting him." He's almost sobbing. "And, this is weird, he – he was naked, and..."

"Toby," grunts the landlord quietly. "It was Toby Kwimper. He's my grandson. We gotta follow him, right?"

Danny nods. Grandpa Kwimper carries the shotgun casually on the crook of his arm. Leads the way back, away from the bridge, past the Big Bad John to where the cliffs close in, the path narrowing and climbing higher. Less a path as a shingle slip deposited by a slurry of rain-washed pebbles. Disturbed in shivering trickles by the earthquake. By the tremor that started it all. Deep subterranean pressures forcing unpredictable surface echoes.

"The Romans were mining here, broaching though into the natural caves beyond. And before them the Celtic Parisi tribe who roamed these hills." A sandpaper voice that rasps at his nerves.

"If I'd known that I'd have packed my pot of wode." The attempted joke does little to restore his self-confidence. And he can do with all the self-confidence he can get. Needs a whole heap of sanity, and all he's getting is one big pile of not-follow. It's a nightmare, no, it's a reverse nightmare. In dreams you find yourself pitched into surroundings that you tell yourself cannot be real. But this place, he almost knows this place. It's teasingly familiar. He's sketched and painted similar rock formations over and over again.

He stumbles and goes down in a shower of shingle. Kwimper reaches out and grabs Danny by the arm. A grip that's scarily strong. Or maybe it's him that's scarily weak? For a moment they pause. "You're a stranger. I guess you've got a right to know. My daughter Holly was sixteen. She was out on the moors. Would never say what happened, or who did it. But she wound up with this kid, Toby. It was obvious he wasn't quite right from the start. She could never adjust, never got over it. She was found face-down in the reservoir. We never registered the birth, that'd open up awkward questions, but what else could we do? We kind-of look after him. You understand?"

Understand…? Sure he understands. If the weird kid doesn't officially exist then he's not liable for his murder, or his grievous bodily harm. He fights down a feeling of resented relief. It's wrong to feel that way. It seems Grandpa Kwimper's moment of uncharacteristic revelation is done, because he resumes the trek, Danny sauntering in his wake. They've passed through the narrowest pinch-point – four paces wide, into a flat enclosed valley, cave-mouths or mine excavations punched into the steep walls. The sound of running water away left, probably feeding the stream by the pub, which is way out of sight. It's almost a primeval landscape below a roof of cloud.

"Toby!" The landlord's call has a dying fall that only serves to make his evening shadows seem deeper.

Danny follows the direction of Kwimper's shout. Yes, he's there. A slouching shape, half in darkness. An animal at bay, shambling this way and that. He clutches his left shoulder with his hairy right hand, where the impact wound seeps. Then, as he watches, Danny can make out a second form beyond, and a third, detaching themselves from shadow, yet still part of it. The hair on the nape of his neck prickles in horror. A circle of carnivores from the dawn of time, closing in on him. Anthracite-black eyes adapted by long troglodyte generations. Through teeth sharp with blood they emit thin high-pitched shrieks that don't resemble language, yet communicate meaning. He startles back in wild shock.

"Hush," says Kwimper. "It's alright. They sensed the sharp stab of his pain. It's drawing them to him, as he is drawn to them. He's returning to his own kind to heal himself…"

How does he know? Is he guessing? Or does he carry that

126

same DNA-trace from even earlier cross-species matings?

Much later, back at the South Wind Danny Fisher sets up his easel. He has his preparatory sketches. He has a series of photos framing interesting stones and mossy rocks. But more than anything else, he has a theme burning bright. Brighter and more luminous than ever before. A million suns pound inside his head. He works swiftly with few corrections, broad strokes setting up the scene, then adding detail, before filling in the spaces with soft washes of pale colour. He's scarce created this way before, carried along by the urgent need to burn the image in his mind onto canvas.

'The Last Neanderthal'. His masterpiece. The best painting he's ever done. He stands back looking at it, taking it all in, can hardly believe it's his own work. The same familiar hills and sky he's rehearsed so many times. As if every painting he's ever done has been a try-out for this one. The formation of rock with its lichen patterns cascading down from the right upper hand. But this time, a sole melancholy figure, sitting, gazing out over the moor. A great sadness suffusing its powerful body. The time of its species drawing to a close.

He hangs it in pride of place in the breakfast room. But will keep it as centrepiece of his display in the society's summer exhibition.

The visitors browse. And move on. They buy paintings of the castle. They buy paintings of the fishing boats unloading their catch along the wharf.

No-one glances twice at 'The Last Neanderthal'…

TERMINATOR ZERO & THE DREAM DEMONS

> What happened the night of the Rooftop Gardens, the Tandoori House, and the studio mix-tricknology? Perhaps it's something to do with the smuggled Khmer statuette, the prehistoric beach, and the return of an ancient evil...

It starts this way. Last night was the Rooftop Gardens, the Tandoori House, the studio mix-tricknology. This morning, the auto-chase – jabbing for the hyperspace button on the dash facia as dawn fades up into day, slamming this ultimate driving machine – this neutrino-powered stretch hover-car with moonroof up through the orbital. 1000 kph, while thinking in pictures. Foot's hard down on the pedal through the lights at red, underjets whining, out into orbit – the unjust *BEWARE!* The bad guys are hunching up hard left behind me in a low-slung Thunderwing Interblock Zoom, the passenger-side zombie's readying a Kalashnikov rifle *NOW.* I hit the kerb. The impact slams me round into the wall, watching the car crumple in around me like some strange beercan in a giant hand. The Renault roof goes convex. Then concave. My stomach implodes. My mind gives a flinch. Then...

Zap. I'm on the shore watching while the tribesmen haul something from the sea. Something huge and drab.

Yes – you scanned it right. And no – I don't understand it either, can't put a handle to it. I want to tell you more, but can I trust you? Probably not. But I'll go ahead anyway. You've seen the *Terminator Zero* film. It's *because* you saw the film at this low-rent Independent Movie Mart and took the time to hunt me out, through long fading corridors and up clanking elevators to this floor that's so high you can look out the window and see helicopters chopping their way beneath you. I don't like high places. I have an intuitive terror of vertical and oblique roofscapes, and this city hugs all the way to the horizon like the ribbed carapace of some gigantic louse. My fear is so primal deep it scares me. And this suite is so high you could fall out of that window and have time to read the entire script of *Blow-Up* before you hit the street. And you came all that way up just to ask me the questions that no-one else has bothered to ask, so I'm going to try to give it to you straight. As I imperfectly understand it myself.

You know my track record, the College Super-Eights and videos? The work goffering for Julian Temple and Derek Jarman (so go *ask* them if you don't believe me!), the bits of promo and commercial work for TV. But it's this one that's got me over the edge and biting my toe-nails. I had to raise the cash myself, some here, some there, some subtle blackmail, some greasing investors, some bridging one to reach the other. And one – just one strategy that's mortgaged my soul. Artists do this for their art. Statistics prove it. I did it. In innocence? – in a sense. Statistics. Interballistics. What the hell. It was something I had to do, you understand? No – so I'll talk a little faster. The whole thing was already developing in the grey cerebral darkroom of my head, so all I had to do was externalise it. I had no choice. I had to have some way of projecting it into a tangible form so I could explain myself to myself.

The wharf is in Sheffield. I'd worked there with Peter Care on the DVA video, and it seemed to fit. The shingle beach with the ocean of reeds is on the seal-coast of the Wash. We stayed over in Boston – me and vision-mixer Pete Benka, we ate at a Chinese, then kept going. And it was so good, so *REAL*, I just couldn't believe it. This place is the image that's already in my head. This is the place where the tribesmen haul something huge and dark from the waves. The wind comes in off the lead-grey breakers like blades of ice here. A night so black that it's a tangible presence, a lurking thing made even more opaque by the pyramid of light on the sea horizon that's so incandescent the tribesmen can't even stare directly at it without shading their piggily recessed eyes. Standing here, feeling that wind cut into me, feels so good. Like at last I'm getting close to those dreams, nightmares, haunting images that have plagued me for as long as I can remember.

Of course, it's not exactly the right place, to believe that is to believe that the Big Bang occurred in the photo-booth on the platform of Sheffield Central. The *real* beach might not even exist anymore. We're talking prehistory. Look at the foreheads, the body-hair! We're talking pre-Conan. A time when the Earth was younger – but already incredibly ancient. The beach could be Pangaea or Gondwanaland before humans had any right to exist *AT ALL* according to Leakey and the rest of contemporary science. I'm talking instinct, and this beach is older than old. But it's close, close enough to spark off an eerie sympathetic buzz, a disorientation, a feeling of eagles flying through the hole in my sock and on up weaving in and out of every node of my spine...

And then there's Venice and the Khmer statuette. I'm there in ninety-five degrees of heat to do a commercial. Films so numbingly dull they could be bottled and sold as anaesthetic. And I've got no creative input, doing strictly technical stuff to do with filters, curly leads, the Sony this and the Nagra that. I know some people get off on slow torture. I'm just not that way inclined, even in a city so ludicrously beautiful it's a cliché. A city of arching bridges and secret alleys, shuttered windows and squares you can find once and never find again.

A break in shooting. I'm watching a turquoise crab no bigger than my thumbnail, webbed into tentacles of weed floating on a lap of canal tide that's washing rotting masonry. Levelling my eyes up from the water's scintillations to the crowd in the square. People darting like water-beetles on a toxic pond. A girl is sauntering by through a benign pigeon-storm and rafts of disjointed voices. She looks to be tensing one gluteus maximus after another in time to her Walkman. The effect is very fetching. Her face is Eastern promise. To me, her very closeness has the effect of a forty-five-minute smile. She stops. Watches the cameras, the sound equipment. Taking it all in, until her attention gradually reaches me. And she smiles…

Her name is Penny, or a close approximation thereof. She's Cambodian. She wants to learn to speak good English. She listens to the crew, and wants to know if the word 'guy' is obscene. When I tell her 'no' she smiles suspiciously, as though I'm sending her up. She juggles tenses in a dislocated blur of language. She asks if we're decamping for London once the job's complete. I tell her that when the stars are correctly aligned I can take advantage of their magnetic flux-fields to levitate across the solar system to Saturn. Does she want to go there with me? She smiles again. Looks down into my peeled eyes, and I decide that even too much sex with her couldn't be enough.

Evening. We're in a low-lit Trattoria. For some reason I'm still talking to her. Her conversation is ethereal, almost intergalactic, while I'm telling her things I've seldom told anyone else. Ever. Like the beach-dreams and how they metamorphosise constantly, but never quite reach a conclusion. About how the tribesmen haul something huge and drab from the breakers, and how the intense illumination from the light-pyramid reflects off it as though it's made of shaped alloy and highly polished. The rope slackens, then springs taut so that jewels of saltwater spin and we pull together so the massive shape gouges a deep trench slowly up the damp shingle. I can feel the calluses on the palms of my hands, small cuts and the indentations of grit between my toes. Sometimes it finishes there. Other times we haul up beyond the highwater-line where mounds of weed make the footing treacherous and the reeds begin to become dense, thickening inland towards the megalith circle and Skull House gleaming ivory-white in moonlight. Mammoth skulls are sunk into the turf, tusks, vertebrae and rib-bones curve up from them to dome the sacred places, skins, hides and daub infilling the interstices. Other skulls – human, reindeer or bear – are wall-hung and the great triple-jawed sea beast over the carved portal doors glowers down at all interlopers. We loose the hawsers as the sound begins. A sound that eludes me once the dream's gone. A sound that's something like John Coltrane playing the Dartford Tunnel with a gigantic reed. To this accompaniment the thing opens, the hatch unscrews. Light, the colours from the inside of stars, begins spilling from its intestines in shimmers of sharp ice... and that's where it ends. I can never get beyond that point.

I suffer migraines, my head an egg-shell through which something is hatching. I have vertigo panic-attacks. There are other less persistent dreams that come with even less clarity and frequency. I'm on a horse. I'm watching a herd of large shaggy animals, bisonoids so numerous they stretch to the horizon. I'm grasping the rough shaft of a spear so tightly my knuckles gleam white and the wood is near-indented with the pressure. Then I'm wearing a metal helm with the visor-grid down, the air thick with a pother of smoke. It's raining black cinder particles. My bare chest glistens sweat with the heat it's exposed to, unpleasantly intense. The city is burning. Somewhere beyond the swirling black to my left I can hear a woman crying. Then I'm trudging through a howling icescape towards a colossal sphinx that's embedded in glaciation. I'm wearing animal furs. The moisture inside my nostrils freezes as I inhale. And on and on…

Apocalyptical dreams, she tells me, are one of the seven signs of the end of the world.

"What are the others?" I ask. A plague of frogs, an epidemic of boils, fish falling from the sky? Hey look – there goes a dolphin!

She says a dolphin's not a fish. It's a mammal.

She smiles. Like a trap. And I leap in joyously. We talk money, statistics, interballistics, movies, and the interaction between the several. I know words are only seven percent of human communication. The rest of the interchange occurs through gestures, smells, poise, tone of voice, smile, intonation, the narrowing and enlarging of the eyes. I know this, yet I'm defenceless before her use of such devices.

On our last night together, with the filming wrapped up ready for the mix-trickery and voice-over vocals to be dubbed on in London by the black soul singer who used to work with the Ike & Tina Turner Revue, me and Penny walk by the canal where the moon's so huge it's like an alien planet from the sky of some fifties SF pulp magazine cover. The moon is pale sulphur yellow. We embrace in its light outside the Hotel Galactica.

She says, "Do you know there's no natural time on the moon?"

I say, "Next time we meet, we'll do it there, so there's no need for partings, because moments never end."

And I walk away from her, stupidly choked, holding the Khmer statuette of Vishnu. Parting. I never knew pain could feel so beautiful.

Things go from bad through worse and beyond. When I get home Peter is dead. Planets shatter, and it doesn't matter. It's the small things that bring the pain of the universe into fine focus. My budgerigar's dead, and it hits me like a psychic clap inside my skull that life is cruel. Peter on her back on the shit-encrusted grit-tray of the cage that imprisoned her all her life. Claws clutching at air absurdly. It's tragic. Flushing her down the toilet takes several efforts. Each time the water settles she's still there, only more sodden and pathetic. Eventually I shove wads of toilet paper down too, and the whole lot vortexes away, and I go back into the lounge with the kind of relief a sex-murderer must feel after disposing of a latest victim.

I look at Vishnu. She said it was Vishnu. Isn't Vishnu Hindu? She should know. I think of Penny, and luxuriate in the pain of memory. The statuette was carved from sandstone in the ninth century. It was then looted from the Phnom Kulen temple complex near the ancient city of Angkor Wat during the last days of Pol Pot's Killing Fields. When Kampuchea fell to the liberating Vietnamese. Now it's an objet d'art smuggled out to finance Penny's émigré family in London. Nothing political. Nothing technically very illegal either. Just a strategy to short-circuit bureaucratic complications and generate finance *FAST* where it's most needed. Penny said that. Nothing the dope-sniffing custom dogs can detect. Nothing to lose sleep over – in fact I can sleep through the entire thing. Cram the statuette deep in among the technical gear and let it find its own way through. I'm a courier, that's all. It's a low-risk operation. It's a last lover's favour. I believe her, but then I'm obsessed with her. Obsessed with a sexuality richer than just bursting cleavage. Her body-talk chatters spools. The aphrodisiac attraction ad-makers would defy the laws of biochemistry to distil and bottle. Even her vaginal secretions taste of the purest mescaline. I have a clear foretaste of marketing stuff like that. It'd walk straight off every shelf in every smart store in the galactic cluster...

And then there's my financial percentage. A not-inconsiderable inducement in itself. Artists do this for their art. Statistics prove it.

But right now the Vishnu makes me nervous. Suddenly, I want rid of it, so I fumble for the Highgate address delivery point she gave me on that last delicious night in Venice. It starts like this. Last night was the Rooftop Gardens, the Tandoori House, the studio-mix tricknology. Now it's 23:15 and I'm stood in front of a stranger's door in the wrong end of Highgate. The nearby highway breathes in smooth gulps of Nissans and Fiats shishing past through a night calm populated by well-spoken drunks. The area is bohemian, alcoholic and sleaze-accented. A place where the dead bury the living. I try to open the door of the flat, a subdivision of a Regency row – or Georgian, or something, but the Yale she's given me won't go in. The door's locked from the inside and the key's still in, jamming it. So someone's inside. I go back to the car and sit there with the radio on for half-an-hour chewing my knuckles.

Vishnu watches me, beatific and passive. The digital time read-out is accelerating towards midnight. I walk round the back of the houses to a small yard. A shiny expensive car (a Peugeot?) stands on a rubble-strewn parking lot some way beyond the yard. It's curiously out of sync with the neighbourhood. I reach up to bang on the kitchen window once, then harder until the glass rattles in its peeling frame. Nothing. The heavy impenetrable curtains are drawn, but it's that torpid bedsitterland where the curtains are always shut anyway. After several attempts the kitchen window slides up. I should wait, bring the statue tomorrow. But I want rid of it *now*. So I hoist up and clamber inside. The heat, the sound and the stink hit me all at once in senssurround. A heavy oppressive heat that fills the dark and prickles my skin with sweat. A low whisper of voices murmurs from the next room (or is it a badly-tuned radio?). But the smell assaults me like nothing I've ever smelled before, a long way beyond anything I *should* have smelled before in my life – at least in this lifetime. A fetid rotten smell swimming in an aquatic-deep heat, thickened by a haunting of scrambled voices.

My heart is pounding up against my rib-cage. There's a laser-knife on the melamine worktop. I pick it up and shuffle deeper into the dark flat like I'm walking on stalks of shattered glass, fumbling for light switches. In the first room there's a crumpled magazine – *Interzone*, beside the toilet pedestal, dropped as carelessly as Andrex, but twice as strong! Myrrh oil in the bathroom cabinet. Next I nudge open the bedroom door with my shoe, reach in, thumb the switch. In a sudden glare of white light I step inside before I've even had time to register what's wrong. There's something on the bed, beneath the tarot cards bluetacked to the wall – the Hanged Man, the Fool. A panic-attack is pounding in my head like my skull is eggshell-thin and something is hatching through it. The smell congests my nostrils and fills my lungs. I want to get out. Back to the car. But I grip the laser-knife and go further in. There's a pair of naked legs protruding from under the duvet, dark tan legs with silky black hairs. They're too immobile for my liking. I don't want to lift the cover, but I do – and recoil. A grotesque face stares back, beaten black, so disfigured and distorted it's some time before I even recognise it as human. This is where the stink comes from. The corpse in the bed, Chinese, oriental – Kampuchean.

I start hallucinating. I try to fight it, to grip the reality of room, duvet, corpse, but the stench of decomposition becomes the pother of smoke and the rain of black cinder particles. I look out through the visor-grid at the flames crawling the walls like quicksilver, a glistening cellophane rippling over the tarots and racing up the heavy impenetrable drapes. I back off, feinting with the laser-knife as if it's a sword, back off into the hallway… and into the enforcers. They're there waiting – heads up, alert, like big dangerous animals, but greying into the dark like spectres from the outskirts of Hades. The first one has aviator shades pushed up, and looks to be heavily into dishing out instant heart-failure.

My bare chest glistens sweat from the heat it's exposed to, unpleasantly intense. The city is burning and somewhere beyond the swirling black to my left I can hear a woman crying. Perhaps she's on the badly-tuned radio murmuring from the next room? My sword comes up, aimed at chimeras, a snarl curdling deep in a throat that's not quite mine. There are three enforcers only a mind-snap away. As oriental – as Kampuchean (?) as Penny is, as the guy under the duvet was. The storm crackles noisily through my head. A strobe begins pulsing crimson. My only advantage is that they seem as stunned to find me here as I am to back into them… I break first, howl like a banshee, bolt into the kitchen slamming the door behind me. And I'm halfway through the window before aviator-shades crashes the door. There's no natural time in this room. The whole thing happens faster than it takes to describe it. For now I'm already slithering sideways down into a painful crouch beneath the window. Haring back towards the car, things come loose in my head and drift off into the night. My Renault is on automatic pilot. Figures leap and howl from the cones of flaring headlights…

A long time later I awake with a hang-over. Stiff-necked and painful. Sourness floods my mouth. The upholstery of the car smells of dead cigarettes, smoke, and vomit. Through the windscreen traffic crawls over a multi-legged fly-over like bugs on a diplodocus, in a silence so clear I can hear it. Last night seems stupid. A hallucination. Someone else's memory with squatter's rights to my head, like the beach-dreams, the burning city, the icescape, the mugging in the Arab Souk. I open the car door so the sound bursts in. I fill my mouth with saliva and spit it all down into the chickweed and dandelion carpeting the waste-ground I'm parked on. The ignition keys first time and I pull into the nearest fast-lane for home. By lunchtime I'm thinking straight again. Straight enough to spend a couple of hours trying numbers, between decaff coffees, in an attempt to reach Penny. Every address I can remember. But it's like she never existed. Something is severely out of kilter.

Vishnu watches me, beatific and passive. He knows. This is no cosy family heirloom bringing succour to ageing Kampuchean émigrés. This is political. This is arms-dealing... or something *BIG* – big enough for rival factions to kill each other over. Eventually I give up on it. I have other commitments.

We – me and Pete Benka, vision-mixer, co-director – go north. M1 out of London. The most striking thing about Pete is his violent enthusiasms, both in working and talking. He spiels with effervescence, shouting as he grabs hold of a conversational theme and turns it into a multi-media event of flailing arms and dramatic eyebrows. I'm able to switch off and be drawn into his slipstream. Boston, we eat at a Chinese restaurant by the river, then keep going, until we can go no further, standing on the shingle overlooking the seal-coast of the Wash. The air is primal clear, so sharp it's purifying. This is the location I've dreamed of. *LITERALLY* dreamed of...

Memory often plays me factually false, especially when I'm trying to recall those days. But later we spent time in Sheffield, a night of slides 'n' electro at the Leadmill, a meet with local muso's in the Crucible bar. Adi's got a new twenty-minute piece, easily the most atmospheric thing he's done since *Thirst*, industrial and hard, dappled with electronic dream demons, but with a surrealistic edge that's transfixing. The label could perhaps be arm-twisted into being interested in part-sponsoring a promo-film to go with it... if we're interested? We go down by the wharf to check out locations... but eventually the days wind down to an end.

You've seen the film. Those who took the trouble to hunt out its screening here at this low-rent independent Movie Mart, and those who either liked or disliked it based their reactions around its fast-cut style. The blur of faces meta-morphing one into the other, superimposed over the vicious rituals on the seal-coast or on the wharf. The jerky speed-bite editing pulsed to Adi's magical sound-fragmentations, the intentional disorientation. All that had fallen into place by that long southward drive back to London through grey veils of melancholy drizzle. We'd already playfully tagged the project *Terminator Zero*, only the denouement, and the final finance have yet to be worked out.

Leicester Forest East Services. Looking down on files of traffic, hunting for omens. The more the distance indicators on the big blue M-way signs countdown towards London the more I'm in need of whatever reassurance I can get. The more real the night of the dead Cambodian becomes. The more it regurgitates from the back-brain limbo I've managed to suspend it in. There's a magpie on the glistening-wet soft verge picking at a crisp packet. "One for sorrow..."

Then later, back beside the car, another one. "Two for joy!"

"Naw," from Pete. "That's *CHEATING*. It's the same bird. It's just flown around a bit and re-alighted *HERE*."

Suddenly it's very important to me that – no, it's *TWO* different magpies.

Nosing back through the dirty spray of London traffic, the statuette is still there on the car rear-seat. What to do with it? A person-to-person call to Prince Sihanouk? A discreet drop-off at the Kampuchean Embassy or cultural attaché? Penny no longer exists. The contact she intended it for *literally* no longer exists. Perhaps if the enforcers had asked nicely I'd even have given it over to them. What about the British Museum...?

In the event we just happen to snarl-up at some lights and there's an Antiques & Antiquarian Collectors shop framed in the windscreen. I say, "Wait," and scrabble out the car. The dealer can't believe his luck when I upend Vishnu on his glass-top counter. Although he tries to suppress all outward signs of excitement it keeps leaking out in little flashfire smiles and predatory glints of the eye. He makes an offer, no questions, no receipts. I instinctively stick out for more which he concedes with only token argument. It's worth more, his every lustfully possessive caress along its sandstone limbs tells me that, but I've got enough for my immediate needs and daren't get further involved in questions of origins or authentication.

Back at the Beka apartment we talk late into the night. We can do *Terminator Zero* now, it's all come together immaculately, the seal-coast, Adi's music, the wharf, the cash from Cambodia. It's past three when I leave and pick up pace looping around the Victorian Park then on down towards home, skirting Highgate almost without realising it. Brought up sharp at the last intersection where there's a Kebab take-away that's oddly still open, a gaggle outside in the luminous glow, a shiny-expensive Peugeot that's curiously out of sync with the neighbourhood. I look at them. They look at me. Something unpleasant crawls inside my gut, a feeling like my intestines are unravelling and being slowly drawn out through my anus. As I pull away they're scampering for the shiny car. Another ten minutes and they might have gone, they've been staking out my flat, possibly for all the days I've been north. After tonight they might have given up, after taking time out for one last Kebab...

This is where the nightmare *REALLY* hits overdrive. Where the voices in the back of my head begin squirming, whispering, shrilling, twitching like shoals of brilliant lizards scuttling on sun-heated pebbles. The Peugeot slides out beneath a wall of identical ad-posters, repetitive – like a Warhol exhibition, but ripped into collage more like Pop Art backdrops in a Godard movie. I'm driving hard against the direction-arrows on the road-surface, tyre-tread shrieking, jabbing for some imaginary hyperspace button on the dash fascia as dawn fades up into day, slamming up towards the orbital, foot down all the way on the pedal, through the lights at red. The bad guy Cambodian enforcers hunching up behind me...

Then I'm on the shore of the seal-coast watching tribesmen haul something from the sea, something huge and drab...

Now I'm in a narrow street where vivid awnings flap and crack overhead in the hot dry wind that gusts in off the desert, haggling over price with two men, Arabs or Phoenicians, dark-skinned Semitic like me, while golden light pours down, deluging us.

You've seen the movie. You know the accelerating blur of faces fragmenting instantaneously into pure screen white-out? A crescendo that brinks over into nothingness. End. Finis. A 'Der Der Der That's All Folks!!!' You want an explanation for it that I can fit into words? But, for me - *THAT* is the explanation. That's how I understand it. I think in pictures, as I was then... On the orbital I'm thinking I might out-run them. But instead they ram me and I hit the kerb. Then I impact a wall, a warehouse or outbuilding by the river. I watch the car crumple in around me like some strange beercan in a giant hand...

I can feel the calluses on the palm of my hand as we haul, the rope slackens, then springs taut so that jewels of sea-water spin off into the luminous night and the massive shape hauled from the sea gouges a deep trench slowly up the damp shingle. I can feel small cuts and the indentations of grit between my toes as we drag it up beyond the high-water line where mounds of weed stink, making the footing treacherous and the reeds begin to become dense...

I smile at the two faces, Hittite, Assyrian, Phoenician faces. We've reached a deal on the transaction. A woman. The nearer of the two grins unpleasantly, revealing the misaligned remnants of shattered black teeth. He beckons in a way that's both salaciously offensive and intimately conspiratorial. The heat-haze teases the eye and bakes all colours into near-whiteness. They lead me through a low decaying arch into a filthy alley with steep featureless walls of pumice-debris bonded with baked-clay infill...

And now I'm spiralling into a black sun helplessly out of control, with choking floodtides of vertigo terror and a nameless crawling horror canting in the deepest pit of my stomach (this is a new one I've not experienced before!). Ahead there's a blacker blackness cut out of the spangled night of deep space, and the projectile encapsulating me is hurtling down into its polished anthracite heart. My eyes move independently and from odd angles on the side of my head as though I'm not quite human. Yet even more disturbing, the intelligence behind the eyes doesn't exactly seem to belong to either me – or it. Instead, it's a cold primitive intellect as ancient and eternal as the stars, willed only by survival...

The car roof goes convex. Then concave. My stomach implodes. My mind gives a scrotum-tightening lurch. The autowreck of screeching grating metals finally quietens to a mere hiss of punctured radiator steam and the tick tick tick of a revolving wheel that's somewhere no longer in contact with the road. I shrug away the shock and burst at the door as the Peugeot growls to a halt nearby. The door won't budge. I hit it again with full body-weight and it groans away from me, tumbling me out onto the concrete. Sounds burst in at me. A bullet sprangs from the Renault-shell, and bent Groucho Marx double I'm haring down between bins and trash through an alley. The river ahead of me. The enforcers behind me, three of them, the first one has aviator shades. A storm crackles noisily through my head…

We loose the hawsers as the sound fades in. A sound that's suddenly clear, high and keening with a poisonously hypnotic beauty, dappled with dream demons, and to this accompaniment the beached projectile opens. The hatch unscrews and colours from the inside of stars spills from its intestines in shimmers of barbed ice. And something squat and hideous swims inside the effulgence, scrabbling and lurching in pain across the rim flopping and slithering obscenely down onto the damp cold pebbles. A frog…?

My head an eggshell through which something is hatching. A grotesque scream from somewhere. From me. I go down holding my head, feeling the hot gush of pulsing blood matting my hair. My attacker grins unpleasantly through the misaligned remnants of shattered black teeth as his kick stoves in my ribs. The other Hittite – or Assyrian assailant impales a curved knife in and across my chest, ripping it open. No woman here. Only betrayal and death. A strobe begins flashing crimson. My head explodes…

Spiralling down into blackness. A planet. Night side. Features separate out from the shadows below. Ink-dark oceans, grey land-masses, the javelled margins between. The atmospheric friction-heat climbs intolerably…

I go down holding my head. Aviator-shades holds the pistol down-slanting at me. I can smell the stink of the river. My head explodes…

The frog-thing, near man-size, is drowning in alien terrestrial air. Its skin gleams with amphibian-green sheen. Its huge eyes move independently. The pyramid of light pours down onto the seal-coast as its head fissures and rips open. An eggshell through which the cerebral parasite is hatching. The frog head explodes…

White-out.

Nothingness.

Finis.

End.

That's the movie. When I come round it's cool dusk and everything's slowed to a halt. I can still smell the river. There's a urine odour too, and an unpleasant dampness beneath me. A dull nagging like hangover or toothache orbits my head like the stun-stars in a Popeye cartoon. There's an airplane gleaming miles above me. A green light pulses on its fuselage as it crawls from the setting sun. I stand gingerly, and walk splay-legged back from the wharf up towards the road, avoiding the bloody mess that's all my brain-parasite left of the Kampuchean enforcers. And as I pace with quickening step past the autowreck and the skew-parked Peugeot the images start coming in neat sequential frames. The visuals for *Terminator Zero*. The primal beach where the starship first crash-lands. The heads that the parasite has lived in down the centuries, since it escaped from the dying frog-alien. Emerging only to protect and ensure the survival of its host. Until it reaches me... where it all ends. Clear at last. At least for now. But worst of all is the nagging thought that remains, that what if the thing I call me – the confused jumble of thoughts, memories, instincts, intuitions and opinions I carry around in my head, are not really *me*, not *really* me at all. What if they are aspects of the parasite? The eternal parasite? I've mortgaged my soul. But artists do that for their art. Statistics prove it. I (we?) did it. In innocence? In a sense. Statistics. Interballistics... into film.

A GROTESQUE ROMANCE

The Art of Secrets. Or just Secret Art? Was Hannibal Mytholmridge a Pop Art iconoclast of squalid multi-sexual bohemian outrage... or an exquisitely perceptive painter of tactile female eroticism ? And what is the nature of his last and greatest work ? Only his wife... and his mistress know, and they tell their shocking truth to just one man....

SENSATIONS...

Autumn. Yorkshire. Her voice in my head. Even now. Now that the shock and horror is over. In my head she's here, saying "there is a time for quietness, and a time for conversation." Yet squirming closer, into body-scent range... it alone teasing me higher than heroin. And I'm there. In that strange flat light. The silence, deep and unremitting. Semi-conscious in a semi-dark room. Olfactory sensors working overtime, itching away at something I can't quite reach. Something important. Something significant. Cobalt and crimson illuminate the walls like high-tech lamination. It's as if I'm sucking in screeds of hallucinatory prose, snapshots of the unconscious, the dreams and nightmares of the three people who've sat, eaten, slept, fucked, and dreamed here, in this impossible place. The artist. The wife. The mistress. The strange weave of relationships binding them. And their secret. The secret silence they hold for all the decades. The secret they reveal to me. And only me.

As *Art Times* critic, the mutational stages of Hannibal Mytholmridge is a long-held fascination. The unique furore thrown up by his original work. His abrupt mid-career shift into other realms of subject-matter. They've variously baffled and intrigued me for as long as I've been doing this, and now – the odd circumstances of his death too. I recall his explosive entry onto the scene in the 1950's as part of the Pop Art generation, the movement that numbers Peter Blake, Richard Hamilton, Dalton Trumbo, Vivian Oblivion, David Jones and Bridget Riley. Rejecting traditional techniques and styles, embracing modern consumerism in a Jacuzzi-whirl of bizarre collage, cornflake packets, machines, rips in bright cloth, SF strips, movie stills, spliced in with cinema tickets, nails, sprockets, then spattered with molten-faced daubs and rich spirals of luminous colours. Aesthetic disruptions and surface fragmentations in haemorrhages of colour. Wordless stories in tides of imagery. Art that floods directly from the spell of the subconscious, subject only to mercurial chance. An intoxicating time. A radical breakthrough in forms of expression by vibrant and angry young art-radicals.

And he was there. I follow his development through the pages of specialist magazines, through short-lived exhibitions in small Beatnik Soho Galleries, and events in Leeds or Liverpool. Occasionally his notoriety erupts into the national press. A large ferociously-bearded Bohemian in blurry photographs taken in chaotic studios piled high with junk and canvasses and invariably with a naked girl, her body patterned in curves and grids of paint. All so deliciously dangerous. An adventure of creative anarchy.

All the things I am not. I never meet him, though I write about him. Always in awe of his reputation. A heavy drinker. Red wine. A narcotic tendency. Roaring days, a dislike of conventional un-cool people. Legendary short-tempered outbursts of anger directed at incautious journalists or unsympathetic critics, lurching down the Frith Street kerb one foot in the gutter. But also a shrewd man, whose contrived awkwardness effectively obscures his firmness of purpose. And his mission is to destroy all he deems stale and conservative in the art establishment, and rebuild it in his own manic image. Quote – "My work is not for the cultural brothels of stuffy art galleries, an aphrodisiac for erudite-vultures whose concept of art is light-years from mine. Nor will you find it in the hallowed enclaves of Bond Street dealers, to whom art is no more than an investment and a cash-generating machine," unquote.

And then... inexplicably, and totally without warning, it all changes. As the 1960's decays into the 70's his work softens. Takes on new erotic qualities and depths of technical expertise his earlier career never hinted at. Dark nudes, always his favourite long-term model, Shelley-Colette. Voluptuous and as richly detailed as a Rossetti print, delighting in the minutiae of pubic hair and subtle nipple pigmentation – glistening open-legged flesh and skin-tones. Distended speechless lips fringed in thickets of pubence. Clammy with desire. Teeth. Thighs. Fingers. Oranges and pinks and golds. A sequence that fits together, frame-by-frame, into a wordless strip-narrative of vivid eroticism.

Shelley seated. A hard-backed chair. Lazy-limbed, curvingly soft. Oval eyes. Half-smile holding secrets. Or painted nails honed to fierce points gripping the sides of a wicker chair, clasped on her lap, or scrabbling at her face under its flicked dark locks. Or resting on her hands. Wheeling stars in her eyes, and the bright dust of galaxies shining in her hair. Inevitably I'm re-intrigued. Just a little in lust too. The mythic life-style has also changed. He's now become something of a hermit. Increasingly rare photos show him as tall, thickset, mane of long greying hair sweeping back from his high forehead and curling untidily over his collar. His clothes a rusty black, stained and spotted with age, neglect and pigment. His nose a beak. His eyes heavy-lidded. His thin mouth a caricature of aesthetic arrogance. A reclusive figure in a solid stone house in the high Pennines somewhere above Harrogate. In an exclusive ménage that consists of his wife Leigh, and his model Shelley-Colette. I guess I help fuel the rumours. Filing features on him for colour supplement back-pages. And review sections.

I work through his agent, patiently, persistently. She knows me. My writings over the years prove I'm more than qualified to write the definitive Mytholmridge bio-profile. It takes time. Until now, when suddenly, unexpectedly, I receive the news of his death. I'm the first – and as yet, the only writer confided with that news. And an invitation to interview his survivors, the executors of his work – Shelley-Colette and Leigh, who still live in that house they'd shared during his life. *Me* – Leigh personally grants *me* the exclusive that must be shared with no other, to see his final – most uncompromising work. And in some strange way, this is my chance, not only to make the entire cycle of his life suddenly more accessible, but to explain myself to myself. Through him.

JUST WHAT IS IT THAT MAKES HANNIBAL MYTHOLMRIDGE SO DIFFERENT, SO APPEALING...?

My cassette machine. A bubble-pack card of new long-life batteries. A selection of clean C90's. And my Honda Civic 1.6 climbing away from the still low murmur of Harrogate traffic, quick glimpses of music heard from passing cars, up into the unknown territory beyond. Where I receive more weirdness than I can ever imagine. I halt a number of times. Make enquiries at a public house called the Travelling Light. Dusk rushes in to swallow me in heavy mauve shadows. Dashboard displays light up like emeralds. The softly intimate tones of a late-night local radio DJ detailing the alleged marital shenanigans of a TV Soap star. A road that is little more than a rutted track. And trees that are dark, hostile and black, with the long witch-fingered grasp of monochrome Arthur Rackham illustrations from haunted fairy-tales. Even the radio reception distorts and submerges as if I'm transgressing time-bends across reality-fractures. I kill the radio, slide in a tape, Cabaret Voltaire's *Yashar*, recorded at Western Works during October 1981. Kirk. Mallinder. Alan Fish of Hula's machine-sharp percussion. "There's 70-billion people out there – Where are they hiding?" spliced into the chill Asiatic sway of proto-electro. Emphasising that I've been extradited to new continents uncharted by terrestrial cartographers.

A distant throbbing above, felt rather than heard, and winking white, red and green navigation lights of an in-bound airliner drifting across my field of vision. Leeds-Bradford Airport. A tree weeps into the river, huge and tragic. Then a building up ahead with time stretching out around it as rich and vast as the sky. A house that must have been new sometime around the mid-to-late Jurassic. Shadows chained to its exterior like so many bicycles. A path overgrown with weeds, muddy and slippery. A front door under an ornate portico, so shielded from the diffused light of the moon. Fumbling to find a bell-push. There is none. A knock. A noise that seems unnecessarily loud.

Leigh. Inviting me inside. "Mr Quist?"

"Er, yes... that's Daryl. Daryl," breath catching at the back of my throat at her tactile closeness.

"Daryl? You're well-featured Daryl."

And 'Oh my god, so are you'. Of course she's now in her late-forties, but radiating a kind of hypnotic pre-Raphaelite beauty that years can do nothing to detract. Her hair, deep auburn, is long. Her dress, in dark paisley print, is long, yet does little to disguise the fullness of her figure. And it is as though she was walking around me, poking and probing into my deepest psyche, turning me upside-down, shaking me quietly, emptying my pockets for small-change, and all without ever once moving.

I stammer out some inanity. She's expecting me. Miles Davis' *Bitches Brew* hisses and sizzles from speaker to hidden speaker. And the house is equally chaotic. A charismatic pile-up of signs and symbolism as I'd always imagined it would be. But still its reality startles and excites me. Book-lined. Masses of thumbed magazines and pulps. Sketches and illustrations thumb-tacked to the walls. A stuffed crocodile glowering with eyes of amber beads. The long emerald tongues of aspidistra. The strong aroma of sensimila and colitas. The scent of joss sticks, or subtle drugs, or heavily spiced food. An aircraft propeller suspended from the ceiling, slowly revolving like a huge fan. Empty wine bottles. And canvasses. Masses of them. An orgiastic banquet of canvasses, where skeins of bright lines fluctuate between writing and drawing, inky little hieroglyphs, incomprehensible script, inverted alphabets from undiscovered alien languages dredged up from the bowels of pre-Lovecraftian time. Fluorescent night creatures emerging from neat black squares. Fiery biological wriggles and curls. Chinese pictograms scudding like tiny tripeds along paths of unwritten music.

...and Shelley-Colette is here too. Darker. Fuller. Somehow more corporeal. A sky full of stars in her eyes too, yet a more earthy primal version of woman, contrasting the more aesthetic style of her companion. Yin and Yang. I feel stupid and clumsy. Wedging myself down into the chair like a climber stuck in a crevasse, using hands and elbows to keep from falling. Yet it's a space too narrow to fully contain me. And all the itemised questions I've written down and rehearsed evaporate in my head. I'm here. They sit close. His women. Watching me. It's already late.

I review my options, thought by thought. It doesn't take long. "Patrick Moore says there's a comet up there," attempting flip.

"It's... er, visible to the naked eye. Unfortunately I can only recognise one constellation. And if the comet's not lurking in Orion then I've no chance of locating it."

"Language distorts thought, Mr Daryl Quist. It's a hopeless medium for communication." The stab of a jewelled finger. "We prefer other access points. Fun. Jocularity. Drollery. Amusement. You remember them, don't you, Mr Quist?"

"But don't worry Mr Quist. We'll cure you of any reputable qualities." Shelley-Colette, in a voice untainted by innocence.

SEVERAL ANECDOTES CONCERNING THE ARTIST...

Outside, the night. Outside, the trees, darkly hostile and witch-fingered. I'm semi-conscious in a semi-darkened room, its clinging shadows sliding across my skin. I imagine at first someone is here in the room with me, whispering enticing obscenities, alluring suggestions. And – although no succubus congeals out of wet darkness – my olfactory sensors are working overtime, itching away at something I can't quite reach. Something important. Something significant. Cobalt and crimson illuminate the walls like high-tech lamination. And it's as though I'm sucking in screeds of hallucinatory prose, snapshots of the unconscious, dreams and nightmares secreted by other previous residents who've sat, eaten, slept, fucked, and dreamed in here, in this impossible place. Ghosts. Ghosts in the real sense of the tangible after-image of past lived-experience which reverberates on in this room. Molecular memories are imprinted here. The hint of its vibrations. My art-voyeur fingers slither across one of the canvasses. Pigment builds up in rough piles, in irresistible rhythms, but always there is the sense of space between the strokes, and the abstract repetition of brushstrokes is somehow frightening.

A bottle of linseed oil. I remember my own first box of oil paints and my first palette the size of a school exercise book. And I'm handling tubes with exotic, distant names, Indian Red, Naples Yellow, Burnt Umber, Raw Sienna. And the mysteriously named Flake White – suggesting a blizzard of snowflakes. Others too – the ones I imagine, jaundice and bruise, livid orange, dust blue, irradiation red, silver sheen. Somewhere out there now is the spectre of Hannibal Mytholmridge. And simultaneously I feel

147

him, dripping, smearing and dragging brushes full of paint across this canvas, watching the material absorbing it. His long slim hands with their encrustations of hashish beneath overlong fingernails. I evaluate. I analyse. He does. But by now I'm laying fantasy on fantasy with an imaginary palette knife, as lavishly as he once cleaved pigments onto canvas with a real one.

"I studied sculpture at St Martin's College. That's where I caught her eye." The next day. Leigh says this with a strange humour, making a deliberate smile that smears across her face for longer than seems natural, as though I'm supposed to read more into the words. "Dates? Totally fuzzy. What do you expect after the life we've led. But those days left visible scars. You want to see? You're here to survey the wreckage, after all. But there are invisible ones too. Those you can't see."

"Me, and Shelly. We hook up almost immediately. Share a room. Sketch each other. At first mutually. Casual profiles, free-handing art with a Bic biro, etching it onto the back of a beer-mat while enduring the tedious chat-up lines of boring beatnik art-poseurs. Or full studies of each other for our own amusement, or for assessment. Often nude."

"She was better than me. Always," adds Shelley-Colette, across from where we sit. Her hair is brush-strokes of night. "So it gets she does the painting, while my talent is to be more passive. I assume poses, furnish curves, light, contours, shapes for her to replicate in oils."

You were lovers too? The air as thick as honey. "Not exactly. We do a bit of this, try a bit of that. Experimenting as feminist awareness dictates, part of what we imagine to be the bohemian libertine milieu. We explore physical limits. The erotic. It's what you're supposed to do, isn't it? It was expected. And we are good together. We function well."

And him? "When I first met him, when we first meet. A student-art event. He is there. I fix my gaze on his back, willing him to turn. He, unaware of the compulsion – conscious only that he has turned, turns towards me. He expresses interest. I'm flattered. He's a star. Hannibal Mytholmridge, a legend. Who would not be flattered? He's charismatic, full of black depressions and huge roaring joys, lean looks and fierce silences, with half-closed eyes giving a perpetually sleepy expression, a confirmed somnambulist air, a highly effective mask for one of the keenest minds in art. Then. And I feel that same sense of bewilderment that Little Dorothy must feel on her first trip to the Land of Oz. He knows how to charm. Practiced in the art of deception. You know it's deliberate. A routine. While at the same time, when it's aimed at you, you're fascinated. Within a week I move in with him. And within a few more, Shelley-Colette follows."

"It was... strange," Leigh continues, as though explaining it to herself. "He's... supposedly, drawn to my art. That's the point of contact. I'd assumed it was my technique, my expression, my brushwork, he admires. The economy of line. But no. Fool that I am. It was the subject-matter. It was voluptuous contours of nude flesh. Her body. Shelley's body. That realisation only came later. Gradually."

Painfully? "No. Not really. He never much cared for the realistic mess of actual feelings. No relationships that went more than six inches deep. But sure, I couldn't believe it the first time I saw Shelley give him head. I suppose it's only then I realise what's going on. But to actually witness it is oddly disconcerting. We are in the studio. I'm working on a canvas and Shelley is modelling. She's nude, of course, sitting on a Van Gogh-style simple chair, her legs wide-splayed. It is evening and although the sky is becoming dusk it merely invests everything with a kind of roseate glow. He, Hannibal – comes into the studio in a silk bathrobe of Japanese print. At first he hardly seems to notice either of us. He paces up and down looking critically first at the work in progress, then at her. Comparing – I imagine, the skin-tone, texture and shading. He doesn't speak. He pauses for a long moment, then crosses to stand in front of her, I don't know what to expect. But slowly he draws the sash and opens the gown. I admit I watch in horrified fascination. My hand gripping the brush so tight my fingerprints must be etched into its shaft. And she's administering a kind of delicate cannibalism. My attention fixed on their point of oral connection. It goes on for a long time. Longer than I believe possible. Then I realise he isn't even looking at her, that he's looking at me. My eyes move upwards with reluctant dread to meet his eyes. He looks at me blatantly, fully into my face. And he smiles a sinister smile of gloating satisfaction as her head dips and bobs. This is for my benefit. He is doing it deliberately so I can see it all. As I wait, patiently, to resume my painting.... what will be marketed as *his* painting. Until he's done. It is an exercise in control Mr Quist, don't you see?"

SOHO, SEX, AND THE POST-SURREALISTS...

Autumn. Yorkshire. Mosses and strange fungus breaking through the plaster. So real I can hear it breathing. Small blue notebooks with sun-faded covers and fray-whitened spines. Larger A4 pads of cream-wove. Open them up, the air fills with a smoky complexity of sketches, diagrams, profiles, wrists with a thick-ribbed pulse of veins, oval eyes with startle-wide pupils. And penises, from this angle, and that. Coiled flaccid. Glistening erect. Carefully studied. Smoky wisps of pubence.

The world shifts beneath me. Something that's been gnawing there at the back of my mind ever since I arrived, suggesting, intimating. Now it is blaring full frontal. And it pitches me over the rim of the known world. So it was you who did his second-phase work? You? You were responsible for it all? He did none of it himself? Still the eyes locked. "Of course." In tones suggesting stating the obvious to an idiot child.

"Artistically, he's running on empty." From Shelley-Colette now. "He'd begun as a fine draughtsman. He could draw representational stuff. He'd been producing commercial line-graphics for advertising agencies – art-work for women's fashion-shoe ads. Then came Pop Art. Collages. Cut-ups. Assemblages. Conceptualism. Installations. Happenings. The art-pubs of Fitzrovia and Soho. 'Gerry's Club'. 'The French House'. 'The Colony'. Old smiles. Old hair-styles. Artists, gangsters and drunks. But by the 70's, when we arrive on the scene, his draughtsmanship skills have atrophied through a decade of neglect and abuse, he's surviving on a reputation that's already exceeded its shelf-life. Repeating, regurgitating, re-jigging, rehashing. If there's any kind of aesthetic left, it is cannibalistic, chewing over the art of the recently warm past. So he uses one of her paintings, of me."

"At first it's meant to be a one-off. He gets an invite to contribute to an exhibition. The Serpentine, wasn't it? He's got nothing new. And I have masses of unseen stuff. So why not? It's a joke. A subterfuge. Art-subversion. Marcel Duchamp inks a moustache on a postcard of the Mona Lisa, creating a new original. Still the Mona Lisa. But it sells as a Duchamp. A brilliant scam with a hidden agenda on the nature and status of art. That's all we're doing. Initially. But it works brilliantly. It was hit. His career reborn. A resurrection. A second Coming."

What about ethics. Remember ethics? "I spent a weekend there. Didn't rate it highly." But surely you must resent him stealing credit for what is essentially your work? "No. I paint. That's what I did. That's what I do. I was never interested in all the hype that goes with it. That's where he excels. He gets journalists and art-critics, from the dodgiest geezers to the smartest suits, into the bilious-green corner of the Soho Colony or some-such, and he spin-spiels quotable quotes, spontaneous aphorisms and contentious theory all pulsing with absolute eye-contact sincerity. He's hypnotic. They are hypnotised. He's done abstract. Gone to the extremes of conceptual non-representation. Now he's coming home. Getting real. Flesh. Body. Gut. Vagina. The stuff of life. It makes irresistible copy. At a push we could still justify it all as a clever scam. I guess. At the beginning. But soon it just becomes a convenient arrangement. He sells it immaculately. Just that he can't paint it. I do that. He needs me for that. That's why I became his wife. And Shelley-Colette is, Shelley-Colette is... full. Generous. He likes that. Lusts after that. Big tits. Fat arse. I'm not built like that, as you can see. I can't compete in that area. That's why he needs her. So Hannibal needs me 'cos I can paint. He can proselytise. Shelley-Colette can pose. We all form essential parts of the collective machine. The synergic body. And of course, the sex fires it up further."

Shelley-Colette shrugs agreement. "She's got everything she needs. She's an artist. She don't look back." The coquette and the existentialist. "We are three. We love equally. Share equally. Although some a little more equally than others. We are moving – we imagine, in the art demimonde. Different. Our morality more flexible. Cool. We are Henry Miller and Anaïs Nin. Sartre and DeBevoire. Augustus John. Genius is not subject to dull social conformity. It defines its own limits. Or it has no limits. So I pose. She paints. He fucks us both. We fuck each other. It works. A game we'll never tire of playing until the universe runs down. Chaotic times. And we are just instruments of the times. But yes, he always *was* sexually voracious. Creative people tend to be highly-sexed."

"Are you... creative, Mr Quist? Daryl?" Leigh leaning forward. Moving closer, within body-perfume range to tease me.

"Creative? ...I wanted to be. Oh yes, how very much I longed to be. During my final school terms I spend lots of time in the Library pawing Art volumes, looking for nude studies of naked women. But somehow their art always escapes me. Their art never reached me. Only their nudity. Then I discover Hannibal Mytholmridge. And here is art that misses or by-passes my conscious mind, yet somehow it seems to wrench something deep down inside me, probing and twisting. He is everything I am not. Everything I yearn to be. But now I know that, at least a part of that, wasn't him at all. It was you. And it was you."

"There is a time for quietness, and a time for conversation." She's moving closer, within body-perfume range to tease me with, "So pray tempt me not into dalliances beyond that, sir."

Is it possible to get a heroin-high merely from the physical presence of another human being? Because I am. I am. I wait a billion years. And yet no longer than a moment.

I WANT TO SPEND THE REST OF MY LIFE EVERYWHERE, WITH SHELLEY AND LEIGH, ONE TO ONE, ALWAYS, FOREVER, NOW...

A magnifying glass, old copies of the *Guardian*, dried-up pots of pigment, empty wine bottles, a pair of broken spectacles with one lens missing, a fly-blown mirror, a plastic figure of Daffy Duck, a tablespoon, a Sri Lankan Buddha, a faded pack of French pornographic playing cards. A shaman's room. His room. I see him standing here, standing back to inspect what is supposedly his latest work. He's stroking his ragged beard and gloating over some previously unobserved detail. A phoney. A cheat. More sperm-star than art-star. Watch. Does this realisation destroy him? Does this free me? Me – who live my life through him? Or what I thought was him. And now know isn't. The fraud, and the defrauded. The deceiver, and the deceived. And I, the more diminished. But no, it just makes me less real. More tenuous. Weightless. After an endless couple of ticks I snap out of my freeze. This place is a theatre of undisclosed dramas. A membrane between image and meaning. You guess. You imagine. Yet it resists interpretation. As impermeable as the pigment. It's only me that has no real substance.

To buy space I'm saying, "What function does art serve? It comes in a dream. The artist's unconscious self standing midway-down between the phenomenon, and the thought. Yet – in itself, it is entirely nebulous. For it is something apart, something between. Something like, and yet unlike each of what it mediates."

"Art is itself. It means itself."

"So it can't be judged in any terms other that its own? In that case, how can we talk about its power to touch us? The hold it has over us?"

"It is the language of the soul. It sees from within. It teaches us to feel all feelings. That is the dialogue it constructs."

Until I can hold back no longer. So tell me, when does this idyllic tryst start going wrong? "Who knows? I don't know. The equilibrium merely becomes lost. Or maybe it doesn't. Maybe it didn't." A pause. A first sign of uncertainty. "The other women he went with – and there are many. They betray our exclusivity. Ceecee Ryder is the first I know of. But there are others. Then there are the men Shelley-Colette goes with. Hannibal encourages it. He sets them up. It amuses him to do that. Then to hear her tell the details. Eustace Plinge is *her* first foray outside our tryst. But again, he insists on many. Yet all the while he is watching me, provoking my reaction. This is all for me. For my benefit. This is about his control – and his loss of control, his power – and his loss of power, and his revenge on me, for what I'd done to him." Her eyes, fully alert to my presence. "For stealing... no, for becoming his creativity. Something that was vital, necessary, and also... unforgivable. You understand?" Nothing hidden or closed. Her raw life roaring beneath the skin, merely eclipsed – rather than concealed, by her smock.

And now, and now...? How does it end? With more revenge? With the final payback? "Art tends to perish and degrade. That's its nature. But it's only a problem. It's not some kind of off-the-peg metaphor for a tragically abbreviated life. It is just what it is. No more..."

"You think it's time to see the final work, you mean? The decisive move into his last, terminal art-phase? Perhaps it is time for you to see..." Now we are climbing narrow stairs that protest.

Across a crimson landing washed by a single suspended bulb. Into a room I've not seen before. Stark. Totally empty, but for two large fluid-filled vitrine tanks. Glass panels inner-lit, and into these I peer. Something at first roughly rounded within, suspended in a viscous liquid, faintly orange, a darker nucleus of many, uncountably numerous parts, and with a transparent skin on which several thin hair-like things look to be whipping and wiggling. I blink. Look again. Baffled. Like I'm semi-conscious in a semi-darkened room. Olfactory sensors working overtime, itching away at something I can't reach.

"I love the smell of formaldehyde in the morning, don't you?" says Shelley-Colette. Formaldehyde? Cobalt and crimson illumination washes the walls like some high-tech lamination. Glints of hard aquarium-green light. Shapes? Hallucinations? But detail is at first lost in feeble light. Instead there's only a twisting forest submerged in the unnatural luminance of alien atmospheres. A dissolving morass of tentacles and copper weed. Fuzzy fronds filtering purple light, spreading in widening ripples of colour. And something else. Something important. Something significant. Something rearing against the density of air. And it's like I'm reading screeds of hallucinatory prose, seeing snapshots of the unconscious, the dreams and nightmares of this impossible place. The artist. The wife. The mistress… and the critic, whose existence is less than any of them. The strange weave of relationships binding us. And the secret. The secret silence we've held for all the decades. The secret we are finally revealing to each other. The deadness is me. And only me.

Formaldehyde. HCHO. Made by the oxidation of methanol. And a severed body suspended within. Head, shoulders and torso in the first. Thighs and legs in the other. But transposed, arranged. Then rearranged. Added to. Subtracted from. Intestines spiral in protective coils. Internal organs wink and glisten. Ornamented. One eye watches from deep inside the navel. The other from the anus. The penis replaces the nose. Testicles fill the empty orbits of the eye-sockets. Feet replace hands, and hands feet… Hannibal Mytholmridge. Our final work.

I guess life goes on.

But sometimes… it doesn't.

She speaks in my head. Even now, now that the shock, and

the horror is over. In my head she's here. And I'm still there. Swaying, brain throbbing with sensations. Abruptly now the Earth has ceased to rotate. Time has stilled, its timelessness seeping into my bones. There is no air. All seasons are winter. Everything is gone. Even the dream. Day is dead. All that's left is the twilight of that strange flat light. With that silence, deep and unremitting...

THIS WORLD HOLDS SPACE ENOUGH

> The equation changed the world in more profound ways than anyone could have anticipated. The very universe itself will no longer be the same.

August 1849

The world was a more strangely different place in those distant past days than we can now imagine. Fleeing the aftermath of the Dresden atrocity, the Czibarovsk family arrived at Gravesend beneath gull-wheeling cloud-tumbled skies. Otto was a tall, bearded man who carried himself with bruised dignity. Self-assured in his intellect and culture, yet tensed for the casual taunts and threats provoked by his race and creed. Hannah was a contrastingly small compact woman, patient and precise in every movement, selflessly devoted to her husband and infant son. They'd stood together at their attic casement and grimly watched Prussian troops suppress the insurrection. Saw them encircling the old 'Altmarkt', splintering barricades and massacring the disorganized rabble penned within. Then, in horror, they witnessed the retaliatory process begin, troops targeting suspected dissidents, with gaolings, beatings and summary executions. Otto was concerned for his family's safety, he'd contributed libertarian essays to the *Dresdner Zeitung* which some would see as radical, so it was in dread urgency that he was forced to ensure their escape to Paris, and from there to the east end of London.

Percy Dove represented an immigrant support network. He was waiting to meet them with practical advice and a matter-of-fact outlook, his outwardly timorous appearance belying his steely resolve. With the world convulsed by change, he explained, it needs a humanist moral pole. And are we not all companions in misfortune? As a free-thinker working through

Church Benevolent and Liberal Reform societies, he helps the family locate cheap decrepit accommodation, apologizing profusely for his inability to find them better. Spitalfields is a vile district of thieves and whores, plagued by crime and ill-health, with the taint of mildew within and the stench of swarming humanity outside. Yet over the following months and years the two men become oddly mismatched friends, sitting playing chess together, strolling and debating the limits and necessity of political freedoms. Otto also spent time in the airless hush of the British Library where he continued writing. Conjecturing egalitarian utopias.

His son, also called Otto, was an awkward unattractive child, sulkily prone to bouts of unresponsive lethargy. He'd sit for hours on a corner chair in the drawing room with his hands over his ears, as if to keep out the sound of the big grandfather clock's slow-ticking, time crawling as though it was wound but once in a century. He is also the most important human being who ever lived.

Otto senior was a stern learned man, who nevertheless loved the fluidity of puns and riddles enabled by his adopted tongue. He was perplexed that his son, with a more inflexibly literal hold on language, was incapable of grasping such verbal-games. So as an intellectual exercise, the father devised a series of mathematical equivalents, number-puzzles involving converting top-heavy equations, algebra, algorithms and prime numbers. Young Otto not only takes to them immediately, he carries them further. They become his toys, totally absorbing them into his inner world.

An introverted child, young Otto frequently falls victim to bullying by delinquent local urchins. Percy Dove was startled to witness one such occurrence, as he traipsed towards the Czibarovsk's tenement. Too distant to intervene he could see Otto being taunted by a group of ragged ruffians a little older than he was. The boy neither resists nor attempts to flee, instead he withdraws into a trance-state that so alarms his tormentors they draw back, and leave him alone. His mind racing, Dove approached the boy. He's sitting on the dirty stone flags, his eyes wide and staring, but oblivious to everything. Until Dove's soothing words and patience brings him out of the trance, smiling as though nothing has happened. It was a small dark face not built for smiling.

From that moment on, Dove was both wary and respectful of him. A strange child with an uncanny flair for arithmetic, who sits beneath the garret window at night hypnotized by the huge frozen moon suspended over grimy London rooftops.

Later academics and speculative researchers debate the likelihood of placing Otto Czibarovsk within the autism spectrum, perhaps a traumatic response to whatever horrors he'd witnessed during the Dresden insurrection? Nevertheless, despite their threadbare penury, Otto Czibarovsk's genius for mathematics, combined with Dove's earnest ability at raising sponsorship from enlightened patrons, earns him a scholarship at Durham University.

It was there, some time around the autumn of 1860, that he devised the equation.

June 1903

Sad-eyed Roald Amundsen set sail from Kristiania as captain of a seven-man expedition to chart the theoretical north-west passage around the upper shoulders of the Americas, and hence through the Bering Straits to the Pacific. Certain geographical societies and universities offer financial incentive, but the trading opportunities such a passage would open up would provide reward beyond measure. Earlier attempts had been made using larger vessels with bigger crews. They'd all failed, so he reverses their logic, relying instead on speed and manoeuvrability. Anticipating a mission of high important that nevertheless holds out the prospect of long periods of deadly dullness.

By late September his seventy-foot vessel, the Gjøa had passed through Baffin Bay and the Peel Sound, to arrive west of the Boothia Peninsula, where they put into a natural harbour on the south shore of bleak snowbound King William Island. As winter closes in they become ice-locked. The team remain there for almost two years, learning from local Netsilik tribes-people, wearing Inuit clothing, wintering in igloos, and adapting native survival techniques while undertaking measurements intended to pinpoint the elusive and shifting location of the North Magnetic Pole. They resume their interrupted journey when conditions ease, making good and steady progress beneath strange arctic constellations, until they finally anchor at Herschel Island, from where Amundsen is able to ski triumphantly into the Alaskan city of Eagle, with unbelievably wild tales of the ice-free shores they'd glimpsed to the far north.

The Gjøa itself puts into shore at Nome in 1906, vindicating Amundsen's earlier strategy, in waters too shallow for a larger vessel to navigate.

March 1908

In response to charts provided by Amundsen, an American expedition from New Archangel docks in a natural harbour of what they term Borealia. They establish a base camp, from which they commence charting the extensive coastline. Norway, claiming spiritual rights, first names the territory Haakon after the king, or Ultima Thule, according to ancient Nordic tradition. Others call it Erebus. The Russian Empire immediately sets up a colony to the east, claiming the Alaskan Purchase of 1867 does not apply to these new offshore territories, and that access through the Bering Strait gives them legitimate sovereignty. Prussia and Austro-Hungary side with Russia while Britain and France support the American claim. In return the British Empire is permitted to establish a penal colony to the west.

Grizzled John Wild looks older than his thirty years. Glowering at his reflection in the shaving mirror he's abysmally displeased with what he saw. He'd scavenged a frugal existence as an itinerant prospector in California, then travelled north when the Klondike gold-rush opened up, but found himself not only again penniless, but marooned in even harsher conditions. It was there he first heard stories of the newer new world further north. And gambles all he has to reach it. Wracked by seasickness he watches the ferry's wake cutting across serried waves, and the spiralling gulls that follow them, skirting ice-floes beneath dark skies, steering towards rocky spines and pinnacle outcrops, where guide-beacons are positioned in lieu of a lighthouse.

Immigration from the Klondike has already expanded the American base, spilling out over the original stockade, into a sprawling city of shanties named Further, from which prospectors are penetrating through soft swirls of snow along the shoreline. As doors rattle and bang in the wind like percussive music down the gusty streets, talk inside the warm gaslight glow of bars and bawdy houses along the harbour-front is of Archduke Nickolai unilaterally proclaiming himself Emperor of the realm in defiance of the Czar. There's some relief that sporadic ongoing hostilities with the United States were suspended, as the imperial fleet is diverted to blockade the Russian city. Within weeks Nickolai is deposed in a coup provoked by the privations of siege, to be replaced by a utopian socialist state, which splits into rival factions who establish separate satellite power-hubs.

It was while playing stud poker in a bar off the Einstein intersection that John Wild first encountered Paul Hackett. As he ate a Reuben sandwich with sauerkraut, it emerges that Hackett is a convicted fraudster and escaped-fugitive from the penal colony. And although Britain has no extradition rights, he considers it wise to evade their reach. So they team up and hastily prepare for travel. They barter for a bad-tempered mule. As they negotiate price, it snuffles restlessly like a dog hinting a walk is necessary. Wild takes that as a positive omen. They name it Napoleon, and once equipped they follow prospector-routes inland towards the austere ramparts of the coastal ridge, where they meander in a vaguely easterly direction along arid screes of rocky shale.

In a detached air of timelessness it's impossible to gauge the passage of hours, even the sun has become a hazy bronze disc suspended in the pale cold sky. Storm coming, the hills shining as the sky darkens. They're forced to seek shelter from sudden squalls, with snow like melting stars swirling into nebulae against stone cliffs and thunder rumbling along the bluffs. By chance they happen upon the entrance to a narrow cleft, that broadens out into a clear pass as they trudge deeper between raw peaks, emerging to overlook a forest gently shelving inland, the dark line of the far horizon slipping away beyond…

For a moment fear takes them unawares, as they lean out over its vast emptiness.

They set up overnight camp in the oxbow loop of a river beneath a stand of tall pines. A river thronged with fish. The forest alive with deer. Feeling the springy texture of the grass underfoot, which Napoleon crops contentedly, the breeze on their faces is cool, but pleasantly so. They drink from the stream, splashing the water up onto their faces. Allowing its freezing, refreshing droplets of ice to awaken their dulled senses. Breathing deeply.

For John Wild and his new partner, their scuffing days are forever over.

October 1913

The first of the Prussian contragrav heliospheres to achieve orbital elevation films further extents of the new continent, glimpsing previously unsuspected woods, lakes and prairies dense with bison. Naval geophysics surveys attempt to chart the coastline, but only find more island groups, archipelagos, peninsulas and land-bridges to yet more land-masses.

A League of Nations summit attempts to resolve disputed claims, while a Geneva Scientific Convention debates the contradiction of its very existence, with representative from journals and universities. Percy Dove, a vigorous 92-year-old arrives to speak about a paper published by the Durham Department of Mathematics. But because he represents only a small network of academics he's denied preferential treatment.

He sits in the rattling public streetcar travelling across the city, carrying his sheaf of documents in a briefcase. He wears a maroon silk bowtie and dark three-piece suit. His shoes are carefully polished. His hair is greying, but still full. He notices the man sitting across the aisle watching him with piercing rat-bright eyes. He has black greased-down hair that seems to sprout from every facial orifice. Dove tries to avoid contact, but the man moves across to join him, and leans close in a conspiratorial manner.

"We must beware. We must be on constant vigil," he hisses.

"From what?" asks Dove warily.

"For crying out loud man, where's your vision? I can tell things about people. I know I can trust you. You're a delegate?" He holds a finger to his lips in a "shhh" gesture.

"In a modest way, yes."

"I'm Fabian Rudd, no doubt you've heard of me?"

Dove attempts to conceal his rising unease. "Never mind the dramatics Mr Rudd, pray make your point."

161

He glances furtively to left and right. Then resumes. "They appear as ordinary people, 'cept for they have no navels. You can stand alongside them in the queue at the telex, or sit beside them on the omnibus and suspect nothing. No-one knows how many of them there are or what are their intentions. They are shape-shifters, vampiric by nature. They come from the New Territories, in slow and gradual infiltration…"

"You'll forgive me for saying this, but I fear your assertion is incorrect," Dove ventures.

"The clock is ticking, my friend – if you could but hear it, we're all a thin step short from genocide, and we're running out of time."

He's rescued from further unwelcome dialogue by the bell announcing arrival at the venue, and manages to lose Rudd in the crowd. Wandering bemused through parades of the full diversity of humankind, and some that seem, through the exaggerations of fashion, barely borderline human. But he finds himself thinking of Rudd. Fearing that his unsettling encounter constitutes an ill-omen, trepidations that are amply borne out by what follows. From the inaugural "Welcome colleagues" it's a fractious conference that frequently devolves into a slanging match, with delegates denouncing each other and storming out of the auditorium.

Dove listens intently, after all, are we not here to talk? To arrive at a consensus? The first speaker asserts that, in order to accommodate the newly-discovered lands, surely the world is the wrong shape, rather than spherical it must be ovoid – resembling an egg? He creates the first uproar. Surely this contention is at odds with all conventional wisdom? So all the maps are wrong. How can this be possible? It can't be. No, there must be more here, another explanation. If he'd lobbed a bomb into the centre of the room he could have asked for no better reaction.

During an intermission he retires to the saloon seeking refreshment. A fellow delegate from the Pan-African republic strikes up an unwelcome conversation. "Listening to each speaker," the burly newcomer blusters, "it's impossible to decide if what they're saying is of great consequence, or complete flim-flam."

"I fear this debate is no longer about the truth," counters

162

Dove. "For there's no longer any such thing. Truth has become malleable."

"Do you realize? You refer to our familiar world in the past tense?" the African points out.

"Because usual can no longer be considered a part of our lives."

"Now, I hear what you're saying, but what interpretation am I supposed to put on it?"

"What, indeed," he concedes.

Their conversation is abruptly curtailed when sessions resume. But Dove watches in dismay as a triumphalist group from the Flat Earth Society seizes the platform, ridiculing what they term "the Great Copernican Heresy". The chair resigns and order collapses into recrimination and disarray. Dove enjoys the situation even less. The inevitable delays are a source of irritating frustration. But formalities must be observed. The corridors are long, his wait seems even longer. The rehearsed words tick inside him. Reminding him of the sound of the big grandfather clock's slow-ticking in the Czibarovsk's drawing room, time crawling as though it was wound but once in a century. Young Otto sitting on a corner chair with his hands over his ears, as if to keep the sound out. And Rudd telling him, "The clock is ticking, my friend, the clock is ticking..."

Eventually his patience is rewarded, even though he's only speaking at a fringe-meeting. Standing at the podium, Dove begins reading from his prepared text, a little huskily at first, but gaining strength and confidence as he goes along, his voice finding depth and resonance. The very significance of the words he's imparting powers his delivery. Almost unreported in the general hubbub, he determinedly succeeds in delivering his paper. Once he's done, he bows slightly from the waist, thanks his audience for their kind attention, and steps down. It's only after the resulting stunned silence that the Czibarovsk equation is first seriously debated, setting up dialogue among academics that will continue once the Geneva Scientific Convention has dispersed and delegates have returned to every major world centre.

Meanwhile, Dove travels from the Conference centre across Geneva towards the railway station home. All the while, the more he strives to dismiss the image of Fabian Rudd from his mind, the more the conversation in the streetcar follows him. He was a little rodent-like man with startlingly bright eyes set on either side of his beak-nose, talking nonsense – of course. His very appearance is suggestive of alienness, of extraterrene origins. But he was scared. He was a symptom. People are unsettled by the changes taking place around them. Unsettled by this new century, barely begun. Sigmund Freud in Vienna deciphering the secret code of dreams. Albert Einstein upsetting concepts of time and space. Otto Czibarovsk showing in vital ways that both are connected, that the unconscious mind affects and alters matter itself. As the Pan-African delegate had said, "Our familiar world must now be referred to in the past tense." Yes, for some, such metaphysical innuendos can be terrifying.

At the same time, the Ernest Shackleton Imperial Trans-Antarctic Expedition embarks from South Georgia into the Weddell Sea. Preliminary supply-caches to equip the venture are laid by the Ross Sea Party across the Great Ice Barrier as far as the Beardmore Glacier. They trudge on until, cut off by extreme blizzards and inter-personnel disputes, the advance party survives only by the unexpected discovery of a thermal fresh-water lake. There, miraculously, it is raining. Not snow, but mizzling rain. Retreat is no longer an option. They set up a camp and prepare to sit out the storm.

Over the following months, with Shackleton's venture overshadowed, further expeditions to the lake establish a permanent base on the wind-scoured shoreline and accomplish a successful circumnavigation of what is redefined as a temperate inland sea, presumably the result of subterranean geothermal energies. Claimed by the British Empire, mineral exploitation rights are established, and immediately contested. Further naval complements traverse the forbidding ice-fields on runners to reach the inland sea, and once a land-corridor highway is established the base rapidly expands. Next, they're tasked with navigating a course to the first major island sighted within the shimmering body of near-tideless water.

The rowing boat splashes towards a shingle beach in a sheltered bay, an eerie quiet lying over the cove as they tack in towards the shore. There's Aldous Rankin, a nervous crypto-geographer, a civilian academic. But Captain Lewis will be the first to set foot on the glistening pebbles where the slap of waves is made up of liquid consonants. A serious man, he'd striven diligently all his life, making a vocation for himself, where his natural abilities outweigh both Puritan parental opposition, and his obscure social origins. An instinctive egalitarian, it seemed natural at first to ease formality and adopt a first-name basis for this seven-man landing party. Now, not for the first time, he wonders if that was the right thing to do. Get too friendly, they assume you're soft and take advantage. At moments such as this, he knows well the mystique of discipline and the fragile basis on which it rests. Now, if ever, they need firm leadership.

Not a man partial to hard drink, he'd nevertheless considered it appropriate to spend his last uneasy Plymouth evening, before embarking, in a quayside tavern with his future crew-members. A girl was singing. Likely a slattern of dubious morals, but a voice of such piercing purity he'd found himself entranced. She sang of a solid House Carpenter whose wife is seduced away by the guile of a Daemon Lover, abandoning her husband and babes three she sails away with him. As the ship breaks in twain, and as it spins three times round she glimpses the dark hills of hell whence they're bound.

This unnatural realm is the hell of which the slattern sang. The shores of death. Lewis tries to fight the superstitious fear rising like puke in his craw. He steels himself to step into the surf, certain it will scald with toxic poisons. Of course, it does nothing of the kind. It is water, no more than salt breeze and silver light. Assembling on the beach the party leave a guard where they've hauled the narrow-boat above the tide-mark, and track up beyond the tundra shoreline. The men joke, spit and curse as they climb towards a ridge of forested foothills.

Cresting the rise, their banter fails as they gaze out across a vast desert extending as far as they can see. Draped against a soft wind they're reduced to a line of small figures silenced by immensity. To those of a certain temperament, the strange nature of the environment is even more disconcerting. Not in any obvious way, because there are no obvious differences. Simply the implications of being there at all. There's something about the supernatural horizon that's wrong. Where the roof of the planet should be, it simply stretches on towards a vanishing point.

The captain lowers his binoculars, and turns to the crypto-geographer. "I feel as though the world is no longer turning beneath my feet, literally, absolutely."

"Yes, I feel that way too." Rankin turns towards Lewis. "There must be certain specific words arranged in a certain order that explain all of this. I suppose. But if so, my vocabulary's inadequate to find them."

"Perhaps there is no answer? At least, nothing we can comprehend. It's just that we've run off the rim of the world." In the back of his mind he hears the entrancing voice of a tavern slattern singing of the dark hills of Hades.

"Yet every question must have an answer."

Captain Lewis opens his mouth, as if to speak, then shrugs…

April 1925

The sparkling Bosphorus sucks hungrily at the wooden piles close by where the hydrofoil nudges still. Shielding her eyes from the midday glare, above the dome of the Byzantium Centre, she can see a drifting formation of heliospheres targeting the cloud-free horizon. She can identify their modified zeppelin-shapes, evolving more into elongated teardrops. Beneath the skyships, among the ancient splendours of minaret towers, smaller gyrocopter danglepods act as local taxis. Yes, in a world confused with imagination and out-weighted by fiction, it was indeed pleasant here. Crossing terminators, Constance Olssen had awoken so early she was sure it was still yesterday. Now she steps with exaggerated care from the gangway onto the jetty, into tomorrow. Her lightest portable camera cased and slung over her shoulder. She doesn't yet know what she intends to snap, but this is one of the world's great cities. Move carefully. Move slowly. That's the way.

"Hoşgeldiniz." Sophia greets her, taking her hand and leading her. "You haven't lost any time getting here."

"As I understand it, we're living in end-days, so there's little time to lose." They both laugh.

A slim sliver of a person, Sophia wears a pale blue silk headscarf, with a matching trouser suit. Her eyes are piercingly bright. The two have corresponded, but have never met until now. She lays her hand companionably on Constance's shoulder. There are some people you connect with straight away, who stand out – from the moment you first fix eyes on them. Today is going to be a good day. Constance feels that certainty, breathing it in with the salt-sea air.

Beyond the quay, the heat-soaked rockcrete is pooled with congealed light. Fluted pennants and banners flutter everywhere, catching the sun. It's the bright brisk morning of an animated day, dense with colour, loud with conversation and music. A sense of urgent excitement pervading everywhere. And a bored line of Janissaries with perspex riot-shields holding back a mob of protesters.

"Why are the people protesting?"

"The people are always protesting about something. The speed of reform is too gradual. The speed of reform is too hasty, you know."

The international delegation of Cartographers and Geographers, what Sophia calls "a scrambling of eggheads", are led past the demonstration, across the spacious avenue beneath fretted minarets, through the luxurious antechamber, and into the dome's even more luxuriously cool interior. The symposium venue is a palace of green liquid-light, a place of harmony, which blends grace, power, fantasy and scholarship.

With her blouse sticking to the small of her back, Constance follows the ticking of Sophia's heels. Up marble spirals to mellow guest accommodation, to her minimally furnished suite. It has a white tiled floor, hand-woven carpets, low futon bed and wet-room. In the corner, a brass telescope on long tripod stilts, with adjustment screws for careful alignment. And a silver tray of refreshments, a dish of couscous, hummus, diced peppers and veg. Later, rested and refreshed, she rejoins the main party, wrangling amicably, settling into lavish upholstery arranged around the fountains and tiered trickle-pools. She accepts a clear glass of Turkish çay from Sophia.

An informal calm flows through the fantasia, encouraging a sense of shared intimacy. "At the risk of provoking ribald laughter, when I was a girl I watched a Hollywood film called *King Kong*," says Constance. "Sitting in the warm movie-theatre darkness, I was entranced. I was fascinated. I knew there were new worlds being discovered at the corners of the known. Previously unsuspected lands. Skull Island could be just another of them. But I digress, and become flippant. That is not my intention."

Sophia rakes her with a hard gaze of appraisal. "No apologies, please. So far as we know, there's no indigenous human presence, or previously undocumented biota in the revealed territories. But people love stories. They love to romance. They've always woven fantasies since Odysseus and Sinbad. To some, the Antarctic island desert is said to hold archaeological remains of vast ancient cities with cyclopean temples dedicated to terrible octopus-gods. There have been alleged sightings of an uncharted Pacific continent – which they name Lemuria, and islands within the Sargasso Sea where Jurassic reptiles survive. But I know what you mean. I, too, have wish-dreams. The world is now infinite. Who knows what is possible...?"

She holds her camera up, framing Sophia's face playfully. "What are your wish-dreams, Sophia? I'd be fascinated to find out."

"This is a place of discovery. We shall see. What is your primary objective?"

Click. Click. Click. Three images freezing her face. "I'm just here to observe, to report on the seminar back to the good readers of Detroit. To ask, on their behalf, where we go when science no longer makes sense?"

"Science does indeed no longer make sense – in western terms. It can't, it makes no sense at all, according to the old physical rules. But that's because you have a fixed view of those rules. The west is tying itself up in impossible conundrums, attempting to reconcile the new physics with the old constants. That's not our way. Christian Europe tore itself apart in a century of doctrinal warfare during its reformation and renaissance. That's not our way either. The Islamic reformation rippling outwards throughout the Ottoman Empire is based in dialogue and respect for other cultures. This is our beginning. This is the point from which the world comes into being."

Constance shakes her head. "No, there's more to it than that. I fear there's something fundamentally skewed, but tantalisingly elusive about the whole business. Maybe I don't understand. Instead, physical laws break down into uncertainty, and become hypothesis. The world has become a mathematical abstraction of approximately infinite size. It defies logic."

"No, we just have to accept it, it merely requires new logics."

Her eyes narrow, watching her very closely. "Think about this. Science is observational. Detached. Yet sub-atomics shows us that the greater part of matter is void. And separation becomes impossible the further you delve, the deeper we penetrate into micro-particles the more they become indistinguishable from energy. The two are interrelated. We are not something set apart from matter, we are of it. We participate, we influence by the act of observing. Zen studies, and peyote-based research both reach pretty-much the same conclusions. Matter is a form of interactive energy that responds to, and can be influenced by consciousness. That is the legacy the Czibarovsk equation gifts us."

A new logic, yes. Later, in her improvised darkroom, new portraits take on form by emerging from photographic developer fluid. She watches images infest the print by tipping trays of silver iodine, pouring chemicals. Old ghosts on paper. Images of a new life clarifying.

Constance turns her head to gaze through the panoramic glass, out beyond the Byzantium dome. To a world crazier on its surface, but far saner underneath where it most matters. There are gardens in tiered wander-ways down to, and along the rim of the wide Bosphorus. Later, they will walk there, together. Constance, and Sophia.

She wonders if anything will ever be the same again. For the first time in her life, she hopes it will not.

August 1938

With the realisation that his marriage was finally and irreparably over, Felix Farrell emerged restless and disorientated from a week's ouzo-binge and determines on a journey from Athens to Paris for no other reason than to do it. He's joined by Velimir Ilic, a musician with a shaven poll and a sinister, rather cadaverous face – sardonic rather than menacing. Almost immediately Felix regrets his choice of companion. A decision made on the spur of blurred impulse in an early hours bar. Yet they make for complementary, if curious companions as they take a leased VW motorhome north. Velimir sits picking his teeth with a slender splinter. He either respects, or fails to pick up on Felix's taciturn mood. They sit in silence, side by side towards Thessaloniki. Beneath an arch in thick Byzantine walls, through the Ano Poli down to the waterfront overlooking the Thermaic Gulf, rank with seaweed and fish-scales.

Standing there, it's as though they're tasting the layers of history, peeling it back like the skins of an onion, Ottoman, Roman, Macedonian, to when ancient mariners set sail from this shore into an unknown Aegean of mysterious islands inhabited by mythical beasts and unpredictable gods. A voyage as strange then, as the new world vistas are now.

"I think of those old maps from classical times," muses Felix softly. "A circlet of land around the Mediterranean. Nothing more. This was all."

"Perhaps that *was* all, then?" Velimir responds agreeably. "I think of the Norsemen island-hopping across the arctic rim. They find a tolerably pleasant island, but to discourage an inrush of migration they call it Iceland. They find a frozen arid island, but to entice colonists to go there they name it Greenland. Then they get as far as Newfoundland, but their colony doesn't survive its first harsh winter. I always wonder, if only they'd pointed the prows of their dragonships south and followed the coastline down they'd have reached the wealth of mainland America. Or perhaps we're wrong? Maybe their Vinland really was the edge of the world, and America was not actually there, not until our collective dreams forced it into existence when expanding population pressures made it necessary?"

"A nice idea. But I don't think the Native American peoples would agree, the Inca, or the Mayan. Anyway, isn't there some evidence of a Phoenician colony in central America?"

"I'd offer a convincing refutation, if I only had your brains and bone-structure," quips Velimir.

Felix smiles. Perhaps this trip will work out after all.

Over the following days they set out across into the province of Macedonia, descending into Serbia and across the Skopje stone bridge, and hence into the fading grandeur of Austro-Hungary. Overhead they see evidence of the new German hegemony. Denied access to colonies in the virgin territories the Berlin-centred Confederation had redirected its industrial energies. The first of their hermetically spacetight heliospheres to orbit the moon, photographed a second, smaller moon, eternally hidden beyond the familiar Luna bulk. A honeycomb globe at a place of frozen gravity. Subsequent spheres determine that Mond Zwei is the site of what translates as numerous 'shift-tubes', which lead to various other points in space-time. There are immediate outbreaks of panic. The object is artificial. It is an incredibly ancient artefact abandoned by a long-dead alien civilization, or a signal-station primed to alert a malevolent living one, now preparing to pounce. Authorities assure the public that no, it is a naturally-occurring quantum nexus. To a world already buffeted and awash with wonder, viewers are astounded by film of a series of linked German habitation modules, blockhouses constructed of compacted rust-brown regolith, in the deep Martian canyon.

"There would have been war, without doubt," comments Velimir Ilic, taking a swig from a curiously-shaped flask as Felix drives. His voice lacks intonation, even to the point of monotony. "Competing imperial powers with expansionist ambitions jostling up against each other on a finite continent. It's a recipe for disaster. There would have been tech-war so terrible we can scarce imagine its ferocity. I know, I've read the speculative fiction of George Tomkyns Chesney and Mr HG Wells. They conjecture it on our behalf. The dawn of infinity has saved us."

"So what world do we live in?" queries Felix truculently. "I do my job, that's all. And that's all that anyone can expect of me. All this talk of discoveries and new frontiers bewilders me."

"We are anti-history, we must de-time ourselves too. We just are, and that's enough." Ilic clicks his fingers to illustrate the point.

"The north I understand, kind of. The land goes on, and it goes on for ever. But the south...?"

"Yes, I agree. It's a paradox. An inland sea, with a single island at its centre. At the centre of the island is an inland sea, with exactly the same dimensions as the original inland sea. It, also, has an island, with an inland sea, which also has an island. Each inland sea is the same size as every other inland sea. Each island is as big as every other island. Again, apparently for ever. It resembles one of those Russian dolls that fit one inside the other. Except all of the dolls are of exactly the same dimensions."

Such thinking puts him in mind of how, following the great Pan-African Congress expulsions, white South Africans had established an embattled enclave on the inner Antarctic shore. How skirmishes broke out with the Imperial Chinese loyalists, exiled from the new People's Republic. And a temporary demilitarised zone lapsed when the new Voortrekkers moved inwards across the inland sea, to the first island, then the next. Where are they now? How deep are they in never-ending contradiction?

"There are ambiguities. It is a very inexact science. If we were any smarter we'd all be crazy. But you do, kind-of, get used to it. Miracle of miracles." There's a seesaw of ideas in his head.

"It's not true to say the old laws of science were wrong, just different. After all, a physical constant is determined by observed evidence. And isn't there some other rule of science that tells us everything is an approximation in a constant state of flux, with everything permanently in motion, things evolve, life mutates and changes, atoms are always moving, sub-atomic particles are in endless random collisions, nothing ever remains stable. If that's true, it follows – as inevitably as day follows night, that physical laws must also be constantly redefining in response to the ever-altering natural realities."

From beautiful time-frozen Salzburg they cross over into Germany proper, the autobahn link-system spanning distances north-south. When the vehicle stops, there seems to be no sound in the world. There are Buch Shops crammed with garish pulps and comic-books in Stuttgart, and meat-easies where retro thrill-seekers can still dine on the corpse-flesh of dead animals. Instead they get drunk in centre bars on Schnapps. Staying sober is not the problem. The need for intoxication is the answer. Felix finds himself wandering the old town alleyways where Cathedral bells ripple the skies. Echoing his wife's name, Carole. How did it ever get to this? How did he ever allow himself to lose her? What is she doing now, watching a TV-soap, doing a word-search in her magazine? Is she thinking of him? Is she happy? Because he's not.

There's something in the air, something in his brain. The fall-out of some noxious vapour, some experimental condensation which releases ideas into the air, so he's inhaling dreams with every breath. He can no longer feel her body-warmth in the night. No longer hear the sweet undulations of her breath. Shut off your mind. Don't dream these things.

He wakes from a grumbling doze. He's not in a good mood. Accelerating into France itself. Velimir is thumbing through

Deutscher Gespenster Geschicten, the vivid cover-art illustrates a screaming blonde having her flimsy gown ripped away by a Borealian fear-beast in a fantastic Gothic city. It's taken their VW motorhome two weeks to come two-thousand miles across united Europe.

"Are you intent on communicating with me telepathically today?" opens Velimir, putting the magazine aside. "If a picture paints a thousand words, you'd be a cartoon."

An uncalculated pause. "My life's been good," muses Felix. "But not all of my decisions have been for the best. It's like we've become fragments in the random collisions of our own lives."

"I'm a musician," announces Velimir. "I play the universe in one long improvisation, shifting time signatures and scales. Sometimes smooth, sometime jagged. Infinity speaks the tongue of beasts and birds. A slow melancholy refrain, with a ground-shaking bass. It used to be notation, now it's free-form."

"Did you really just say that?"

"Did I say what? I said nothing. Nothing at all."

"And the result, we are at peace. We live in a perfect world. What could possibly go wrong...?"

Velimir is still restless. He wants to go further. To London, southern capital of the British Federal Republic. There's the Czibarovsk Heritage Centre. And Westminster where they forever debate the merits of teetering on the brink of European accession.

Felix sits on the South Bank looking out over the Seine. He toys with a glass of red wine. The pale sun is warm on his skin. There are lizards in the grass. A girl in a blue denim dress throws sticks for a black collie to chase and retrieve. The dog waits, tensed in eager anticipation for the next throw.

Felix feels only immaculate desolation. He phones his wife in Athens. Carole refuses to take the call.

June 1985

Elmore Priest looks out from the forty-fifth window-balcony over the greening city. That green has its own voice, its own life-echoes. The forests have come back to the world. The gradual crawl of wild vegetation already erasing huge areas to north and east towards where the river has flooded into sparkling lagoons.

Clouds of waterfowl swirl over wet-ways that were once orbital freeways. He tries to imagine the kind of horror you can't wrap your mind around. Squint, and the birds are swarms of bloated bluebottles, attracted by bodies abandoned to rot in the streets. Too many to count, too many to imagine. A mustiness that settles everywhere, like invisible silt. No matter what happens in years to come, this dark shadow of tragic survivor-guilt will always remain. Remorse. Recriminations that eat into your soul.

Academics and speculative researchers still debate the origins of what later generations call "the winnowing". Investigative work by Paris-based virologists link its source to earlier outbreaks of encephalitis lethargica in the 1930s, but the two pandemic waves of June and October 1945 involving the H1N1 influenza virus became the most deadly natural disaster in human history. With no society left intact, and an 85% fatality rate. Panics and riots were sparked by rumours that the infection originates in the recently-opened regions, despite being discredited by epidemiological evidence. They result in the massacre and torching of homebound crews and anyone connected with newer land-surface expansion. Insanity born of fear, too, is contagious.

The near-extinction event probably proves things, typifies things, symbolises more hubris and irony than he can bother to think of at one time. You try to read meaning into each day, and fail. Yet to live is so precious. Now we try to cure ourselves, to heal the scars.

He steps back from the balcony edge with an unreasoned sense of relief. Into the faint scent of geraniums and flowering cacti. Inside, nothing has changed. The pale watercolour pictures on the wall, the plush arc of couches, the tinkling mobile, the plants in terrariums. The sound of the big antique grandfather clock's slow-ticking, time crawling as though it was wound but once in a century. To some, familiarity represents boredom. But Priest has a love for his suite and its geography that comes from intimacy, connected with his mindset, his need for some kind of stability. Gaining strength from everyday repetition.

"Memes," the dictapad says to Elmore Priest. "There have been periodic memes which rewire the cerebral cortex into new configurations, although social in nature, they nevertheless induce physical evolutionary changes within the brain itself.

174

That's what we have been observing here. Language was maybe the first. The separation event of our species from other hominid groups. The sophistication of a cultural development that became an inherited trait. I'd hazard that numerology and print-literacy had similar effects on the brain. Print-literature consists of words arranged into sentences that build by a logical process, one step connecting to the next, into paragraphs and so into text. Routing thought to replicate the method, into stage-by-stage reason and methodical logic, a dialogue of thesis and antithesis into synthesis."

"So where does that relate to what we've seen here?" He enjoys his solitude. Yet he speaks out loud, to hear the sound of his own voice.

A new flotilla of spheres had reached Mars after a gap of forty years. The original German installations were still there, still performing their oxygenating function, even though there were no bodies. Search parties yield no results as colonists set up a city of spires, soaring into the thin air. But there are persistently whispered stories. That the Germans, abandoned and isolated on the hostile planet as the home-world collapsed into pandemic chaos, had retreated into deep cave systems where they'd survived on rations for five... maybe ten years. And yet there are alleged sightings. Every now and then, a new ripple of scare-stories. An insubstantial ghost-presence. Or emaciated troglodytes still lurking in trackless caverns far beneath the surface, emerging periodically to cannibalistically feed.

But their original work bore fruit. The atmosphere in the lower valleys is breathable, barely, and there's modified vegetation – up step-by-step from simple spores and mosses, which are accelerating the process. While the web of orbiting helioshields, deflecting intensified sunlight surfacewards, is raising the temperature by tolerable degrees. Is Mars also infinite? Is it feasible that two infinite worlds can exist in the same continuum? And if so, what of Venus where the Chinese are said to have established hovering cloud-cities?

Elmore Priest had visited the new northern territories to negotiate business. From the John Wild oxbow tributary down into the widening river, towards the new city of Beyond. Vehicular trails remain fairly rudimentary, there will be a railway – eventually, but despite regular air-shuttles the most

175

popular mode of travel is by leisurely paddle steamer. Sitting high on the rear-deck of the Shangri La he has to keep telling himself they're travelling north, when every sense insists the opposite, as the increasingly lush vegetation along the river's edge conceals alligators, storks, terrapins and beaver. With giant man-tall ants-nests glimpsed through gaps in dense forestation.

Beyond proves to be a confident ebullient city, largely unaffected by the 'winnowing', and determinedly transforming itself from its pioneer settlement roots by the addition of a university complex, sports stadia and marble-fronted art centres. The intellectual talk here is of enigmatic fossils. If these are new lands, why do prospectors excavate fossilized remains hinting at millions of years of prehistory? And if the lands were here, but merely hidden by a wrinkle in space-time until the Czibarovsk revelation, could not other accidental crossings have occurred? When the Bering Straits was a land-bridge enabling human migration from Siberia across to Alaska, could that bridge not have extended here too?

Horror-films and trash-literature have already envisaged lost tribes and decadent civilizations ruled by beautifully evil high priestesses, hidden in folds and secret valleys of the still-unexplored mountains that loom further down the river's slow flow, their dazzling summits wreathed in cloud. The very implications of such agoraphobic vastness fills Priest with an uneasy sense of dread.

He's tired. His eyes ache. It's a thing of the blood rather than the mind, the same reality-afflicted nausea felt by the first to reach the Antarctic realm. It's with a profound feeling of relief that he returned to the familiar changelessness of the old world.

"The Czibarovsk equation," the dictapad tells Elmore Priest dramatically. "It was the next meme. Not the complexity of the math involved, although there is complexity. Indeed, there had been partial hints, glimpses through number theory, alchemaic incantation, positive and negative integers, ritual codex, differential calculus, heretical catechism, numbers rational and irrational. The paradigm is that understanding each process of the equation induces physical change in the soft parts of the brain itself. Opening up new channels, new possibilities. Messing with the brainwaves. Those incapable of adapting died in the great winnowing. It was not only a natural occurrence, but an evolutionary one. We adapt to survive. Those of us who came through are stronger, by inheriting the adaptation."

Yes, it's not as though the world's out there waiting for us, stretching away forever. That is not its nature. It reacts to consciousness. It is magicked into being by our presence. Infinite, no, not quite. Potentially infinite.

Priest paces across the global etherstream suite. All the vast electronics of the world now feeding barely a tenth of the population, left with the greatest wealth in world history. While he has seen no-one in person for – how long? Five months. As long as that? Yes, as long as that. Evidence of some kind of neurosis?

"Yet I have been struggling with the basic math underlying the equation. I don't understand it. I'm making poor headway. What does that mean? Where does that leave me... an evolutionary throwback?"

Priest sits down opposite the array, rubbing his hands together. He addresses the dictapad: "Are you real?"

"No," it replies.

He looks away. I must persevere. I must work harder. I must follow the equation through. I must...

September 2040

As soon as there's a lull in the shooting, she knows what she must do. Tensing for less than a moment, she launches herself from the highest point of the Martynov Bay Hotel Tower, Sevastopol and plummets down towards the earth eighteen floors below...

The world is a city. Yet even the greatest cities have districts-gone-bad, areas it's not wise to frequent after nightfall. The world might be a city, but there are still niggling territorial squabbles, turf-wars which collapse into chaos before UN arbitration can intervene. Arna Laswell can see the smouldering city scars as she checks her fall, levels off and flies above them. All that same old tumbling-rumbling makes-no-sense strife, same old conflict-sounds hit-by-hit. Drones can do this. And they're here too, visible as streaks in the still air, thin lines of brightness. But she does it better. Arna, winner of the 'Constance Olssen' newzatrix award, renowned for her capability and resourcefulness. As tough as they come. This is piss-easy, these clips will sell to the media, snatched live, as it happens. Despite rival cross-channel attractions.

Otto Czibarovsk's two-hundredth birthday is cause for universal celebration across the human worlds and continents. A naturally reclusive and uncommunicative man by nature he consents to appear on-screens. Curiosity levels are unprecedented. The sequence fades in with background scene-setting, retelling his story. Although everyone already knows it. Then zoning in on his Tibetan habitat-complex, through colonnaded cloisters with fountains and pools of bright fish.

Arna sets down on her balcony, shrugs off the suit and runs her fingers through auburn hair released from beneath her helmet. She downloads her new visuals. Yes, they look good. With a little editing they'll be better. She's not interested in new geographies. This is the here and now. She'd been born long after the controversies. All this absurd melodrama is the dusty concern of vanished generations. Enough past-times. Let's see action. The world is here. As it has always been here. The new lands are merely a part of her life. Yet as she dries her hands she glances across at the rolling news.

He's totally hairless. His thin papery skin is fibrously brown, the same hue as old well-seasoned leather, resembling that of a Mummy from a Universal horror-film. But his eyes are bright and sharp with undimmed intelligence. When he speaks, clearly and distinctly, there's still a trace of accent, retained across two centuries from Dresden. No, he never intended to change the world. That was never his intention. That was not even a consideration. Not a distant possibility. It was a game. An intriguing puzzle. No more. Never more than that. He'd done so little. And what he'd done, he'd done unintentionally. Yet its implications have done so much. Everything that has occurred since is totally incomprehensible without the formulation of that equation. It alters the rules. His very survival is proof of that itself. Longevity is a matter of choice.

That some might consider this strange is a thought that hadn't struck Arna before. After all, the world was more strangely different in those distant past days than she could imagine. Already she's thinking of how soon this Crimean conflagration must be closed down. Maybe it will be internationalized, like Jerusalem or the Vatican museum? Before that can happen, she has clips to capture.

A rich orange and white flash smashes against the sky in a sharply-evil blossom of sound...

July 2049

Carson steps from the 154th floor into the flitter. It drifts him across the Dresden greenway. With the sun bursting down over the eternal horizon of a perfect world. What could ever go wrong? How can this change? The flitter – the seamless black of a beetle's carapace, docks and he passes through into the skydome. Walter Coerns ushers him in. Carson self-consciously checks the hang of his long robe. A group of people sit around watching the vid-sphere. Awaiting the great announcement. Some of them look up and nod greetings. There's a party atmosphere. And yes, she is there.

When a man reaches the sombre maturity of thirty-and-nothing, and literally nothing ever happens in changeless isolation from one year's end to the next, he gratefully embraces this opportunity for human contact. He finds a space close enough to be close to Melody Wednesday to sit down and wait. He wants to speak to her, but can't find the words. Would it be a tad too fast, too pat? They've interacted in various virtual ways, but he's never been close enough to detect her body warmth, as he can now. The world is strange, and stranger than known, but people are deeper, more unknowable. They are exploring each other, tentatively feeing their way. She smiles as though she's rehearsed it, her hair a golden haze. He swallows. His throat is dry.

Otto Czibarovsk is about to announce his second equation. All the world is standing still. As Carson waits for an opportunity to speak to Melody Wednesday. That is the one thing on his mind...

...AND THE EARTH HAS NO END

> Why does the earth breathe beneath his feet?
> Why are there two suns in the sky?
> For Copernicus-2 the world he finds himself in is a confusing place...

AGAINST HELIOCENTRICITY: THE GERMINATION

The ground breathes gently

Copernicus-2 opens his eyes and the sky screams purple at him. It was riddled with erratic clouds that resemble maps from childhood legend, shifting island clusters, peninsulas, with navigable straits and channels between. He traces imaginary journeys. His fancy taking walks in the sky. At other times they reconfigure into tantalisingly human shapes, erotically amusing. He lies on his back, trying to decipher what they mean, watching retinal rods and cones dance as he stares into the brightness of sky. And all the while the ground breathes. It undulates in regular rhythms like tide. Rippling away over the plain of softly crumbling ochre to where it melts into horizon.

For a long while Copernicus-2 lay, enjoying the sensation of his heartbeat, the pulse of blood in his veins, the drowse of warmth falling on exposed areas of skin. There were richly scented currents of air moving lightly through the heat, smelling of fresh earth and other odd things, as the ground rose and fell in the waves of its exhalation. At length he reached out, and pressed his index finger into the soft ground, as deep as it would go, past the second knuckle. The ground felt damp. Almost sensually, organically warm. After a long moment, he slid his finger out of the ground leaving a small circular hole. The finger was covered with slime, like the trail left by a snail. He crouched to examine the finger, and the slime that glittered facets as he twisted it in the light.

In his squatting position he found the undulations of the ground more than a little disconcerting. His eyes refocused beyond the slime-covered fingernail. From where he crouched, halfway up the gradually breathing incline, he could see a phosphorescent pool of water some distance below him.

He wondered where he was. A defective tooth ached unpleasantly...

BENEATH THE TWO SUNS

He first glimpsed the Advocate silhouetted against a different sky, with a huge moon less than a stone's throw above them. He was a rangy man sitting hunched beside a small fire among wild bracken. A rangy man who poked the fire-embers with a whittled stick while humming tunelessly. The gleam in his eyes exactly matched the colour of the flames they mirrored.

Copernicus-2 slammed his eyes shut. The whole universe blotted out, and the soot-blackness beneath his eyelids was scary. As if, when awareness of everything external is taken away, there's nothing left inside either. He could taste blood. A salty metallic taste. And an incongruous thought came to him – "So the dead feel pain? So the dead taste blood?" It spilled from his mouth, down his cheek, streaking the wind-blown dust that grimed his face. He wanted to close his eyes, but they were already shut. And there was a web of sound across the soot-darkness, a lace of crimson blood-vessels quivering, shifting, screaming. He was aware of perspiration trickling freely down his back, beneath the collar of his white shirt.

His eyelids flicked open. The Advocate was partially hidden by shadows, humming.

"Where am I?"

"Where are you? You only have to look around to see that. See the plain? See the bracken stretching to the mountains? See the yellow flowers flecking the bracken like spray, the yellow mist hanging over the water? Doesn't that answer your question?"

Copernicus-2 shook his head, as much to clear it as in attempted reply. Would it be ill-mannered to say no, to suggest that the reply didn't really answer the question? He needed more. Would the stranger be offended? Instead, the Advocate just laughed a flinty laugh. "Conserve your strength. We have a long walk ahead of us. We must reach those mountains before the enemy try to stop us."

"Yes, of course." He lay back. Could feel the coarse grass, the unyielding soil beneath him. Hard. Real. A reality that was comforting. He dug his fingers into the dirt. Held himself to the earth. Its warm contact was sensual. The dirt beneath his nails gave him animal satisfaction.

At length the Advocate gestured for him to rise. He rose obediently. They walked. "Shouldn't we douse the fire?" He turned. There was no fire. There had never been a fire…

ANATOMY OF THE EYE

The glassy pool below Copernicus-2 reminded him of one half of a pair of spectacles. It was an elongated lens, rippled as the breeze grazed its surface. The sky lent it a faint mauve hue, or perhaps it was the other way around, and its colour was tinting the sky? Tall fronds of grass and reeds resembling pubic hair sprouted around the water's edge, sometimes wading out like long-legged bodiless birds into the shallows, at other points receding politely leaving miniature coves and sandy inlets. Growing from the pubescence at the pool's far bank was a bizarrely-sculpted rock formation. An immense arm, with veins and downy hair, ending in a long single finger that coiled endlessly about a huge phallus growing out of an empty eye-socket. The blind eye formed the other half of the imaginary spectacles formed in tandem with the pool of water.

For a while Copernicus-2 switched focus, and his attention, between the pool, and the glittering finger he held before him. Intrigued by the focal blur he could induce by such a simple exchange. Eventually, without any real motivation or decision, he picked up his brolly in his right hand, his briefcase in the left, and began to amble down the incline. The cloud formations above him boiled and imploded in insane choreography. The ground beneath him gradually grew soft downy hair mottled with clumps of the wispy grass that grew as aimlessly as smoke. As intricate as baroque. Until tall fronds of grass surrounded him, swaying irritatingly up against his legs in the breeze.

He brushed his finger clean across the groin of his neatly-pressed pin-stripe trousers, leaving a streak of ground-slime. The action had been unconscious, and its results were annoying. He carefully pulled a clean white handkerchief from the breast pocket of his jacket, saliva-damped it at the corner near the embroidered blue initial 'C', and attempted to remove the stain with short decisive strokes down the thigh. The smear was gradually replaced by an elongated patch of spit-damp.

Resuming the easy stroll he soon reached the pool's edge. Knelt down beside the water. Copernicus-2 was thinking, with amazing clarity, of seed catalogues. Suburban English gardens in coloured half-tone photographs on imitation gloss pages. Neat lawns edged with rose bushes, floribunda, Ena Harkness, Hybrid Tea Roses, the carefully planned clusters of Hydrangea, Hortensis, Clematis, Hibiscus, the borders of Sweet Williams, Michaelmas Daisy and Delphinium. Beyond the contoured privet hedge and the crazy paving pathway was a shallow concrete pond with a few plaster gnomes, eternally fishing.

He could feel the dull ache in his defective tooth.

He tried to fit the tantalisingly familiar, yet irritatingly unspecific mental seed-catalogue pictures into the context of what he was seeing. To what botanical genus did wispy pubic hair grass fit? He could arrive at no satisfactory explanation. He looked down into the water. As the landscape breathed, the pool rippled, sending shivering wavelets to lick and die up against the shingle at its edge. Looking back at him from the bed of the pool, distorted by ripples, was the reflection of a feline face. Feline, but humanoid, in a hybrid kind of a way. And didn't his hair consist of grass? For a long second they exchanged stares. Slit yellow cat-eyes hypnotically penetrating, effortlessly condescending. He thought 'The Cheshire Cat'? without knowing why.

Eventually, Copernicus-2 broke the duel by deliberately looking away from the apparition, then edging his attention surreptitiously along the pool's bank. And then back. The water was clear now. It reflected a human face that he supposed was his own. He didn't recognise it, although it seemed vaguely familiar. Clean-shaven, respectable. The torso beneath it was fleshily middle-aged, with an unhealthily developed paunch. He ran his fingers over his gut, just to check. Yes, it's me. He realised that he was carrying a briefcase. Why would he need a briefcase? He watched the reflection. Pulled exaggerated expressions at it, which it dutifully returned. He cupped his hands, thrust them into the stingingly cold body of water, felt it boiling up between his fingers, heard its secret whispers. Then he raised his hands to his lips, leaving long strands of spider's-web water. It trailed from his fingers arcing back into the pool. The water was slightly salty, treacle-thick, but strangely refreshing.

His reflection gradually reformed, jostled by the vortex of colliding, eclipsing ripples and neatly ascribed expanding circles. He watched the reflection. It watched him. He smiled. The reflection smiled. He frowned. The reflection frowned. He stuck his tongue out. The reflection thumbed its nose. Copernicus-2 laughed, and was painfully reminded of his aching tooth.

He was thinking of a stuffy-hot science room in a modern comprehensive school. His text-book was open at a chapter explaining optics. A diagram of a lens and a mirror with dotted lines representing light-rays transmitting an inverted image to the retina. The retina received an exact image of the object it reflected. Deviation was not permitted. Beneath the diagram it said 'Fig 139'.

THE BRUTALITY OF FACT

"Why are there two suns here?"

"Is two not enough? Would you prefer more?" The Advocate led the way slowly up the bleak gradient amid fields of growing ears, mostly they were human, but other species too, tall flexible rabbits' ears, horses', cats', pigs', bears', silvery, pale, flesh-coloured, many as small as coins, others as large as cauliflowers. He was aware of inner diagrams of eardrums (tympanic membrane), incus (anvil), stapes (stirrup) and auditory canals, but tried to resist them. As they passed, the ears switched in their direction, as though listening. He felt exposed. Vulnerable. Although he didn't know why he should feel that way. There are forces at work here that he did not understand. His senses were under attack. The bracken appeared to be rising towards him, the fern-like leaves beckoning in a swaying tide. Even though there was no breeze. The sky clawed beneath his retina.

"Berkeley," said the Advocate suddenly. "There was a thinker named Bishop Berkeley. He pointed out that we do not actually see, feel, hear or taste. Not really. What we do is experience the sensation of seeing, feeling, hearing or tasting. They are not the same. The two things are different. Sensation is experience translated through the senses. And the senses are fallible. See those points of light in the sky?" The Advocate continued talking as they walked. And yes, there were stars, so it must have become night. "Centuries ago people thought the Earth was flat. They thought of the sky as some kind of protective upturned dome, and that those points of light were pinpricks in the ceiling of heaven filtering down divine light from the domain of gods. People have believed all kind of crazy stuff. Crazy, illogical people – right? People who only used their eyes to believe. People who knew only what they saw. But have you ever wondered, have you ever thought – what if they were right? What if – for as long as they believed that the world was flat, it was flat?"

Intricate diagrams of heliocentric solar systems crammed his mind with blinding clarity. Great elliptical orbits journeying through the depths of space. Each orbit neatly labelled with small sans-serif lettering. Mercury, Venus, Earth – spangled asteroids herded between Mars and Jupiter. A stray comet wandering in from the edge of the page. A small boxed key indicating the diameter of each planet, its distance from the sun, length of year, number of moons. The closer he scrutinised it, the more the text became blurred and indistinct.

The Advocate was talking. Out in this wide-open space, Copernicus-2 felt the need to connect, but found it difficult to concentrate. Beyond the mental vista of the astronomy text-book there was an idea struggling to emerge. A memory of awakening into a surreal Salvador Dali landscape of tall wispy grass and bizarre sensual rock formations. A memory – or a premonition. Yet it was happening simultaneously, like the other half of a schizophrenic personality. It was happening now. It was happening to him.

"Then there was Ptolemy" continued the Advocate. "He thought of the Earth as some kind of sphere. That the moon and the stars and the planets and suns and all that cosmic stuff revolved on curved tracks around the world. Revolved around us – the human race. Crazy concept. Illogical concept. But could it be that he was right? Could it be that for as long as people believed in Ptolemaic cosmology, it was true?"

Copernicus-2 attempted to thrust the astronomical graffiti from his mind to concentrate on the intimations of a third layer of images tugging for his attention. The recurrent fleeting vision of two people on a wild wide beach. One of the people was him. The other was a girl. There were tall cliffs. A wide tideless ocean. They were waiting, anticipating… something. He knew he was watching himself. A future self? He sensed that this was some kind of prophetic dream. As though time had become disrupted, as well as geography. As though, at that moment, time had become unglued from its place in the universe. As though the force that stuck it there had paused, held its breath, and that whatever spun loose had become the events of these strange dislocated hours. But the image was fluctuating, an insubstantial thing that refused to clarify, leaving words that played around his head as he watched, "an infinite Earth, the Earth goes on forever…"

AGAINST HELIOCENTRICITY: TRIPTYCH

His tooth gnawed belligerently. He opened his mouth and prodded at it with the nail of his index finger. It tasted salty and the pain intensified. He pressed his eyes closed until the pain ebbed back to a more tolerable level. For a long moment he stayed rocking back and forth on his heels, then opened his eyes. He was looking along the edge of the pool to where, about a hundred yards away, a youth dressed in a dhoti, with grass for hair, was returning his stare with open curiosity.

Copernicus-2 looked away in embarrassment. Concentrated his attention on the microcosm of lapping water just beyond the toes of his well-polished shoes. A beetle was sculling across the surface of the Lilliputian inlet from reed to reed. He watched its painstaking progress. Watched its long angular hair-legs skimming the ripples, its blue-green shell catching the light.

But all the while, he was aware of the youth's lizard-eyes watching him. Copernicus-2 tried to sneak a glance at the newcomer without making his intention too obvious. And the more detail he determined, the stranger the youth appeared. For no reason he could adequately explain he was reminded of a painting, *The Martyrdom of Saint Sebastian* by Andrea Mantegna, a Paduan renaissance artist. He'd seen the painting in a gallery in Italy, or maybe just in a book of art-reproductions? Like a painting, he was well-muscled, standing with his weight on one

186

leg, like a statue. He was breathing heavily, his naked hairless chest gleaming with sweat, mottled with wind-blown dust. His hair was a mass of tousled black curls that cascaded about his face and shoulders. His arms were folded behind his back and appeared to be pinioned there by highly polished chains. At first, from his sideways glimpse, he saw what he took to be a long flexible penis coiled up around his left thigh, its head apparently embedded in his anus. At a second glance, it became an umbilical chord extending from his navel, coiled flexibly around his left thigh and embedded in his spine.

As he watched, the youth began to move slowly, indecisively along the water's edge towards him. Copernicus-2 concentrated with growing desperation on the area of dirt, shingle and water between his feet directly in front of him. The water-beetle had disappeared, leaving him alone to face the new stranger. He resented its desertion. There was flickering movement at the corner of his eye. He tried not to look, but it was impossible not to. He sneaked an occasional glance at the approaching toes until they stood close enough to touch. He could hear the youth's laboured breathing, could smell the musk of his body.

"They're after me." The disembodied voice came from somewhere above the toes. The intonation was odd, heavily accented, but recognisable.

"And that affects me, how?" mumbled Copernicus-2 at the toes. "My tooth is aching. I don't know where I am. Why should I concern myself with your troubles? Go away."

"We are at war. You are part of that war." The toes clenched into the dirt, leaving two sets of five furrows. Copernicus-2 watched with interest as they unclenched. Then looked away, to the left slightly, then down. Although there was no longer a sun there were long blue-tinged shadows pointing sometimes this way, sometimes that, or else just pooling in hollows. He could see the tall outcrop of organically shaped rock on the far side of the pool, see where the primeval moss-slicked stone curved gently, protectively down to eventually submerge itself in the tall wispy grass at the point where it grew most densely, garlanded by overgrown vines and rotting leaves. "If that's true, you could always hide over there, in the grass," he hissed conspiratorially, relenting a little.

As he looked up, the youth smiled weakly. There were

perfectly-formed tears of sweat on his forehead and tangled like dew in his grass-hair. As he watched, he began bounding in the indicated direction, his hands secured behind his back with highly polished chains, the penis-umbilical swaying as he moved. The martyred Saint Sebastian from a medieval oil-painted original, a statue sculpted from some unknown marble. Copernicus-2 was relieved, pleased that the interruption to his solitude was over. He had things to do, ideas to sort. He watched the youth's receding back, his muscles moving like liquid beneath his skin. The fleeing figure circled the border of the pool where grass eddied around his knees, then he was brushing his way through the caressing fronds of taller grass where it grew to the height of his chest. Until he squatted down and was no longer visible.

Copernicus-2 crouched by the water's edge. There was a reflection of the back of his head in its glittering mirror. "This is irrational," he thought.

He could see manifestations of surreal madness printed in colour plates, paintings, found art, assemblages, collages, all set into an elaborately detailed library book of Twentieth Century Art. He could see the textual comments and dates in parenthesis, Paul Eluard (1938), Joan Miro (1925), René Magritte (1928), Yves Tanguy (1938).

His ears picked up the thrumming of hooves somewhere…

YOU CAN WATCH REGINA DANCE…

The man and Regina walked along the margin of beach beneath a sky that was pregnant with storm. They walked for a while with even, measured steps. Then they ran, chasing their lengthening shadows into the approaching darkness. Finally they danced solemnly on the sand, beside the endless tideless ocean. It started out as a light fandango, mutated into a tango, then became the twist, until – laughing, they collapsed into the sand to regain their lost breath. Clawing it thirstily from the thin, chill air, when their eyes met, and fixed together. And they were frozen for an eternity locked in each other's gaze. "When I was a child," she said, "and it rained, I used to stand as tall as I could, open my mouth, and let the fresh rainwater trickle down my throat."

"It will rain… soon," he promised, "and when it does, the

188

war will end, and the world will never change again." The sea was waiting. The cliffs were waiting. They ran through surf that rose all around them in shimmering lace, and fell slowly in dream. Stinging with sensual fingers of liquid ice. Then they lay on the moist sand, cool to the touch, and dried their clothes until they were dry. They didn't even talk. They breathed and they watched their breath disappear into the still air.

They walked some more. There was a concrete pyramid in the sand. It was taller than she was, not quite as tall as he. It pointed an accusing finger of umbra and penumbra at them as they strolled towards the gathering storm. It was the remains of an ancient lost coastal fortification. But to them it was a citadel. A giant squat spaceship from Jupiter. "Jovian gravity is so much greater than Earth," he mock-lectured. "Therefore the people will be shorter, their spacecraft more stub."

She laughed, "I wonder how we look to them. Tall?" She stretched on her toes until the sand beneath her crumbled away and she lost balance. "No, it's a windmill, see its sails," her arms moved in a slow circular motion.

"How can it be? There's no wind."

Her vision dissolved, and she threw sand it him. "But there will be wind. Come the storm."

Time dripped away. The storm built...

DIALOGUE CONCERNING THE TWO CHIEF WORLD SYSTEMS, PTOLEMAIC AND COPERNICAN (Galileo Galilei, 1632)

"Think of it like this. To destroy the Ptolemaic universe, it required a Copernicus, right?" argued the Advocate. For that is what Advocates do, they argue. "It required a man who viewed the universe as rigidly sun-centred, with the Earth as part of its planetary retinue. A man, not only of will, but with a belief in universal stability of sufficient strength to move his contemporaries." As he talked, they continued up the gradient, the bracken thinning, giving way to unhealthy moss and lichen. And as they walked, subtle differences were taking place. Outlines were becoming vaguer. The very landscape was disturbingly unstable; he sensed it shifting like smoke when he wasn't looking at it directly. As though it was dissolving around him. Time itself

189

coming unglued.

Copernicus-2 forced his attention back to the rangy stranger.

"Some people believe in magic. Believe in magic so strongly that it works. People believe in universal systems of logic, and for centuries the Earth lives beneath the benign smiles of reason. Others believe in gods. Belief has always been more about belonging than about truth. What use is truth to your everyday life? What good does it do you to know truth if it sets you at odds with your fellows and makes you a lonely outsider? No good at all. Going to the temple, mosque, church, synagogue, marks you out as belonging, gives you a social network, you share family, community, village, you are a part of something, and that makes you more comfortable. You don't deny, it never occurs to you to deny, why should you? That only sets you apart. No-one likes that. Don't get me wrong, I'm not mocking. I'm not even suggesting they're wrong to live that way. Only that belief is more useful than truth. Belief is a social thing, a belonging thing. And because of that inter-connectivity, it creates and reinforces its own zone of truth."

"I don't get it. What are you saying...?"

"Saying? What am I saying? I'm saying that perhaps every group of people in history, any group who believe in anything strongly enough, maybe they are right. Perhaps for the duration of their belief, the universe is exactly the way they believe it is. What if the human mind is the creator of world form, and not just its interpreter? Perhaps reality twists and reshapes itself. Perhaps it's really as pliable as smoke, and conforms to human dreams and ideas as they change. You think that's a crazy idea? You think it's illogical?"

"You're saying that this is true?"

The Advocate's eyes fix his attention, laying bare the mind beyond in a moment of sudden peace. "Me, I'm not saying anything is true. But I'm not denying it either. Things are not what they appear. But then, neither is the reverse necessarily true. I'm merely suggesting a hypothesis..."

'UNIVERSAL MIND DECODER'

His tooth ached. His thoughts began to clarify like chemicals separating in a test-tube. "This is illogical," he thought, with growing conviction.

The sound of hooves grew, drowning out the train of thought. Two riders appeared over the crest of the hill from which Copernicus-2 had so recently descended. At first they seemed to shimmer like slender columns of smoke in still air. Or like mist moving over water. Then, for the briefest of moments, they reigned their mounts and were silhouetted against the purple back-wash of sky. Clouds like legendary continents boiling around them. The mounts were coaxed into a slow canter towards the glassy pool. The horses were sweating visibly. Their legs ended in human hands. The riders were tall, statuesque. As they approached, Copernicus-2 could see that they were dark-skinned, as the youth had been. Yet their features were Caucasian, in an indistinct way. One of them was evidently female. Both were ornately costumed. He thought of Samurai, then of Mogul tribesmen.

Copernicus-2 looked around for the rangy stranger. He was nowhere to be seen. It was these riders he'd been scared of, the Advocate had been trying to reach the mountains before these riders stopped him. He felt vague tremors of fear, yet was also detached – as though he was not directly involved in what he was seeing, as the riders cantered to a dusty halt before him. The female dismounted. Her face, shoulders and arms intricately etched with complex tattoos. She moved with a grace that made Copernicus-2 feel clumsy. "Where is he?" she demanded.

Without hesitation Copernicus-2 pointed into the tall grass. The second rider drew a long serrated blade from a saddle-scabbard, urged the human-handed horse forward into the nearer edges of the tall wispy grass.

"You are Copernicus-2," said the girl. A statement, not a question. She stood beside him, not quite as tall as he was.

"Yes. I'm pleased to meet you." He extended his hand formally. At that moment there was a shriek. The youth leapt terrified from concealment, wild hair flailing insanely, eyes wide. He took a step backwards, stumbled. Lurched forward towards the water, his body gleaming, as the rider bore down upon him.

"You may mount. We don't have far to go," commented the girl softly. Copernicus-2 felt a little embarrassed. He went over the necessary actions for mounting a horse, his imagination viewing himself from various angles. He had never mounted a horse, but had vivid mind-pictures taken from an archive of western-movies of the accepted procedure.

The youth sprang with the agility of terror into the water, it danced like fire about his knees, clinging, colliding into rivulets down his thighs and legs. The liquid rose and fell in slow motion as he ran.

Copernicus-2 smiled, approached the horse. An empty stirrup dangled to his rather exaggeratedly rotund waist-coated stomach. He turned to find that the girl was watching him expressionlessly. He felt puzzled, transferred his briefcase from left to right hand, his brolly from right to left, then back again.

The rider tore into the pool as the stumbling youth emerged up the shingle of the opposite bank.

Copernicus-2 gritted his teeth, placed his foot in the stirrup, swung himself up and over the beast's broad back. The contact was solid and pleasingly warm.

The blade glimmered in the light of three suns. The chase was short and brutal. The youth, face contorted, eyes pleading, scrabbled up the shingle as the rider approached from his rear, bending, aiming, as expressionless as his companion. The blade pointed, impacted the shoulder-blade. The youth's eyes stared wide in disbelief, he staggered forward. The bloodied blade re-emerged above his right nipple. His chest shattered with an eruption of bright crimson that exploded in long forming tears. The youth shrieked soundlessly, fell to his knees. The rider had withdrawn the blade, reigned the horse back and dismounted in one liquid movement.

The girl swung up in front of Copernicus-2, his body tight against her robe, his arms around her waist.

The blade arced and fell, the youth's back imploded in bloody welts. A tethered arm somehow came free, jerking grotesquely. He rolled over onto his back, coiled, screamed in a blur of crimson. The blade drew life and rhythm, slashing, thrusting, gouging, until the youth was unrecognisably still. His body exploded into a spray of droplets. The severed umbilical chord lay free, it squirmed languidly, serpent-like, then divided up into several identical lengths which flexed in identical movements. Copernicus-2 thought of garden earthworms. As if at a signal they insinuated themselves into the breathing ground and slithered out of sight.

The bloodied grass wavered. The rider carefully wiped his blade on the grass. Re-sheathed it and mounted. "All deviations from true-form must be cleansed," he said by way of explanation.

"Of course," agreed Copernicus-2 with a slight twinge of guilt over his betrayal of the faun-boy. And anyway – they rode human-handed horses, had they forgotten what true-form was? The rider smiled across at the girl, then urged his mount into a canter up the slope. Copernicus-2 and the girl followed. The pace was easy. No-one spoke. He found it difficult to decide whether it was the motion of the human-handed horse, or the mental replay of the butchered youth that produced the disturbing sensation of nausea in the pit of his stomach. The images of slaughter were interspersed, and frequently juxtaposed with clear line-drawings of human intestines from a biology textbook. Lungs in exploded diagram, neural patterns, bone-structure, the digestive tract, the reproductive system, respiratory system, cerebral diagrams, the epidermis in neatly stratified cross-section, glands neatly lettered or numbered referring to the explanatory keys, occasional colour-plates of magnified blood-cells, cancer-cells, single strands of hair.

At length the storm of images ebbed. Copernicus-2 recognised that his eyes were registering the view from the crest of the hill from which he'd originally descended. The point from which his memory – his life? – went back no further. It was as if that had been the very first moment of time, and for him it was. There was no memory of yesterdays before that to give him identity. It should have frightened him. But it didn't. He could see, at the exact location of his genesis, the imprint of where his body had lain, pressed into the spongy ochre ground. And was as though he'd woken there from sweet sweet sleep…

GIRL WITH THE UNQUIET MIND

They stood on the beach together. For the briefest second, night was turned to day. Distant thunder seemed to be applauding the death of time. Snaking twisting retina-searing light fell from the leaden sky to freeze the beach to a silver photograph. The lightning was violent. A pistol-shot to startle the world to awareness.

"The storm." Regina's were filled with dawn. They were stars, bright binaries absorbing all of the silver sea, silver cliffs and silver sands greedily into them.

"It is now." He breathed in huge gulps of air. For a moment he was cloaked in a mist of spray that caught and held him in its silver fingers, then dissolved and died. Rain followed the lightning, it struck at the sea. Spinning vortexes grew, merged, vanished, were instantly replaced, until the frozen sea was frozen no more, its surface pitted and scarred.

Her eyes danced, alive with fire. His eyes picked up and reflected that fire. They laughed, the cliffs screamed laughter back at them. The rain fell, gently at first, as the first thunderhead scars of light faded from the sky. Then lashed more violently, encouraged by the cover of twilight, tearing her hair, plastering their clothes to their skin, outlining their ribs. Making glistening skull-caps of what had been hair. Stinging their eyes, pit-pattering across their faces. Their hysterical laughter increasing with the rain's fury. They jumped to catch it before it could reach the sand. Eyes burning, mouths wide, heads flung back, hair dancing casting spray into the rain.

They'd met in the insect city. They'd escaped together, heading in what he assumed to be a northerly direction along the coastline. At a safe distance he laid the briefcase on a smoothed square of sand. Flipped it open to reveal the circuitry within. He'd uncoiled the electrodes and she helped clamp them to his temples. He took the brolly and slid it open. Taking it to the maximum fully-opened position, but he kept pushing it up beyond that point, inverting it, until it formed a dish open to the sky. With three rapid twists he unscrewed the curved handle, then inserted the shaft into a socket in the circuitry, and turned it until it was secure. The electrodes would transmit his mental patterns into the amplifying circuitry, which would then be broadcast into the gathering sky. Altering the nature of reality.

"It's happening," she told him, although he already knew, "can't you feel it? the world is about to never turn again…"

THE CREATION OF THE SECOND COPERNICUS

"So tell me more about this 'hypothesis' of yours." They stopped walking. The mental images were gone. There was just the slope

194

of the dune they were standing halfway up, its striated greys, roses and beiges deepening in the low evening light into reds, violets and golds. A vast openness of bracken and breeze, huge and silent, all detail pared to the skeletal. The breeze dithered, whispering hushed secrets from the horizon as it threaded around enormous and unfathomable formations rising like hallucinations around them, sandstone columns leathery in texture widening at the base.

The Advocate seemed to be considering, a sad preoccupation behind his eyes as he gazed off into the far distance. "Just suppose that the idea that everything must have an end is merely due to poverty of thinking. And that, for sake of argument, people have stumbled through centuries of fearful confusion without realising their full potential. They've blundered through ages of famine and drought, storm, war and chaos, without realising their ability not just to interpret the world, or the universe, but to recreate it. The mind keeps secrets. And it keeps secrets from itself. There are worlds beneath the visible one, where odd things happen. Theoretical physics, quantum mechanics, stuff like that, they provided early clues, suggestions, intimations. Discrete subatomic particles were seen to behave in unexpected ways. That such particles existed, or ceased to exist, had momentum and moved in patterns determined by the fact of observation. Werner Heisenberg, Niels Bohr, they were in at the fumbling beginning. The realisation that the observer could influence the uncertainty of matter, at the point where matter and energy become indistinguishable. So what do you imagine came next?"

He shrugged. "The next step was the realisation that the world itself is plastic, that it shapes itself around people's collective conception of it. Consciously, or not. If you conceive peace, order, stability – collectively, you get a peaceful, ordered, stable world. But the opposite also holds true. You believe in the vengeful medieval god, you literally get a Hieronymus Bosch vision of Hades, the circles of hell, sinners flung into boiling tar-pits by tormenting demons, transformed into bleeding thorn-trees, locked in ice or wrapped in devouring serpents. Strength of will gives that a terrible reality. For as long as they believed in all that, it was true. When the consensus belief was of a flat Earth, with the sky a protective upturned dome, and those points of light as pinpricks in the ceiling of heaven filtering down divine light from the domain of heavenly gods above it, that also was true. For as long as the idea predominated, it was true. Yet for thousands of years all of that occurred on a subconscious level. Universes were created, then forgotten, as ideas changed and evolved. People were doing it, without realising they were doing it. They were grubs burrowing into an apple. Hidebound by the laws of inflexible physics. Materialism won them a global civilisation, but also barred them from any secrets not explicable through charts and diagrams. Until the true nature of reality was discovered. Then suddenly, 'Oh, it's not fixed, it's malleable'. Well, you could view that with naïve optimism, or as unrepentant stupidity, according to the state of your liver. But what kind of world would result from that discovery? Racial shock? Racial fear?"

"A paranoid world? A world of paranoia incarnate?" He realised the idea was amazingly familiar.

"Precisely, a universe where the Earth levels off into a vast endless, infinite plain of never-ending variation. Inhabited by races of people who twist their sections of the never-ending world into their own dreams, their own utopias, their own nightmares, their sexual fantasies, stalked by fears, guilt, crazy gods with absolute powers, and magical forces made real by the intensity of their belief…"

"People would be afraid. Some of them would long for a return to order and stability. A return to the myth of heliocentricity."

"Yes. It's becoming clear. They needed a second Copernicus. A man who could shape universal concepts by the sheer force of his will and his ideas. A second Copernicus to return to the concept and the reality of the universe of a sun-centred planetary system with neatly ordered understandable worlds."

"And if those people longed passionately, intensely enough, for such a man, focusing hard and believing with enough fervour…"

"They would bring into being…"

"A second Copernicus!" The rangy stranger was watching his reactions closely. Framed by the vault of sky, tinged mauve with clouds. The world stretched away over the breathing plain, grey and white in geological stratum, until it merged with the horizon. All was clear and three-dimensional. The second Copernicus switched his attention back to the Advocate. "Yes. That makes sense. But what is your role in all of this?"

"We are at war. Two great empires in opposition, tearing each other's universe to pieces. The empire of order. And the empire of chaos. You are the doomsday weapon that can decide its outcome. To determine which world will vanquish the other."

"Me…?" A flinty laugh.

"Your creators will come to claim you. Those who want all of this to end. To reduce the world back down to its old limitations. But there are others, and we don't want that to happen. There are people who find the infinite Earth exciting. Those who find the incarnation of dreams, the possibility of creating realms through the intensity of will a stimulating challenge. Together, we can realise the innate god-potential of humanity. So there's a need to thwart the second coming of Copernicus by undermining his will to accomplish the mission he's been created to fulfil. Perhaps, just as you represent closure, I've been abstracted to embody aspiration? That's why we, you and I, must reach those mountains before they come for you."

"You want to thwart… me?"

AND THE EARTH HAS NO END: END

His tooth screamed angrily at him. The two horses cantered over the hill beneath a low scud of cloud. The crest was densely forested, allowing only a thin opening showing glimpses of a ribbon of mountains receding in the distance, impossibly vast mountains. They were backlit by penumbras of golden light so they too appeared varnished to gold, with a curve into shadows as gradual as a bloom of mould. But descending the gradient on the far side, the gleaming landscape instead sloped away gently grassed to a distant sea-shore. The vista was exciting. Copernicus-2 imagined that ocean crossed by voyaging ships on Odyssian voyages of discovery to new shifting island clusters, peninsulas, with navigable straits and channels between, leading to new continents that stretched away for infinity. An unimaginably vast theatre of an Earth that literally went on forever. Where does that sea end? Where is its mysterious edge? The idea fascinated him, despite the defensive screen of cartographical diagrams, heliocentricity and astronomical space that resumed within his mind's eye.

The half-memory of the rangy Advocate receded. 'The Martyrdom of Saint Sebastian' youth too. In their place was the premonition of the silver shore, the storm, and the girl Regina, which gnawed tantalisingly at the edge of his mind. He was gently nudged back to the present as his mount descended through spiralling wisps of winged seeds and shoals of dragonflies into a more immediate forest, but what a forest! The contorted boles ascended inconceivably high towards the brightening sky, three times the height of any trees he recognised. There were gaudy flowers washed across the undergrowth between the ancient, absurdly distended trees. The ground no longer breathed. Copernicus-2 registered that the landscape was no longer erotic, but magical. There was a huge ringed moon silvering trees and half-glimpsed figures to soft tinsel. They cantered without pause through the forest where leaf-cover created an aqueous twilight splashed by gobs of leaf-filtered moon, to emerge a kilometre closer to the shore. Across an expanse of rolling countryside Copernicus-2 could see the city that he knew instinctively was their destination.

The city was shaped like a silver insect, a grasshopper rearing at least two kilometres from the ground, faceted with scintillating domes of crystal or inlaid stained glass. From the 'head' extended a number of long cables attached to comparatively miniature giraffes, each twenty times the size of the human-handed horses, made of semi-transparent metals filled with what appeared to be swirling multicoloured smoke studded with glow-worm lights and half-formed shapes. The phalanx of giraffes was frozen in the act of hauling the translucent insect towards the shore. The horses cantered towards the city.

"In that insect city," thought Copernicus-2, "these people will try to use my pre-programmed convictions, and the tools they've provided me with, to destroy this magical, endless planet. But, although there's nothing else to come, this is not the end. I'll meet Regina here. Perhaps, maybe… just possibly, we could take a little time out to explore first. We'll start by heading in what's most likely a northerly direction along that coastline." He smiled. "It might take a while, it might take years, it might take us forever…"

The horses rode into the shadow of the city. "Perhaps we won't ever return," he decided. "There's a hell of a lot to explore…"

Parallel Universe Publications

THE WINTER HUNT AND OTHER STORIES
by Steve Lockley & Paul Lewis
ISBN: 978-0-9932888-9-0

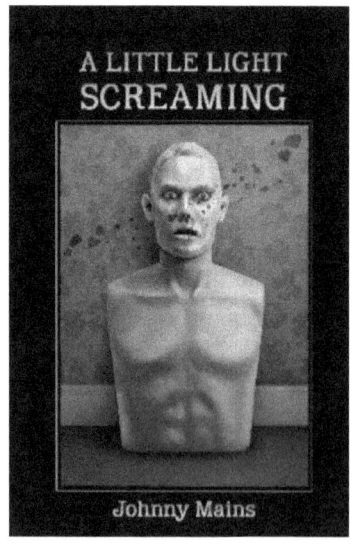

A LITTLE LIGHT SCREAMING by Johnny Mains
ISBN: 978-0-9932888-5-2

ENGLAND 'B': 90 MINUTES OF HELL by Richard Staines
ISBN: 978-0-9932888-7-6

AND NOBODY LIVED HAPPILY EVER AFTER by Kate Farrell
ISBN: 978-0-9932888-8-3

FISHHEAD; THE DARKER TALES OF IRVIN S. COBB
ISBN: 978-0-9932888-6-9

KITCHEN SINK GOTHIC: Selected by David and Linden Riley
ISBN: 978-0-9932888-3-8

WILL ANYONE FIGURE OUT THAT THIS IS A REPACKAGED FIRST COLLECTION? by Johnny Mains
ISBN: 978-0-9574535-7-9

BLACK CEREMONIES by Charles Black
ISBN: 978-0-9574535-5-5

HIS OWN MAD DEMONS:
DARK TALES FROM DAVID A. RILEY
ISBN: 978-0-9574535-8-6

THEIR CRAMPED DARK WORLD by David A. Riley
ISBN: 978-0-9574535-9-3

THE HEAVEN MAKER AND OTHER GRUESOME TALES
by Craig Herbertson
ISBN: 978-0-9932888-2-1

GOBLIN MIRE by David A. Riley
ISBN: 978-0-9574535-4-8

THINGS THAT GO BUMP IN THE NIGHT
selected by Douglas Draa and David A. Riley
ISBN: 978-0-9574535-6-2

CLASSIC WEIRD selected David A. Riley
ISBN: 978-0-9574535-3-1

MOLOCH'S CHILDREN by David A. Riley
ISBN: 978-0-9932888-1-4

Check our website:

http://paralleluniversepublications.blogspot.co.uk/

www.ingramcontent.com/pod-product-compliance
Lightning Source LLC
Chambersburg PA
CBHW070008260626
47159CB00005B/1728